HOMECOMING

FURY FALLS INN • BOOK 6

BETTY BOLTÉ

www.MysticOwlPublishing.com

Also by Betty Bolté

Becoming Lady Washington: A Novel
Notes of Love and War

FURY FALLS INN
The Haunting of Fury Falls Inn
Under Lock and Key
Desperate Reflections
Fractured Crystals
Legends of Wrath

SECRETS OF ROSEVILLE
Undying Love
Haunted Melody
The Touchstone of Raven Hollow
Veiled Visions of Love
Charmed Against All Odds

A MORE PERFECT UNION
Elizabeth's Hope
Emily's Vow
Amy's Choice
Samantha's Secret
Evelyn's Promise

About

Homecoming

Fury Falls Inn in 1821 Alabama. A place for ghosts, witches, and magic. A place of secrets and hidden dangers. A place Reginald Fairhope built to keep his family safe from vengeful witches.

The inn was supposed to be a haven, a place where Reggie's powerful magic would protect both his wife and daughter. He trusts a young innkeeper to care for them while he travels on urgent business. He returns exhausted, longing for peace and quiet along with a stiff drink, only to find his wife murdered and haunting the inn, a witch hunter on the loose, and his witch daughter, now engaged to the interim innkeeper, kidnapped. With his world falling apart, what must a fiercely powerful warlock do to find the peace he craves?

To my husband Chris for all his loving support

Dear Reader,

This story completes the series of six supernatural historical fiction stories set in 1821 northern Alabama.

I'd like to thank my beta readers—Sue, Alicia, Danielle, Crystal, Mandy, and Chris—who read a prepublication version of *Homecoming* and provided invaluable feedback. I appreciate your time, observations, and suggestions for improving the story!

I'd also like to thank readers like you who continue to inspire me to write stories with joy and passion. I always enjoy hearing from my readers, so please drop me a line at betty@bettybolte.com any time.

If you enjoy this book, please subscribe to my newsletter via www.bettybolte.com to be informed of other books I'll write in the future. You can also learn more about me, my other existing books, and read excerpts of each book at my website. You may also enjoy learning more about the behind the scenes research and recipes included in this story at www.bettybolte.net.

Again, thanks for reading! I hope you enjoy *Homecoming*.

Betty

Chapter One

Northern Alabama, October 1821

The familiar lane leading to the Fury Falls Inn finally came into view, welcoming and yet portentous. Reginald Fairhope trudged beside the lead pair of oxen, urging them with a goad stick as they hauled home the carefully wrapped, custom furniture in the battered wagons. He could have used his magic to transport everyone and everything but doing so would worsen the situation he'd soon confront. Caked in dried mud, the massive caravan lumbered onto the lane. After all he'd been through, he meant to insure the safe arrival of the goods as well as the people, his family, behind him. He eagerly anticipated his daughter's happy welcome. The journey home had proven far more arduous than even he'd thought possible. Through rain and mud and steep mountain passes they'd struggled and slowly made their way home. But he'd never seen a sight look so fine as the two-story roadside inn at the far end of the dirt lane stretching up toward the Appalachian foothills. He reached out with his senses and frowned. Many souls resided there, some from the beyond. Including his cherished wife, haunting the inn. He tightened his grip on the long stick and urged the oxen onward. A chill foreboding permeated him with each step toward home.

The home he'd constructed to protect his family as he built a new life for them. He knew every length of lumber, every spike and nail used to create a haven for his wife and daughter. The structure expanded upon the typical dog-trot style of home popular in the region. He'd chosen the layout for its familiar appearance but on a grander scale. The idea pleased him, of having two halves of a whole with a covered porch between to encourage air flow for cooling on hot summer days. On the left side he'd built the public inn with a large working kitchen and an even larger dining room complete with a beautiful bar and immense fireplace. A mahogany square piano stood on display in the front corner, payment from a talented young piano maker passing through on his way to Boston and fame. The upstairs boasted seven comfortable guest accommodations as well as a welcoming sitting area by a rear window. The specially crafted furniture secured in the wagons of the caravan would replace the plain beds, chairs, wardrobes, and other small pieces to elevate the appearance to meet his vision before the esteemed senator's upcoming visit. He'd made it back just in time.

Zander Simmons rode his horse alongside Reggie, matching pace with the slower oxen. "How's it feel to be home again?"

Reggie nodded at Zander, recalling his surprise at the man's sudden arrival in Savannah. The young man had accompanied his father Sheridan, the inn's renowned cook, when the older man had learned his enslaved wife worked in Savannah where Reggie had finally found her. Apparently, nothing could prevent Sheridan from traveling to the coast to be reunited with her. The three of them had managed to raise the exorbitant amount the slave owner demanded to set her free.

"I cannot describe it." Reggie clicked his tongue. "Come up now, boys." Reggie kept the oxen moving with his abrupt command and a tap on the rump. No slacking off. He longed to see his daughter, but more so his wife. Despite knowing she'd died and now her ghost haunted the inn, he must see her. If only he could touch her one last time. Since that was unlikely, he'd settle for seeing her, speaking to her of his love. He'd set up a séance if need be. "Do you think they've spotted us yet?"

He squinted up the lane, hoping to see his daughter, to see Cassandra hurrying out to greet him. He probed for her but didn't detect her. Where was she? He saw only a myriad of other coaches, carriages, wagons, and men on horseback coming and going along the wide lane. At the far end, he noticed what looked like white stone on the ground in a circle around the entrance. Flint had been as busy as he'd been told.

"I bet they've heard us by now." Zander tapped his wide-brimmed hat more snugly on his brow. "We're not sneaking up on anyone."

Reggie glanced over his shoulder at the string of wagons pulled by horses and oxen, the enclosed coach-and-four where the women rode in relative comfort, and several men on horseback behind him. The rattle of harness, the squeak of leather, the stomp of hooves creating a low-lying cloud of dust announced their slow progress. He turned back to look up the lane, waiting to see a familiar face on the wide front porch. Only to be disappointed.

"I don't see anyone looking for us." He pulled his hat off and smacked it against his thigh to dislodge the layer of dust on the brim. Then he put it back in place as he continued easing closer to a cold ale and a comfortable chair.

He heard dogs barking and peered more closely. The household pack of dogs gathered in the circular carriageway, welcoming the new arrivals with sharp yaps and deep barks. "At least someone is glad to see us."

He prodded the oxen again with another encouraging command, a spring in his stride he hadn't had moments before. He'd missed the Labradors and the Cocker Spaniel more than he'd realized. Their friendly overture would also alert the rest of the household of their arrival. Sure enough, young Flint Hamilton emerged onto the front porch and stood there, hand to brow to determine what the dogs were making a fuss about. He looked respectable in his dark trousers and matching vest, a white shirt glistening in the weak sunshine. A second later another young man joined Flint to watch the caravan's progress. Reggie lifted the goad stick in salute, receiving a wave in return.

Several minutes later they halted off to the left of the lane, near the stable and the paddocks where cattle, horses, and swine grazed and snuffled about. He'd maneuvered the caravan out of the way of the flow of guests while they sorted out where to store the furniture, boxes, crates, barrels, all strapped down and covered to protect everything from the fickle, hostile elements.

"Mr. Fairhope, welcome home." Flint trotted across the drive toward him, his black leather shoes crunching on the stones. The other man hesitated on the porch before easing down the steps.

Reggie peered at the young man. He stood tall and dark blond, his bright blue eyes studying him with reserved curiosity. He displayed the physique of an active man, strong and supple in his movements. The stranger took a position next to Flint without saying a word.

Reggie addressed Flint and then shook hands with his substitute, noting the changes in his demeanor and appearance. The youth had matured into a fine young man. No wonder his daughter had fallen in love with him. Reggie had not anticipated the two young people would become attached when he'd invited Flint to oversee the operation during his absence. Cassie's letters had clearly indicated her growing desire to marry the man despite her mother's protests. Now he understood. "Mr. Hamilton, it's grand to see you again. I'm afraid I don't know your companion."

"I'm glad you've returned as well. As to my companion..." Flint glanced to the other man. "This is your son, Silas.

Taken aback, Reggie peered closer at his son and noted the warm humor in those startling eyes. "Silas? Is that really you?"

"Yes, sir." Silas nodded slowly and stuck out his hand. "How have you been?"

Reggie clasped the strong grip and then pulled his youngest son into an embrace. He held it for perhaps a second too long but his joy at seeing one of his son's couldn't be denied. "Welcome. I'm glad to see you looking so fit and fine."

Silas tightened his grip on Reggie's hand and then eased back. "I'm glad to see you, too. I'm sure the others will be happy to reunite with you as well."

Flint surveyed the line of vehicles behind Reggie's

wagon. "Everyone safe and sound?"

The others. His other sons were here. His joy ballooned in his chest but now wasn't the time to rejoice. First he had to get everyone and everything unloaded and settled. Reggie followed Flint's gaze, watching his brother Beck dismount and lead his horse toward him. "Tired and hungry, but in one piece, thank goodness. Where's Cassandra?"

"She's...safe." Flint glanced away and then back to him. "Um... Mr. Fairhope, there's something you should know." Flint's eyes glittered with worry.

Reggie peered at him, seeing that something deeply troubled him. Something he didn't want to know. "Not yet, son. Let's get everyone settled with something to eat and drink, then we can talk about whatever issues may be at hand." Reggie didn't have patience enough to deal with problems when he hadn't even had the chance to sip a cold beverage. His grip on his volatile temper slipped a notch with each passing moment. He'd longed for home and now that he'd arrived, he simply wanted to enjoy his return. Knowing Cassie was safe meant he had a minute before he need worry about her. The dust lining his throat made it a chore to speak. "I want you to meet several people. Come with me."

"But..."

Reggie leveled a glare at him. His patience evaporated, his fingers itching to silence the man with a flick and a wave. His expression must have warned Flint of his brush with a dangerous magical force. Reggie. Flint hesitated only a second, firmed his lips, then followed without another word. Slowly, Reggie allowed the growing surge of power to abate as he turned to face his brother.

"Hey, Beck, I'd like you to meet Flint Hamilton and my son Silas. Flint's been managing the inn while I've been gone, and doing a fine job from what I hear." Surprisingly so, if he were honest. He hadn't expected for the young man to work so hard to make everything shine and welcome guests. Even the crushed stone carriageway proved innovative and useful. What else had Flint accomplished around the inn? The answer to that question would have to wait a spell. "This is my brother, Beck Fairhope."

Beck leveled a stern, understanding gaze at Reggie but wisely held his tongue. Reggie tamped down the remainder of the anger brewing inside. Reclaimed control of his temper with an act of will. Emotions ran high at the inn, triggering his instinctive reaction to the others. He wanted a drink before he had to handle any of the worries swirling around him. Was that too much to ask?

Flint extended a hand and firmly shook with the older man. "Welcome to Fury Falls Inn, sir."

"Nice to make your acquaintance, Uncle Beck." Silas clasped hands briefly with him.

"Just call me Beck. I expect we'll get to know each other quite well over the next few weeks." Beck's green eyes flashed with mischief. "My brother says there's some trouble we need to address."

"Yes, I was going to tell him about it..." Flint let whatever else he was going to say remain unsaid as Reggie glared at him again.

"I just got here, Flint. Give me a few minutes, all right?" Reggie dragged his hat off and raked a hand through his hair. He simply wanted to settle in after the weeks on the trail. He couldn't count the number of broken spokes, wheels, yokes, and straps they'd had to mend or replace. The stone bruised horses they'd had to replace with fresh horses. He tapped his hat on his head with an exhausted sigh. "Let's get everyone inside and then we'll catch up."

"Mr. Hamilton, how are you? It seems like a donkey's ear since I last seen you."

The deep voice drew Reggie's attention to the strong older man he'd called cook and friend for several years. Sheridan escorted his wife, Pansy, toward where the men waited. Reggie couldn't stop the blossom of happiness inside to see the couple walking together. He'd do anything for Sheridan. The man deserved all the happiness he could lay claim to in this life.

Although Sheridan was of medium height, Pansy's head barely reached his shoulder. That she'd made the entire trip without one complaint endeared her to Reggie all the more. The woman had endured so very much and yet didn't belabor her own misfortunes. Indeed, she'd been overjoyed to be reunited with her long-lost husband. Reggie strived to improve the lives of those he employed, and he felt great satisfaction to have done so for Sheridan by bringing him together again with Pansy.

"It has been a long time, Sheridan. I'm pleased to see you well. And this must be your wife I've heard so much about." Flint half-bowed to the petite woman. "I'm pleased to me you, Mrs. Drake."

"Pansy is fine, young man." She aimed a crooked, weary smile up at him. "My Sheridan tells me how much you've supported him despite some...differences of opinion along the way."

"We figured out how to work together." Flint grinned at her forthright comment, slanting a wink at Sheridan. "And this is Silas Fairhope, Reggie's son."

Silas nodded a greeting to the petite woman. "Nice to meet you."

Reggie had heard more than once how Sheridan and Flint had butted heads at first, Sheridan resented not being left in charge just like Mercy had when she'd gotten home from a shopping trip with Cassie to find her husband gone. But Reggie had not wanted to burden either of them with the day-to-day decisions and problems Flint must have faced. Sheridan's talent remained his cooking ability, transforming everyday vegetables and meats into something delectable the guests relished. While Mercy had her own tasks and pastimes to occupy her days. She didn't need worrying over where to purchase the best candle wax, or the finest oils, or even the softest linens. Besides, she had her hands full with Cassandra. As loving and dutiful as his daughter might be, she also balked at her mother's heavy hand. A hand there to protect her from dire threats whether she had realized them or not.

"I heard you've been doing an excellent job in my absence." Reggie studied Flint's somber features, battling inside with his desire to be pleased with his need to have been missed, needed, or at least welcomed home by his daughter. "I'm back now so we'll see how accurate that portrayal might be."

"Yes, sir." Flint lifted his chin as he stiffened his posture, indicating some level of affront at the implication behind the jibe. He gazed down the lane. "Who did you bring with you?"

Damn. His temper made him lash out for no good reason. The man had run the inn for him for four months and all Reggie could do was put him on defense. What was wrong with him? He thought he'd be missed, that things would suffer without him around which is why he'd asked John Baker to supervise for him. To visit the inn frequently and send him reports. Cassie had begged in her candid letters for him to return, implying she desperately needed him home. Now that he'd shown up, everything seemed to be running smoothly. He shouldn't feel disappointed but somehow he did. *Get a handle on yourself, man.* Reggie shifted to see to whom Flint smiled a greeting. "Ah, Scarlet."

"Reggie, dear, you simply must introduce me to these bright young men." His sister, dressed in a long, tan dress with white sash, a floppy tan hat on her head, strutted up to join the group. "I've heard so much about Mr. Hamilton. How perfect he is and all. Which one is he?"

He adored Scarlet despite her flippant ways. Her attitude belied her forty-plus years. Still slender and sassy, she lit up the room when she strolled in. More impressive, at least to Reggie, were her magical abilities. She could flick a finger and enact her will as easily as smile. She'd begged him to stay in Savannah, to move the children there after his beloved wife lay buried out back of the inn. When he'd refused for that very reason, she did an about-face and announced she'd move to Alabama instead. To help him instruct his children on how to finesse their magic. Her smile, energy, and devotion filled him with pleasure beyond words.

"Now, sis, don't fluster the man." Reggie shook his head, but a slow smile spread on his lips. "Flint, this audacious miss is my sister Scarlet."

He nodded once at her. "Nice to meet you, Miss Fairhope."

"Oh, please, since you're about to be family..." Scarlet

angled a glance at Reggie with an arched brow.

"That's likely true." Reggie had shared with the group Cassie's intention to marry. From what he already knew about Flint, along with the fine impression he made upon his greeting, Reggie saw no reason for denying his daughter the future she envisioned. A warmth spread through his chest as he considered calling Flint his son. "I'm sure of it."

"Then please, call me Scarlet." She held out her hand for Flint to take. "I'll call you Flint, yes?"

Flint clasped her hand gently. "As you'd like."

"And now who is this handsome gentleman?" Scarlet angled her head, her floppy hat brim shading half of her face.

"Silas Fairhope, ma'am." Silas half-bowed to her. "Your nephew."

"What a pleasure to finally meet you." Scarlet draped her hand in front of Silas, who took it gently in his own. "We shall get along famously, I'm sure."

The rattle and thud of an elegant coach-and-four cantering up the lane halted the conversation. Well, well. He'd anticipated seeking out John ere long. Here he appeared as if by magic. He suppressed a chuckle at his lame joke as he strode toward the advancing equipage.

The footman leaped from his post and yanked open the door. John quickly stepped down to the ground. As usual, he was dressed in fine attire befitting his elevated status in the community. He strode toward him, an anxious smile tugging his lips.

"Welcome back, Reggie." John halted with a quick nod to Flint and the others. His beaver top hat glistened in the morning sunshine. "I'm very glad you're home."

"Yes, finally. I'm glad to be back." Reggie searched

John's hard expression, reached out to sense his emotions with a quick probe. Then stiffened and braced for the worst. "What's wrong?"

"I'm sorry, old friend, to be the bearer of bad news upon your arrival. But you need to come with us to Riverwood." John shot a worried glance at Flint. "Immediately. Cassie informed me of your approach so I could collect you as quickly as possible."

"Can't it wait until I have something cold to drink?" He'd thought of nothing but easing his thirst and relaxing his tired muscles. Reggie opened his senses to John's feelings and then relented. Cassie was in trouble. Reading his mixed emotions and concerns made it difficult to assess the level of threat, but the fact Cassie wasn't home pointed to a deep concern for her safety. He had no time to refresh himself. "No, I guess not. Very well. Flint, Silas, please see to the others' comfort and refreshment. I'll return as quickly as possible."

"Yes, sir. That is what I was trying to tell you, that Mr. Baker would require your assistance immediately." Flint braced his fists on his hips. "I'd have handled the matter but only you can. I'll take care of everyone's needs here. But please, sir. Hurry back."

Flint's deep concern and fear flowed into Reggie, making his pulse beat in his ear. The man feared for his fiancé's life. He met Beck's probing gaze, sending a silent message. Beck clenched his jaw but kept his expression neutral. Having his warlock brother on hand meant Reggie could go retrieve his daughter without worrying about the others remaining at the inn.

"I will bring her home soon." Reggie indicated the coach his friend had arrived in with a wave of his hand. Despite his wishes, he had to ensure his daughter was safe. Bring her home where she belonged and where he could protect her with all of his considerable might. "All right, my friend, fill me in on the way. Let's go see what needs doing, shall we?"

The coach rolled away, leaving behind a cloud of dust and a lot of concern swirling in Flint's chest. Conflicting thoughts and accompanying emotions roiled inside him as the vehicle turned onto the highway and disappeared. What had Reggie meant? Had he disappointed him in some way? He'd done all he could think of to make his boss pleased with the job he'd done. Why did he have the feeling he'd let him down?

Silas attracted his attention with a shift of his position. "I'll go in and inform Matt of his parents' arrival and see that there's something cooking for their refreshments." He started for the steps without waiting for Flint's response.

"That's a fine idea. Thank you." Flint called after Silas as he heard a familiar voice behind him.

"Flint, good to see you!" Zander strode up to clap him on the back in a half-hug. "You're looking well."

Flint greeted Zander with relief and pleasure in his heart. He had been impressed by the man, who'd managed to overcome so much adversity to focus on the positives in his life. Once a slave, Zander still carried harsh memories Flint could never fathom of his life on the Louisiana plantation. Cassie's oldest brother, Giles, had saved him and his brother Matt from further abuse and ensured their life going forward could only be a vast improvement. When Zander and Matt had accompanied Giles home at Cassie's request, they discovered Sheridan was their father. With Pansy's recent freedom, the four of them could be a true family again.

Flint returned the manly embrace and then stepped away, positioning himself next to Scarlet. "I see you survived the trek as well. I'm sure Giles will be glad to see you when he gets back."

"Where is he?" Zander surveyed the inn's bustling front yard as if he hoped to spot his close friend approaching. "I thought he'd be here."

"He's with Cassie. I'll explain later." He'd not reveal too many details standing out in the open where anyone might overhear. He suspected the very bushes had ears. Knowing Giles stayed at Cassie's side was the only reason Flint had not ridden over to Riverwood himself. He had other obligations to attend but his heart ached for his woman. He gazed at Beck's attentive expression and then at Zander. "Over a pint?"

"Sounds fine." Zander looked at the tall man standing nearby. "Flint, have you met Beck?"

"We've been introduced." The man matched Flint in height, his pale green eyes bright and curious. Muscular shoulders filled out his leather jacket and his stance suggested he was comfortable and confident. Flint assessed the weary faces gazing at him. "I'm glad you have arrived in one piece. It sounds like you had quite a journey."

"Indeed we did. Reginald wouldn't permit me to assist our travels or we'd have arrived weeks ago. He insisted we not draw attention to ourselves." Scarlet tossed her head, her long ebony curls flirting with her shoulders. "He didn't believe I could work my magic and no one would know the difference."

The woman drew attention with the slightest movement so it was no wonder Reggie had insisted she try to keep to mundane modes of transportation. "He can be particular. Now that we're all here, shall we go inside? I've asked my hostess, Mandy, to help you get settled in."

"Oh, that would be nice." Pansy glanced at Sheridan and then met Flint's steady gaze. "What of our bags on the coach?"

Flint flicked a look at the coachman who had finished unloading the bags and boxes from the top of the coach. He nodded to the sturdy-looking fellow as he climbed the steps of the coach and took up the reins. The vehicle rattled and thumped past the group, interrupting their conversation.

"I'll bring them in." Zander waved them inside. "You go on."

"I'll give you a hand." Beck followed him the several yards back to the pile of luggage.

"Then let's get you ladies inside." Having two more strong men added to the number already in residence calmed some of Flint's concern. Knowing Beck possessed magical abilities also comforted him. The more the better as far as he was concerned. He wished yet again for some magical power to add to the mix. A futile wish. All he could do for the moment was what he'd been tasked with. "Right this way."

Flint ushered Scarlet and Pansy, still holding Sheridan's hand, across the carriageway and up the steps into the public side of the inn.

"Sheridan, you and Pansy can go on up to your old room." Flint motioned toward the door to the right that led across the covered passage to the family side of the structure. "It's all ready for you both."

"If Pansy don't mind, I'd like to see what all you've been up to while I was gone." Sheridan arched a brow at him. "Y'know, check on your work."

"Not that you'd have any real say in the matter." Flint leveled a stern look at the man, then let it melt into a grin. Just like old times with Sheridan pushing his own ideas to challenge and improve upon Flint's. Man, having him home was mighty fine. "But I'll show you if you'll keep your unwanted opinions to yourself."

Sheridan chuckled. "If you insist."

Flint led them down the short hall into the new addition, perusing the nearly finished rooms with pride. They'd almost succeeded in having the additional space ready and waiting for their arrival. Only a few more finishing touches to put the project to bed. If there were a bed. Those were on the wagons waiting outside to be unloaded. The furniture had better live up to the long wait.

The rooms stood ready to accept the wardrobes, tables, and beds. Curtains hung at the windows. Pretty and serviceable carpets on the wood floors. That thought reminded him of the fine carpet he'd ordered for the family's parlor, which should arrive in a matter of days. One last detail he intended to complete before any discussion arose of his future at the inn. So many details had occupied his mind in the course of defining and building the new rooms. If only he had a quality carpenter to handle the final little flourishes he envisioned. Unfortunately, they were all engaged and he'd have to wait weeks until any could see to those final touches. But the rooms were finished well enough to receive guests once the new furniture had been placed.

"What lovely accommodations." Scarlet brushed past him to waltz into the first room where Flint had stopped. She spun slowly in place and then grinned at him. "All it needs to be a comfortable retreat is some of the beautiful furniture we hauled all the way here."

"Indeed. I will see to that as quickly as possible." Flint half-bowed to her as Mandy sidled up next to him in her uniform of white blouse and dark blue skirt. "In the meantime, Mandy here will show you where you can freshen up. Then come to the dining room, the one we passed on our way here, and I'll have tea waiting for you. Luncheon won't be for another couple of hours."

"Mandy, is it?" Scarlet squinted at the young woman, appraising her attire and expression with a proprietary air. "I see we have some work to do, my dear, but never fear. I will be happy to assist you."

Mandy blinked several times as a slight frown pulled down her brows. "Excuse me?"

Scarlet waved a hand to and fro. "It can wait for now. Please show me where I can remove this layer of dust from my person."

Flint shrugged at Mandy, silently advising her to be polite. The young woman stared at him for a second and then drew in a breath before pasting a smile on her face.

"Miss Fairhope, if you'll follow me?" Mandy gestured toward the open door.

"I'd be happy to." Scarlet wriggled her fingers at Flint as she passed him, trailing after Mandy.

Sheridan smirked from where he stood with his wife in the hallway. "Never a moment without some kind of drama when she's around."

"Was it like that the entire trip?" Imagine dealing with

such self-assurance from the woman all the way across country. At Sheridan's knowing grin, Flint shook his head. "No wonder Reggie is relieved to have finished the journey."

"Father, you're back." Matt strode purposefully down the hall toward where Flint stood with his parents.

Sheridan accepted his son's handshake and then pulled Pansy forward. "Matthew, this is your mother."

Matt grinned at Pansy, searching her shining eyes with interest. "Mother."

The loving expression in the young man's eyes as he perused Pansy's entire being in one swift glance brought a lump to Flint's throat. The two hadn't seen each other in many years, since Matt was separated from his parents when a boy. The plethora of feelings Pansy experienced crossed her face as she smiled at her son.

"Son." Pansy extended a hand, palm up. "You've grown into a fine young man."

Matt ignored the hand and rushed in to give her a long hug. His quiet voice emerged muffled and choked with his own feelings at embracing his mother. "I didn't think I'd ever see you again."

The emotion displayed on their faces, tears streaming down Pansy's face while Matt closed his eyes against her neck, choked Flint. He hadn't seen his own mother now in weeks, but that was no time at all compared to the many years this mother and son had been separated. Not knowing what had become of the other. All the wondering, hoping, worrying. When he compared his own worry over Cassie being gone merely a day, he realized how fortunate he was. He knew where she was, that she was being protected. Pansy had no such reassurance for far too long. A lump clogged his throat the longer the two clung together, Sheridan watching in bemused silence.

Matt eased from the tight embrace, his hand lingering in his mother's as he smiled at her. "I'm going to fix you all a feast to welcome you home. Let Flint here settle you in and then come to the dining room back yonder. I'll fix you up fine."

"I'd offered them tea."

"Tea? This calls for a celebration." Matt glared at Flint, challenging him to deny him the pleasure of preparing a special repast for his mother.

Flint shrugged with a grin. "Have it your way."

Sheridan clapped Matt on the back, drawing him into a short embrace. "That sounds fine, Matt. We'll be there shortly."

Matt nodded his head vigorously as he glanced between them. "Right. I'll go get busy." He spun on the ball of one foot and hurried away, whistling.

"He's such a sweet young man." Pansy gazed after her son, a soft smile lighting her eyes. "Oh, Sheridan, I'm glad to see him looking so well."

"He's as fine a cook as Sheridan, too." Flint winked at Sheridan. The comparison should raise a cockle or two. "Isn't he?"

"Not even close." Sheridan braced his hands on his hips. "I guess I'll need to whip my kitchen back into shape again, now I'm home."

"Your kitchen? I thought you said you and Matt tied in your last cooking contest." Beck came up beside Flint, carrying a bag under each arm and in each hand. He didn't gave Sheridan the chance to respond before addressing Flint. "Where do these go?"

Zander sidled around Beck and nodded at the collection of matching luggage in his hands. "These are Scarlet's."

"She's in there." Flint pointed to the room nearby. "She's off with Mandy at the moment, but I expect her imminent return."

"I'm sure we'll know when she's on her way." Zander slipped into the room. The thud of several bags hitting the carpeted floor followed before he popped back into the hallway. "Beck has Sheridan and Pansy's things."

"Here, let me take those." Sheridan held out his hands, but Beck backed away.

"I've got 'em. Just show me where you want 'em." Beck juggled one bag to a more comfortable grip. "Lead the way."

Sheridan crooked his arm for Pansy to take hold. "Thank you, sir. Come, Pansy, I'll show you where we'll rest."

"As long as it's with you, I'll be fine." Pansy squeezed his elbow and let him escort her down the passage toward the entrance hall.

One day soon Flint and Cassie would walk together in just such a fashion. Despite having been apart for so many years, Sheridan and Pansy's love for each other was evident and inspiring.

"Would you look at them?" Zander gazed after the couple. Then he cleared his throat as he faced Flint. "Am I still bunking with Matt?"

"Yes, that's your bedchamber." At the moment, that's where he'd stay but Flint would follow up with him to see if he wanted to change things around. "As long as you want it to be."

"Then I'll go with them." Zander tipped his fingers to his

brow. "See you for that pint in a few minutes."

The party strode away, Beck bringing up the rear. The Drake family reunited. The Fairhope family slowly pulling together. But his bride-to-be still kept from him. He'd give anything to have his woman at his side. Surely, Reggie would bring her home safely. But man, how he wanted to ride to her, to ensure she returned home where she belonged. He couldn't protect her when she wasn't near to him. Hell, he worried he couldn't protect her when she was. But one thing he knew: he'd do all in his power to keep her safe.

The blasted coven continues to grow, to expand and accept ever more witches and warlocks. The string of wagons and coaches, of mounted men, of wicked women, all announced the arrival of more creatures. I could no longer put off the inevitable. I must end this. Witches and warlocks showed their true stripes to me ages ago. They wreak hell and havoc on mortals with every breath they take. They lie and they connive. They cannot be trusted.

I know John Baker has betrayed me. He's chosen his side in the fight of good versus evil. He'll pay for his actions right alongside the young witch. Look at all of them, even a new witch and warlock to threaten me and mine. Once I locate the young witch, then my men will act. I'll see to their demise. It is time for the finale of the Fairhope coven.

Chapter Two

Rage hadn't consumed him in a very long while. Reggie glared at John, unable to deny the anger burning inside. Kidnapped. Threatened. Cassie in such danger she wasn't safe in her own home. He'd sensed the undercurrent of hate when he'd stood in front of the inn but hadn't pinpointed its source. He detected simmering fear and purpose combining into a vengeful spirit overshadowing the property. Not the welcoming spirit he'd been anticipating on his return journey. And where did his ghostly wife hide herself? Why didn't she greet him? He'd expected a warm welcome, an expectation left in disappointed shreds.

"It won't take long and you'll be with your daughter again." John met his glare with a knowing look.

Reggie had been out of sorts the entire trek home. Every obstacle, and there were many, rattled him. Rivers swollen over their banks to ford, some requiring days of delay until the level subsided. Mountains to climb, with narrow trails petering into even smaller paths. They'd had to unload the wagons and lead the animals single file at one point and lug the cargo up and over the tiny path to the other side where they could hitch the oxen and horses again. In addition, the rugged trail, littered with rocks and boulders and riddled with washed out ruts, broke wooden wheels and snapped spokes.

"It's been months since I've seen her and I do not wish to delay our reunion any longer than necessary." Picturing their reunion had kept him going. Kept him anchored so he didn't succumb to the temptation to snap his fingers and be home, lock, stock, and wardrobe.

"She'll be glad to see you, I'm certain. After everything she and her brothers have discovered about themselves in your absence, I mean." John glanced out the window with a nod. "Won't be long now."

"They probably have questions." Ones he'd put off answering for too many years.

Riding in a coach proved far more uncomfortable than being mounted on his own horse. He winced as his tail bones bumped on the thin cushion. The jouncing and jolting of the vehicle over the rough and tumble dirt roads after days of walking and riding did nothing to soothe his joints nor settle his anger. Reggie held himself stiffly to mitigate the side-to-side jostling of the rocking coach. What he really wanted was a steaming hot bath, followed by a shot of whiskey and a hot meal. But John's warnings had taken root in his brain and he had to see to his daughter's well-being before any other consideration. Needed to quell the wrath in his soul before someone paid the price.

"Almost there." John turned back from peering out the window. "Your daughter is very keen on having you home."

"She's written to me about the situation but I hadn't grasped the enormity of it." Feeling John's deep concern for his daughter fueled his fury. He had to calm down or relive the kind of harm his powers could cause in the blink of an eye. Literally. He didn't have much time to manage his anger, either. The glimpses of the passing forest through the flapping curtain helped Reggie gauge their proximity to Riverwood. His host regarded him in silence for a moment. "Who is with her while you came to get me?"

"Giles and Haley are both keeping her company along with my wife." John pressed his palms to his knees. "She's perfectly safe at my place, Reggie. No one knows where I secreted her. Stand down, man."

Reggie studied John's tense features, sensed his underlying unease. His anger surged again, flaring inside like a wind-fed wildfire. His palms sparked, his blood singeing his veins. Fisting his hands, he struggled to prevent accidental injury or worse inside the coach. "You don't understand, my friend. I'm not sure I can control myself at the moment. If whoever is threatening her shows himself, he'll die. No questions. No qualms. I won't be able to stop from ending their threat to humanity at large and my daughter in particular." Reggie rubbed his jaw with a hand, hoping the movement would help defray his taut nerves. "I've spent a lifetime trying to wrangle my anger."

"Are you saying you've killed someone unintentionally?" John tightened his lips as he regarded Reggie. "I would never have thought you capable of such behavior."

"I didn't mean to hurt anyone but I was beside myself with rage." He shook his head and gripped his kneecaps through the fabric of his trousers. "Like now."

"Reggie..." John hesitated, simply staring at Reggie for

several seconds. "You've nothing to be angry about at the moment. Cassie is perfectly safe at Riverwood. You'll see."

Studying his calm expression, Reggie forced a deep breath, then another. The memory of the bastard who'd attacked him, used his inferior magic to attempt to coerce Reggie into breaking his personal code of ethics by haranguing witches, swamped his mind. The black-haired sorcerer employed dastardly devices to badger and harass Reggie until he'd retaliated in kind. Until the building anger exploded in a rage of epic proportions with the merest wave of his hands, which forever vanquished the other warlock. They never found a trace of his body after the smoke and ash cleared. When Reggie's anger dissipated like the black smoke, he'd realized with horror what he'd done. His father advised him to leave for a while, to let tempers cool. He took the Montgomery Coven's annual summer gathering as the perfect excuse for a journey and left for Montgomery. Where he met Mercy, and her kindness, guidance, and optimism helped to stabilize his emotional state so he could control his anger.

Until now.

"I can't make any promises as to what will occur until I know more." Reggie grasped his knees, leveling his unwavering gaze on John. "Whoever is threatening my daughter must be brought to light. That's all there is to it."

He'd trusted John to oversee Flint but never thought the two of them couldn't handle whatever might arise. Looking back, he could see why that wasn't a smart decision. Once he realized his brother ran the carpentry company he'd hired, he should have trusted him to fashion the classy furniture he demanded rather than staying. His sisters could have seen to the accompanying furnishings without him continuing to put his daughter at risk. But he didn't trust anyone to create his vision without his supervision. A fatal error. One he'd not in any way repeat. He'd never be with his wife again as a result of his lack of understanding of the bigger picture.

"I can see you're distraught at your daughter's situation." John crossed his arms. "But I promise you she is unharmed and will stay that way."

"I'll see to it that whoever is responsible will not go unharmed. Count upon that."

He clenched his jaw as the driver steered the vehicle onto the lane leading to the plantation manor. At the sight of the landscaped verge of the drive, he leaned toward the window and lifted the curtain out of the way. Bright blue sky provided a sharp contrast for the white puffy clouds floating east above the ordered and shaped bushes and distant trees. Sparks erupted in his core, flashed from his fingers. Soon he'd see for himself his daughter's condition. Then he'd decide his next move.

"Those bedsteads go in the new bedchambers on the upper floor." Flint moved aside as a pair of neighboring men carried the first of many bedframes into the inn. "And, Daniel, if you'd kindly show these men where the dining tables go, that would be a help."

Moving day had finally arrived. All of the time he'd mentally arranged and rearranged the placement of the anticipated quantity of tables, chairs, sideboards, wardrobes, bedsteads, and more, he'd envisioned this moment. Flint's many years of perusing the hostelry-related magazines and newssheets, especially the pictures of award-winning accommodations, established the vision necessary to create pleasing room compositions. He'd feared Reggie would insist on doing the groupings. A twinge of guilt flushed through him. Reggie's required presence off-premises left Flint in charge of removing the old and adding the new furniture. A task he relished more than he'd thought possible. With luck, they'd finish before his boss returned. Another feather in Flint's cap. He shooed Daniel on with an impatient flick of his hand.

"Right this way, gentlemen." Daniel waved him off as he led the group of men carrying the table tops into the inn.

Parts and pieces of finely crafted wood furniture surrounded Flint: table tops, legs, headboards, frames, and stacks of dresser drawers to be carried in. He'd carefully inventoried the contents of the wagons as they were unloaded onto the carriageway. Beck and Abram had assisted him with sorting what went in which rooms while Daniel and Silas directed the workers on where to take them. Another pile grew by the stable, that of the old furniture removed from the rooms to make space for the beautifully turned and finished pieces.

After Reggie and John left, Flint had put out the word to several regular guests that he needed help immediately in order to swap out the furniture and furnishings. While Reggie had arranged for the vast array of items, Flint needed to decide what to do with the old furniture. Some could be repurposed into the family residence but most of the existing pieces would go to new owners. Daniel suggested offering it to another hostel or a boarding school, good suggestions he'd take under advisement in due course. For the moment, he focused on ensuring the new pieces were optimally placed.

He trailed a hand over the smooth surface of the oak dining table waiting to be carted inside. The rich honey color warmed beneath his touch, a smile lifting his lips. The choice of oak ensured a sturdy table or chair as long as it was properly joined. He inspected the workmanship, the seamless surface of the pegs inserted at strategic joints to secure the wood. He could barely see the difference between the round peg in the span of wood. All of the misery he'd endured without his boss around had been worth it. The beauty of the finish, the feeling of the wood, combined to yield a fine work of art, not merely a table. Where had Reggie located such a craftsman?

"You like it, hm?" Beck paused beside him, a brow lifted. "I hope so, after the trouble of lugging all of this here."

"It's beautiful. I've never seen anything like it." Flint skimmed the clusters of furniture dotting the front yard of the inn. "It's all so unusual, expertly joined, and perfectly proportioned. Incredible."

"Like magic, isn't it?" Beck winked at him.

The uncanny resemblance between the newcomer and his boss stopped Flint as he nodded slowly, unsure exactly how to respond to the question. Did Beck know that Flint knew about the family being witches and warlocks? Should he reveal his own depth of awareness to this relative stranger? Beck may have been told everything on the long, difficult journey home. Much could be shared walking along at a slow pace to prevent undue damage to their precious cargo.

In fact, Reggie had gone to Savannah to have the furniture specially made. A town where his family lived. Could it be? "Did you help make it?"

"Help? I should think not. It's my business." Beck widened his stance and crossed his muscular arms over his broad chest. "My workers and I made it, with a little—very little—help here and there from my brother."

"You do superb work." Flint scanned the wardrobes huddled together to one side of the steps. "The detailing is elegant and refined beyond belief."

"Thank you." Beck snapped his mouth closed, pressing his lips together.

What more had he wanted to say but decided against? More lurked behind the shuttered eyes of Beck Fairhope, of that he could be certain. Still, the senator would be duly impressed by the classic yet inspired design of the furniture Reggie brought back to grace the interior of the inn. The regular guests also stood to benefit from the upgraded appearance of the inn. The man shouldn't feel ashamed.

Between Reggie's new contribution and the improvements Flint had made over the preceding four months, the caliber of the property had grown more impressive while still welcoming. The homey touches of the pieced quilts and flowered carpets, vases of flowers and fronds, as well as the excellent food and entertainment all made the experience of dining at the inn or staying for a night worth the time and expense of their guests. As the weather cooled, more folks would take advantage of the hot springs along the falls to ease their aches and pains and seek relief from ailments. Even the view of the gold, rust, and brown draped foothills drew people out to relax with a cup of tea on the back porch. The inn's reputation spread far and wide and with good reason.

"You're quite talented at making furniture." Flint moved to stabilize a leaning armchair, settling it on all four exquisitely turned legs. "Where did you learn your craft?"

"Which craft are you referring to?" Beck frowned intently and walked around the stack of table tops to check the finish on the nearest of several sideboards lined up at the bottom of the steps. He licked a finger and rubbed a spot, then shined it with his shirt sleeve.

"Woodcraft, what else?" This conversation danced around the common knowledge they shared as if it were some huge secret. "Is there another kind you use to make furniture?"

Chuckling, Beck straightened from his inspection. "Sure. Witchcraft."

"You used magic to make the furniture?" He blinked, trying to assimilate what the man implied. "You didn't use regular tools?"

"Of course we did." Beck shrugged and then lifted his brows. "Oh, I see. You're not a warlock so you don't understand."

Was it so obvious? How frustrating to know his lack of magic could be discerned so readily by witches. He'd thought it was his secret by and large. Obviously not. "What don't I understand?"

"Flint, it's all right. Honestly. You do not need to feel inferior simply because you cannot use magic like the rest of us."

Like that statement helped. He folded his arms over his chest. "Thank you?"

Beck studied him. "I mean it. You have other fine qualities. I can sense them."

"So tell me how you used magic to make furniture." Anything to steer the subject away from his own shortcomings in the Fairhope family eyes.

His personal struggle with his self-confidence meant he didn't want to advertise his unworthiness as a potential family member. Sure, Cassie had told him he belonged but did he? Really? He had no magic, only the lame ability to see and talk to ghosts. But then so did all of the witches and warlocks surrounding him. His expert management skills useful in running the inn didn't stand a chance stacked against the magical ability to change shape, skip through time, or work magic in any number of other ways. The gun on his hip didn't stop any magical creature from doing anything. So what good was he to the family? To Cassie? He shook away his doubts to focus on what Beck was saying.

"Everything a witch or warlock does contains at least some residual magic. The flow of power doesn't completely stop even when I'm not thinking about using it. So each piece I touch contains some measure of my magic inside."

"So the wood harbors traces of your magic. Can you invoke it later?" The concept of magic lurking in the fibers of each chair and wardrobe unsettled him. His imagination took flight along with the vision of the chairs dancing or the drawers opening and closing on their own.

Beck guffawed. "Could be. I've never tried to reconnect with any hidden powers."

"Well, don't try it until after the senator has departed, please."

Beck exaggeratedly bowed to Flint. "I will do my best to honor your request."

Could he trust the man to do as he said? Flint gazed at him, trying to assess whether he'd been in jest with his overly formal response to his flippant request. The formal bow had poked fun at the idea of Flint's concern with the unleashing of magic from within the newly acquired pieces of furniture. Yet it seemed a very reasonable plea. Beck did not act with the same solemnity Reginald exhibited, so his levity should be factored into the equation. Flint chose to accept his word at face value. After all, he had no yardstick with which to compare his attitude.

Flint straightened his spine and nodded. "I appreciate your cooperation."

The matter was settled, except for the shadow of a grin on the other man's lips. Doubt ricocheted through Flint's chest, leaving a trail of worry behind. He'd simply have to keep an eye on him. As Flint turned to go inside to inspect the positioning of the tables and beds, he had the sneaking suspicion there was far more to Beck and his furniture than appeared on the surface. Could he trust the man? The question echoed in his brain. As his boss' brother, he'd have to.

The driver halted the coach at the base of the steps leading up to the manor at Riverwood. The footman opened the door with a flourish as John carefully descended to the ground. Reggie gripped the seat beside him, noticing tiny purple sparks around his fingernails. He dragged in a breath and let it out in a rush when his way was finally clear to exit the coach. He landed with a thud as his feet hit the dirt and then he stared up at the façade of the building, trying to temper his furious energy despite feeling exhausted from his trip. He peered at the front door as it opened, a young lady in a familiar calico dress stepping into the late morning sunshine.

"Pa!" Cassie hurtled herself down the steps, feet

pounding and blond hair flowing behind her, to throw her arms around him.

He steadied himself and her with a step into her assault. Her soft hair filled his nose with a light floral scent. "Cassandra."

The rage inside lessened with each breath. Holding his little girl, now a grown woman, in his arms again after all that had transpired in his absence made his heart bump his ribs. She was safe. Right there in his arms. He wrapped them tighter around her, every fiber of his being on alert to protect his only girl child from harm. His fatherly defenses and anger melded into a strong embrace. Everything John had told him on the ride from the inn to the plantation spun in his mind. At the top of the steps, Giles stood gazing down on the reunion. My how the boy had grown into a massively strong man. The flap of wings above Reggie's head startled him into clutching Cassie closer.

She pushed against him as she looked up. "That's Allegro."

"Allegro?" The blue-gray falcon swooped around their heads, diving and climbing in turns. She'd written to him about her familiar. He eased his grip on her to let her separate from him. "Your falcon."

She called to the bird and soon the Merlin falcon perched on her shoulder, peering at Reggie with interest gleaming in his dark eyes. Angling his head to one side, the bird assessed him with an unblinking eye. The falcon was a shade bigger than a Kestrel and out of its natural habitat along the coast. His mother had once bonded with a Merlin as her familiar, another shared characteristic between his daughter and his beloved mother. Their names and their familiars. Reggie returned the inspection, discovering the affinity the pair shared when he reached out with his senses to sample their feelings.

"Pa, I didn't know you were an empath." Cassie blinked at him slowly, tentatively probing his emotions.

He reflexively raised his inner defense. "There is much about me you do not yet know."

"Whose fault might that be?" She crossed her arms, the smile transforming into a frown. The bird flapped its wings, clutching her with his thin yellow and black claws. She shifted her stance, raising her chin with a defiant and accusatory look.

"Let's discuss that later. We should go inside." John interrupted the tense exchange. "Come. We'll have tea and make a plan."

He anticipated Cassie harbored a good bit of resentment over being kept in the dark all this time. He hadn't counted on the heightened level of mistrust flowing from her. He deserved it, since he had insisted on splitting up the family to protect them. The idea went against common conventions to be sure. The father should protect by bringing the family together, not sending them away. But the dire predicament they'd survived proved his solution the better option. Even if they couldn't yet see the reasoning. Perhaps one day he'd have the opportunity to explain it to his children, but today was not that day.

Once everyone was seated in the small, tastefully decorated parlor at the rear of the house, Reggie took a moment to assess the feeling of the room. John's daughter Haley, on guard and wary, occupied a seat by her mother's side as the older woman charmingly poured tea for everyone. Cassie had raised her defenses so he couldn't ascertain her feelings, but the expression, or rather lack thereof, on her face spoke to her inner state. Reggie didn't need to probe John as he could see the tension in the man standing by the fireplace. Giles proved the most interesting of the bunch. When he looked at Haley his heart raced but he shut down his response to her. What might they be arguing about? Or at odds over? Something stretched as taut and yet as fragile as a spider's web between them.

"Now that you're home, Reggie, it's high time you do something to fix things." Tabitha stirred her tea with a small spoon, then placed it on the saucer. "We've all been waiting for your return."

"So I understand." Reggie put his cup to his lips to delay saying more.

He'd yet to face his wife's sisters, Hope and Faith, camped out to badger and cajole Cassie into following them, which she refused to concede. Something to dread but he could handle them and they well knew it. They'd avoid him until he forced their hand. Which would happen ere long. The bigger concern, the witch hunter, was another matter. He'd vowed to never use magic on nonwitches because he had an unfair advantage. It wouldn't be a decent fight to wield magic against mortal means. Yet whoever was behind the witch hunt had targeted his daughter which made the whole thing extremely and dangerously personal.

"Pa, what can you do about the killings?" Giles stood beside Cassie's chair, within protective reach of her. "Ma seemed to think you'd have the answer."

Giles, the family Guardian, fairly vibrated with tension. Reggie tapped into his son's emotions and found dissonance. His emotional presence fought to unite but remained divided. Some grief, or fear, was tearing Giles in two. Reggie couldn't concentrate on resolving the larger threat until he helped Giles resolve his inner conflict. More importantly, neither could Giles concentrate on the dire matters at hand while fighting with himself. Reggie probed harder, Giles wincing as he locked eyes. Apparently, the young woman played a central part.

"First we need to clear the air between you two." Reggie glanced at the young lady sitting primly beside her mother. "What seems to be the problem?"

Haley straightened her back, the porcelain cup tinging in its saucer. "I'm sorry?"

Reggie closed his eyes to open himself fully to her emotions. Ah. There. He opened his eyes and studied her slowly blushing countenance. "You love him, yes?"

She nodded but remained mute.

Reggie looked at Giles and arched a brow. "You love her?"

"That's beside the point." Giles crossed his arms over his muscular chest. "She deceived me."

"No, I–" Haley snapped her mouth closed at Giles' sharp glance.

"Yes, you did. You said you wanted Cassie to come here to talk wedding plans but in fact you wanted to trap her. To let your father kidnap her, for goodness sake. You knew what he planned. You know how I loathe deceit, especially after discovering the many family secrets kept from me."

"I didn't know..." Haley placed her saucer on the table at her elbow. "I promise, Giles, I had nothing to do with it."

"She's right, Giles." Tabitha fixed somber eyes on the burly man. "John didn't even propose the idea until after Haley had left to do some errands in town. Haley couldn't have known."

"It's not like John would have harmed your sister, Giles. He's always been a loyal friend, one whom I trust with my life. And my children's." Reggie frowned at his son. "I don't understand why you'd be worried about Cassie visiting here. John is a friend."

"Is he?" Giles glared at the older man. "He's been mighty chummy with the gang of men we suspect is behind the death of so many witches."

"But Giles, remember that my husband confessed he's always known Cassie is a witch, as are Haley and I, and did what he could to protect all of us. He'd never harm his friend's daughter."

"I realize that now, but it doesn't change the fact—"

"It does. Think it through." Reggie stood and paced closer to his massive son. "Cassie wasn't in danger here. Haley didn't trick you. She didn't know what John intended. You're mistaken. You should apologize to her."

"I know you were surprised, Giles, but I didn't want to tip my hand or I'd lose my inside track to information about who might be targeted next." John splayed his hands for a moment and then held out one to Giles. "I promise you I'd never do anything to hurt your family. Especially since our families are about to be united through your marriage."

Surprise washed through Reggie at John's statement. He pinned his son with a stern look. "You're engaged to Haley?"

Giles stiffened. "We were."

"You should still be, son. She's done nothing wrong." How could he break off the marriage contract so easily? Especially with such a beautiful and loving woman. His own feelings for Mercy would have prevented him from giving up on her no matter what transpired between them. His son couldn't turn away from the love of his life over such a minor matter. He wouldn't let his son make a colossal mistake. "Don't throw away your happiness on a misunderstanding."

"Giles, please." Haley rose slowly from her seat, a hand pressed to her waist. "Listen to your father."

Time hovered in the room as Reggie witnessed his son weigh and assess what everyone had said. Reggie had worn those shoes himself many moons before. Making life-changing decisions based on known facts never seemed easy. Hindsight provided the real truth as to whether the decision was the right one. At the time of deciding, though, judging the nuances of each option, each opinion, each path forward could prove difficult. If Giles had grown into the man he had the potential to become, then he'd only need a moment to determine his own choice.

Giles hesitated, faltered, and steadied himself all without making a move. He regarded Haley for several moments with shuttered eyes. Then he met Reggie's encouraging nod with a brief dip of his head. Crossing the room to take Haley's hands in his, he searched her eyes. Reggie held his breath, sensing the shifting emotions, the changing atmosphere of the room. He hid his fatherly grin of approval.

"I'm so sorry, my love. Haley, can you forgive me for acting like a child?" Giles peered at her growing smile. "I should have never thought unkindly of you. You'd never do anything to hurt me, would you? Will you forget all that and marry me?"

The young woman searched Giles' eyes for several moments. Reggie sensed her slow acceptance of his apology just before she decided on a new course forward. Relief filled her as much as her love for his eldest son. She'd made a decision and aimed her serious eyes at him.

"On one condition." She pulled one hand free to hold up her forefinger as her smile grew. "That you'll trust me in future. Know that I'll never do anything to hurt you."

"Absolutely."

"Then, yes, Giles. I will marry you."

With a whoop of joy, he picked her up and spun her in a circle. Setting her on her feet, he bent to kiss her lips. "I promise to cherish you and trust you forever."

She kissed him back and then snuggled against his side, one arm around his waist. "I will cherish and trust you as well."

"Then we should set a date and make some plans." Giles leaned his forehead against Haley's for a moment. Then searched her eyes. "How soon would you like to marry?"

"I know a minister who could perform the ceremony." Haley glanced at her mother. "Do you think our minister is available?"

"Name the date and we will be sure to ask him after services this Sunday." Tabitha smiled lovingly on the happy couple.

Cassie crossed the room to clasp Haley's arm, Allegro balancing on her shoulder. "Sincere felicitations on resolving that disagreement. I thought you may never speak again." She pivoted and smoothed her skirts, gazing at her father. "Now that you've returned, take me home, please. That's where I need to be."

Reggie also stood. His daughter's mature assessment of the situation filled his heart with pride. Like his wife had always believed, the family would be stronger together.

Especially now that they could unite without fear of discovery. "Yes, it's time for all of us to come together and decide what we'll do. Let's go make a plan."

49

Chapter Three

The inn had once seemed her prison but now her haven. How times had changed in such a short few months. As soon as the coach stopped, Cassie hurried up to her room to change into a fresh dress before going to the dining room to resume her usual routine and put some normalcy back into her life. She tucked a stray strand of hair into her loose bun as she left the bedchamber she shared with Mandy. She longed to stretch out on the comfy bed, to rest on the quilt and process everything she'd learned over the last two days, but it was nearly time for luncheon. She had to find Flint, show him she'd safely returned and kiss him for good measure. Then she'd take her position at the piano to entertain the guests. Her leather shoes sounded on the wood steps as she scurried down to cross the parlor and on to the public side of the building.

As she shut the door into the inn's entrance hall, she heard a voice behind her.

"Miss Cassandra, it's good to see you looking so well."

She knew that voice, its deep timbre and vibrato blending into a special musical quality. She spun around with a happy grin on her lips. "Sheridan. It's wonderful to see you." She rushed to give him a quick hug of delight at seeing her friend and confidant standing safely before her. She'd missed his counsel and guidance over the past months while he'd been away. Somewhat reluctantly, she released him and composed herself as she addressed the petite, dark-skinned woman beside him. "And this must be your wife. Welcome to the inn."

"Pansy, this is Cassie. She's Mr. Fairhope's daughter I told you about." Sheridan's brown eyes twinkled as he introduced the two women.

"I'm mighty glad to finally meet you, Miss Fairhope." Pansy inclined her head in greeting and Cassie returned the gesture. "I'm also mighty glad to be out of that coach. It was a very long trip."

"I'm sure I cannot fathom the extent of the trials you faced in order to get here." She'd heard the guests talk, of course. Steep and narrow trails traversing the mountains. Boulders and rocks to dodge around. Ditches and rivers to cross. Lame horses. Bandits and chiselers. The list of dangers went on and on like the seemingly endless miles between the Atlantic coast and the Appalachian foothills. "I'm glad your ordeal has ended."

"The ladies rode in the coach which didn't seem any smoother a ride than being mounted." Sheridan grinned at the two women. "I think I'd prefer the saddle."

"Neither Reginald nor Beck would have permitted us to ride horseback all the way here, I fear." Pansy flattened her lips with a shake of her dark curls. "I did become better acquainted with Miss Scarlet along the way, though, so that was nice."

"I have yet to have the privilege of meeting my aunt and

uncle, but I understand they are quite an interesting pair." She'd been deprived of seeing them since she'd been away but now that she'd returned she looked forward to the moment when she'd encounter them. To see for herself how much of an "interesting pair" they might be.

Meeting relatives she didn't even know existed until a month ago might yield insights into her father as well. What had his life been like before he married her mother? She had so many questions. Questions about why he left his family behind. How he met her mother. What his family thought of them marrying and then staying apart for years. Why his family never visited him. Exactly what kind of relationship did they have? Knowing her secretive parents, though, she may never discover answers to any of her questions.

"There you are! Cassie, I'm so glad you're home." Wilma rustled across the floor in her long ruffled dress, holding out one hand as if to detain her. "Where have you been? The guests have asked about the music."

She loved her future sister and her enthusiasm. She beckoned to her to come to her side. "Wilma Hamilton, I'd like to introduce you to Sheridan Drake and his wife Pansy." Cassie nodded to Wilma, indicating her gaffe in interrupting the conversation so abruptly. The slip of a girl had more strength behind her than her appearance indicated. An expert with bow and arrow as well as with managing Daniel's moods, Wilma could hold her own among the Fairhope clan. Well-read, alert, and insightful, she'd be a grand addition to the family even if at the moment she'd made a misstep with her manners. "Sheridan and Pansy, Wilma is my brother Daniel's intended."

"Oh, my apologies for interrupting." Wilma nodded an

embarrassed greeting to Sheridan and Pansy. "I fear I forgot my manners in my relief to see my friend."

"It's nice to meet you, Miss Hamilton." Sheridan smiled at the young woman, obviously trying to put her at ease.

"And you." Wilma smiled her thanks and then met Cassie's amused grin. "As for you, I'm sure you're wanted in the dining room. Your father is in there, as is Flint. The guests as well, of course. You should go."

"Yes. I'm heading that way now. If you both will excuse me." She briefly waved a hand to the couple and turned toward the dining room. Wilma paced at her side, glancing fretfully at her. The girl needed to settle down. "I'm fine. Sorry to worry everyone by disappearing for a day or two."

"Flint said you'd only be away for a few days, but he seemed uncomfortable with you gone." Wilma peered at Cassie as they crossed the entrance hall toward the dining room. "At least that's how it appeared to me."

"I'm sure he'll be back to normal now." She entered the dining room and went straight toward the mahogany bar where Flint poured a variety of beverages for the guests, Wilma following.

Her father leaned against the bar, chatting with Flint while perusing the room at large. As she neared the gleaming wood bar, she detected an unusual quiver in the vicinity. She gripped the edge of the counter and tried to concentrate on what Flint was saying. Still, she sensed more souls around her than she could see with her eyes. A strong undercurrent hummed and flowed around her, beneath her, through her. As if dozens of people lingered on the verge of her awareness. Allegro came to her, recognizing her turmoil, and perched on her shoulder. Flint may be back to normal, but the inn certainly was not.

Flint bolted from behind the bar to wrap her in his arms, planting a kiss on the top of her head. "Thank goodness you're home."

"All safe and sound." She eased away, heat in her cheeks. "You're embarrassing me in front of so many."

Flint retreated back behind the bar. "I apologize for my actions but I couldn't refrain from ensuring for myself your well-being."

The conflicting emotions in her beau confirmed his plea for her understanding. He'd been beside himself with her away against her will, even though she'd grudgingly agreed to the necessity.

"Cassie, my dear, do you want a cider?" Her pa patted the counter in front of her. "Flint assures me he's ordered it from a neighbor renowned for the freshness of his product."

So he'd followed through with his idea of negotiating supply contracts with surrounding neighbors. As the guest list lengthened, what the inn's property could supply for itself had been stretched to the breaking point. The time had come to reach out to others in the community to provide the quantities of produce, meat, and beverages necessary to feed everyone. He'd bolstered the property's business and income through all of his clever ideas. Her beau demonstrated a unique talent for seeing to the comfort and needs of not only his family but of everyone who enjoyed what the inn had to offer.

"Thank you." Cassie met Flint's curious gaze with a brief lift of her lips. "I'm glad to be home again."

Beyond mere words. To the deepest recesses of her soul. The place called to her as if it needed her presence. Since her powers had been freed upon her ma's death, her connection to the very ground she trod had strengthened.

Centering herself, aligning her energy with the earth around her, came more easily each time she employed the meditative steps. The property seemed to bring out the best of the people, her family, who put down roots into its soil. Even Wilma, not a Fairhope yet, seemed more alive and skillful than when Cassie had first met her. Could the property invoke and enhance a person's abilities and talents? She chuckled to herself. Such a prospect wouldn't surprise her one iota after all she'd recently learned.

Flint slid a glass of cider toward her. "I may never let you out of my sight again."

"You'll have to get behind me." Giles strode up to stand at the end of the bar, grinning at Cassie and Flint. "At least until this mess is cleaned up."

"Where have you been hiding?" Cassie hadn't seen him since she'd disembarked from the carriage that brought her home. He'd ridden his horse beside the door all the way from Riverwood to Fury Falls Inn. As soon as they'd arrived home, she went to her room to change while he'd taken care of his horse. Having a few minutes alone kept her on her guard even as she enjoyed a few breaths without a witness. She indicated her pristine white blouse and dark blue skirt, the uniform she and Mandy had created for the waitstaff at the inn. "Of course, I didn't need your help to change my clothes, so all is well."

"Which is why I took the opportunity to do a walk around the property." Giles accepted the glass of whiskey Flint handed him. "Now we need to make a plan since Pa is home."

"I'm sorry it took me so long to have the furniture made to match my vision." Reggie sipped at his ale and set the glass down. "Beck was being Beck."

"What does that mean?" Cassie swallowed a mouthful of cool apple cider, washing away the road dust from the short trip home. "Uncle Beck had a hand in the furniture?"

"In a sense, yes. But now that I'm back and Flint has seen to the furniture being placed where it belongs, we can take care of the entities threatening you and others." He gripped the glass with tense fingers as his hard eyes traveled around the small group at the bar. "I could deal with all of it with a curl of my pinky, obliterate the men behind the murders, bind my wife's sisters' powers so they'd never harm anyone. Be done with all of it."

Cassie gasped at the possibility. He possessed far more power than she'd imagined. She had no idea her pa was such a potent warlock. If he had such magic at his fingertips, why didn't he use it? He'd closed down his emotional barrier so accessing his true feelings proved futile. The glitter of his eyes and set of his jaw spoke to the simmering ire he controlled with an effort. But he hid something else. Something he didn't speak about but needed to express for his own sake.

She squinted at him. "But?"

"I learned a long time ago to be circumspect with my powers." He tapped a finger on the mahogany. "I'd be just as bad as them if I used violence against them. There are other means to end their evil ways."

Flint wiped the spilled ale and cider off the bar with a clean towel then tapped the butt of his flintlock pistol. "I'll end their evil ways if I get half the chance."

Reggie blinked at Flint's claim but turned his sober gaze to his son instead of replying to him. "Giles, you said the sheriff is on to them, right?"

Giles nodded. "He wants us to stay out of it. But how

can we when they sit right over there plotting against us day after day. Against her."

If only they didn't all believe she had no means of protecting herself. Once, before her mother's spell broke, she relied solely on others for her safety. Now she had her own capabilities, ones that grew and expanded daily. Her ma had said her powers would grow as the family came together. She'd experienced it for herself. A new power would present itself when she needed to accomplish a specific task. Like when she'd been attacked and blasted the man away from her, knocking him to the ground. And doing the same to Mr. Baker when she'd felt threatened by him. She lifted her chin and stiffened her back.

Cassie felt the weight of everyone's gazes landing on her. "I can protect myself from them."

"History suggests otherwise." Wilma shrugged lightly. "As long as it doesn't repeat itself, you should be safe."

"My powers have grown as well." The surprise she'd felt when she'd knocked John on his back at Riverwood still echoed inside her. She could ward off an attacker with the wave of her arms and knowing so gave her more confidence. Coupled with her protection songspell, she could handle whatever came at her. "Daily, it seems."

Reggie nodded at her but his expression remained grim. "Now that we're all back together, your brothers' powers have united to bolster the strength and array of yours."

"Stronger together." She hadn't fully comprehended what her ma had meant by her oft-repeated phrase. A phrase at odds with having scattered her brothers to the four winds, but she was slowly beginning to understand the motives for her parents doing so.

"Exactly. And therefore more detectable by others." Her

pa stared at her and then sipped his drink, delaying his next words. "The reason why your mother and I had to break up the family to protect you all."

"From Grandfather, right?" Giles huffed as he crossed his arms over his chest.

Cassie recognized her brother's defensive gesture, the one he made when he didn't like the conversation and its implications. "My aunts want to continue his legacy with me at the core of a trinity. I can't be part of their dark magic, Pa. Make them stop insisting. Please?"

"That's something we'll work on together." He took a long draught of his whiskey, rolling it around in his mouth before swallowing. "I can't do that alone without resorting to force, which I will not do. But you have more power to stop them than you realize. Don't worry, I'll help you."

"Help my niece do what?" Uncle Beck's booming voice announced his arrival, diminutive Scarlet at his side. "Surely, she's strong enough and wise enough to not need your pathetic assistance."

She would recognize her father's brother anywhere. Not in personality but by similarity to her father's appearance. Uncle Beck matched Flint in height but otherwise was nothing like him. His black hair brushed his shoulders, not pulled up into a queue as many men wore their locks. Pale green eyes shone with merriment despite the intense conversation he'd barged in on. He laid his hands on the counter and she noticed the tip of his left middle finger missing. How had he lost it? Perhaps one day she'd learn more about his past, reveal any other lurking family secrets. What was one more secret among family, after all?

Flint raised his brows as Reggie guffawed. "What's so funny?"

"My brother, always the jester." Reggie punched Beck on the shoulder. "Scarlet, keep him in line, will ya?"

"I can only try." Scarlet slid onto a chair and primly folded her hands on the bar. "After all, I'm merely a witch not a miracle worker."

Cassie shook her head slowly, trying to determine where the joking left off and the truth began. She smiled at her aunt, taking in her vivacious nature as well as her petite appearance. One might even liken her to an elf, but she knew two other elves who didn't look anything like Scarlet. Like Beck, she had black hair, but hers hung to the middle of her back. Also like her brother, she flaunted the societal expectations by leaving her hair loose and not pulled up into a bun. Cassie patted her own loose one, but refrained from pulling the pins out and letting the curls cascade down her back. Perhaps later, after she'd finished her chores and entertaining of the crowd. Scarlet's nut brown eyes aimed her way, humor sparking in their depths. Cassie greeted her with a smile as she reached out with her senses to discover acceptance and curiosity aimed her way. As a result, Cassie was anxious to find time to engage her aunt in conversation. But that would have to wait.

She had one other question which required an immediate answer. She sidled around to her pa and laid an arm over his shoulders to draw his attention to her. "Pa, I've waited months to ask you this."

He peered at her in silence, studying her expression. "I think you comprehend my answer."

"Since Ma disapproves, I have to ask." She needed with all her heart and soul to finally hear him say it. A flick of a glance at Flint confirmed he understood and waited patiently for her to ask and her pa to answer. She swallowed her discomfort and addressed her pa. "Father, do you approve of my engagement to Flint? Will you give us your blessing?"

How did he feel about her question? Surely he knew she'd ask. Unable to stop her curiosity, Cassie reached out to her pa with her senses only to strike against a fortress inside of him. Not merely a wall, or a brick wall, but a castle's soaring stone edifice with a moat and snapping alligators on guard. She searched his suddenly closed expression but he'd shut down. Only for a moment. Slowly his eyes met hers and his Adam's apple worked in his throat. He nodded once and the clouds in his eyes dissipated. Coming home must have awakened painful memories, but of what?

Having evoked her mother with her question, she realized she hadn't seen Mercy since her pa's return. Why was she staying away? Surely she'd want to see her husband after all these months and the shocking subsequent events. Allegro shifted his claws on her shoulder, flapping his blue-gray wings half open and then closed to stabilize his perch. Cassie surveyed the dining room, seeking out any tell-tale shimmer in the air. Any hint her mother loitered nearby without fully making herself known. Nothing.

"My dear Cassandra." Reggie took hold of the hand draped over his shoulder. "Not only do I give you my blessing, I think you shouldn't put off your marriage any longer than you desire to."

Sweet relief surged through Cassie, flooding her with happiness and hope for her future. Scarlet and Giles both smiled at her, sensing her reaction to her father's declaration. Reggie stood and pulled her into a fatherly embrace as tears smarted her eyes. He approved. She couldn't believe the sense of relief, of joy, of excitement his simple statement caused inside of her. After all the worry, the longing, the hope, *he approved.*

"What do you say, Flint?" But she knew without even having to look at the eager light in his eyes. His joy gushed through her. "Shall we get married soon?"

Flint came around the bar to pull her into a more amorous embrace. "As soon as we can make arrangements."

"I'll start tomorrow." Cassie reached up to kiss him, uncaring who else witnessed their happy moment. Her father was home and approved of her choice of a husband. Planning the wedding could begin, but she was not quite ready yet. She squeezed his fingers and then looked at her pa. "First, I think I should help Pa take his things to his room. He might appreciate a little rest before luncheon." And her physical and emotional support, given his expression at the suggestion.

He'd resisted the moment as long as he could. Avoided contemplating it most of the way home. Climbing the stairs up to the bedchamber reminded him of crossing the mountains with the oxen-pulled wagons. Every step difficult, fought for, a challenge. His heart slowed, dreading turning the corner and crossing the threshold into the heart of his marriage. The room he'd shared with his loving wife for so many wonderful years. No longer.

"Are you all right, Pa?" Cassie waited on the upper landing.

She poked at his inner defense, a gnat easily swatted away. No one would ever know the depth of his feelings as he faced the bedroom he'd shared with his wife. His lover. His best friend. His most treasured and most private thoughts, memories, and emotions must remain his alone.

Now, he must be strong. He steeled himself as he opened the door and went inside, jaw clenched against the anticipated emotional onslaught. He glanced over his shoulder where his daughter hesitated at the open door. "Come on in, dear. I'm fine."

She stepped into the room, resting a hand lightly on his upper arm. "I know this is distressing for you."

"I'm fine." Whether he wanted to or not, he'd behave as though nothing had changed. He moved farther into the room, stepping onto the bare floor as if he might fall through the wooden boards.

The room hadn't altered much, except for the absence of the flowered carpet they'd brought with them from Montgomery. The quilt her mother had given them, that they'd snuggled under together, lay on the four-post bedstead, with its bold tree of life in the center. The wardrobe where their clothes hung side-by-side, much like they'd walked through life, still occupied a space at the base of the circular stairs leading up to her private enchanted attic. How she'd delighted in creating her own secret quarters where she could disappear, escape, meditate, and conjure. Over by the lone bedchamber window, her dressing table stood with its oval, mahogany-framed looking glass. Trinkets and boxes scattered across the table, futilely waiting for her sweet fingers to lift them, admire them.

All so familiar and yet the room felt foreign. Cold and barren. Holding its breath. Nothing like the warm and comforting space he'd left months earlier. When Mercy had kissed him farewell before she and Cassie went shopping in

Nashville. When he'd said goodbye not knowing he'd be obliged to journey to Georgia within the following days. Gone for months with every expectation of returning at any time. Then hearing of her death. Right in their bedchamber. Knowing she had died, that she wasn't waiting to greet him with open arms and kisses, staying away was far easier than confronting what he now faced.

He kept his eyes open, forcing himself to act normal. Inside, though, he fought for control as he spotted the dark stain on the boards at his feet. At times such as this, being a powerful warlock with the inherent abilities and ways of knowing could be seen as a burden. Like now, as his inner eye replayed what had transpired in the room, the horrific events leading up to the moment the awful, tell-tale stain appeared on the wood. Blood soaked into the deepest strands of the wood like a horrible memory about to be awakened. Mercy's last minutes formed a kind of terrifying story unfolding in his mind.

Mercy surprised in the parlor below by three men, the fear in her throat as she realized she was alone and no one would come to her aid. Being manhandled, hurt, tears on her cheeks. His stomach clenched at her terror. Taken up to the bedroom, whimpering as one man held a gun to her temple. Watching them ransack her private room and its belongings, stealing the precious, irreplaceable magic keys, before attacking her. Demanding her treasure despite her pleas of not owning anything of value. The pistol muzzle digging into her forehead before she wrenched away, only to be shot moments later. Left to collapse onto the flowered carpet. Left to die alone. He choked and sniffled before he mastered his reaction to what he'd mentally witnessed.

"Pa?" Cassie gripped his arm, then started humming

softly.

"I'm fine." Forcing the echo of her death out of his mind, he drew in a steadying breath. He scanned the rest of the room around them, seeing in his mind's eye Mercy seated at her table brushing her long flaxen hair. Mercy laughing as she helped him select a proper shirt from the large wardrobe, the immense cabinet that had been a right bear to wrestle up the steps in the first place. Mercy puttering about the room, straightening the curtains, rearranging the items on her dressing table, crossing the room to wrap her arms around him to kiss his lips. A kiss as prelude to more intimate moments they'd shared. No matter which way he turned, his wife's presence lingered. Still, he hadn't seen her ghost yet. Was she as nervous to see him as he felt? Cassie's humming increased and he aimed his attention at her steady regard.

"What's that?" He focused on her concerned expression as he tried to place the tune. "Greensleeves?"

"Yes and no." A shrug and curve of her lips preceded her sigh. "I've changed the lyrics to make a calming spellsong. Do you like it?"

"I believe it's helping. Good girl. I always knew you had talent." His gaze kept roaming the room, searching for Mercy. Not finding her, he met Cassie's expectant eyes. "I don't know that I can sleep in here. Not without your ma."

"Oh, Pa, I can't imagine how hard this is for you." She wrapped him in a hug for a long moment before pulling away. "I don't know why Ma hasn't made an appearance yet. She's usually quick to pop in unexpectedly for the startle effect."

"Sounds like my love." Reggie chuckled and slowly shook his head. "Let's go upstairs, shall we? Maybe she'll be more comfortable seeing me there."

"Perhaps." She fished in a skirt pocket and withdrew a set of keys, jangling them in the air. "Let's go."

He spotted the flying owl key and firmed his lips. "You've been exploring I take it."

"What?" She followed his pointed gaze to the owl key then nodded. "Ma has told us about everything. Well, I think so anyway. It's hard to know with her."

Reggie guffawed, despite his anxiety about entering her private attic. "She does like to surprise people."

A few minutes later they unlocked the attic door and eased into the shadowy domain. She crossed to the small table by the window and began lighting the oil lamp resting on the surface. He lingered at the door, surveying the contents and arrangement of the room. Books on shelves on one wall, Mercy's resources for all her incantations, simples, spells, rituals. The group of trunks they'd hauled north from their former home in Montgomery, filled with artifacts, magical implements, letters and papers, and most of all harsh and often horrid memories. Memories he'd hoped to have left behind but she insisted on keeping them under lock and key until an appropriate moment. Like there was such a thing. Then he noticed the clasp open on the small trunk entrusted to secrete and protect those papers and stiffened.

"What's wrong, Pa?" Cassie stopped in front of him to gaze up at his frown.

"Who's been in that trunk?" He marched over to lift the lid and rummage inside. After a moment, he sighed with relief. "Doesn't look like anything's missing."

"I'm sure Silas wouldn't remove any of those papers without telling us." She eased over to stand closer to him.

"He's been working on writing the family history, even though Ma objects. But then she tends to object to everything."

"I need to speak to her." He scanned the room, hoping against hope she'd hear him. Come to him. He'd longed for and dreaded the moment he'd see her because he felt so bad about not being home to protect her. But he had to have her in his heart and soul. Needed to know she still loved him despite his flaws, faults, and absence. "Where is she?"

"One way to find out." Cassie smirked at him with an arched brow. "Ma!"

"She's not a dog to call in for supper." His wife would not take kindly to be summoned in such a tone.

"It's the only way to get her attention.' Cassie hugged her waist. "Give her a moment."

"Do you really—"

The air shimmered beside him and then his beloved wife appeared in the light blue dress he'd given her for Easter, his final gift to her, hovering a few inches above the carpeted floor. Translucent and lovely, she regarded him with a careful countenance. Not wary exactly, but cautious. He could do something about that.

"Mercy, my love. I've come home to you as I promised."

"I've been waiting for you, Reggie." She smiled at him then, a secretive meaningful message just for him. "You've been gone a long time."

"Too long, I'm afraid." His arms lifted of their own accord, welcoming her into his embrace. "I'm sorry."

"Oh, Reggie. How I've missed you." She shimmered again but then her ghostly form became less see-through and more substantial as she shifted toward him, wrapping her arms around him in a hug.

Every fiber of his being felt at home in her arms. Holding her again brought back so many memories of their life together, their love for each other, their hopes and dreams for their family. All gone. Too soon, she pulled away. Or more precisely, her arms lost their substance, returning to their ephemeral quality.

"Ma, I'm glad you came when you did." Cassie sidled closer. "I'm glad you could hug Pa, too. I wish I could have one as well, but I know how difficult it is for you to hold a material form."

Reggie became aware of his daughter's probing into his emotions, his inner defense having slipped while he focused on reconnecting with his wife for the last several moments. He reached out to her with his own emotions and thoughts.

Don't share with anyone what you saw, what you experienced. Understood?

I won't, but I had no idea of the depth of love between you two. I wish you'd shown me that earlier. It's so sweet.

It's the past now. We both need...to move on.

No matter how much he longed for life to be normal, it would never be. How could it be normal without the love of his life? His reason for living? Suddenly, Reggie's anger flared bright at the realization he'd have to endure the remainder of his life without his best friend, his lover, his wife, all because of some ignorant, greedy, violent men. Men who'd already paid the price for their actions—one with his life according to what Flint had written to him. Killing his wife deserved retaliation. If he could get his hands and his magic on the vagrant he would. Let the hanged man's ghost show its ugly face and Reggie would wreak his own vengeance on him.

"Reggie, darling, don't look like that." Mercy shifted side to side, her worry plain in her ghostly eyes.

"I am so sorry about everything, my love." He could never fix the past. Could never make amends for his failure to protect his wife. His utter disregard for her safety by abandoning her in the wilds of north Alabama. "Can you ever forgive me?"

She shimmered as she drifted closer to him. "My darling Reggie, there is nothing to forgive. Now that you're home, everything will work out as it should. You'll see."

Mercy's ghost wavered until she was nearly invisible, until he feared she'd disappear into the air and never return. He reached out a hand as if he could possess hers in his grasping fingers but only clutched smoke. Wisps of her spirit flowed coolly across his palm. "Mercy, my heart."

"Reggie." She regarded him with a slight lift of her lips to convey her love. "I must go now."

"Oh, Ma." Cassie sniffled where she stood near the square table, a witness to the love between them as Mercy's haint disintegrated into nothing more than a memory. "Pa, I'm sorry."

He'd journeyed for days with the idea of seeing his love, of confessing his sins and asking her forgiveness. Of being with her once more. All of which happened in far less time than he'd imagined possible. She'd said she had to go. For how long? Would he see her again?

"Cassie, my dear, I think it's time we meander down for luncheon." He motioned to the lamp and snuffed it out as he assumed a more decisive attitude. No point in being morbid about his wife's passing. Others needed him to be strong, and so he would be. "Shall we?"

"Of course, Pa." Cassie hurried to catch up to him, locking the door behind her as he started down the circular stairs.

He'd returned home to what Giles had called a mess. Indeed. Questions abounded from all sides. Where exactly were Hope and Faith? He hadn't run into them yet but he sensed their presence on the property. Along with the other souls hovering and lingering out of sight. The men hunting witches dared to organize on the very property where the coven existed. Why? What did they really want? Then the upcoming marriages. When might they be wedded? What were they waiting for? Him? So much uncertainty swirled about him.

And yet there was one thing he knew for certain: he needed a drink and fast.

$$Chapter\ Four$$

How he'd missed the peace and quiet, the view of the foothills behind the inn. Reggie breathed in the nearly forgotten aromas: wood smoke from the laundry shack nearby, whiffs of the tang of fallen leaves, and the ever-present, drool-inducing scent of bread baking in the oven. His favorite place to be still and calm. He fought the downward spiral threatening to make him spin out of control and seek his own form of revenge on the men who snatched his wife from him. Clutching a warm mug of ale, he stared at the fall-draped mountain and tried to ignore the urgent impulse to go find those men, alive or dead. He'd deal with them on his own terms, in his own way. Creative and painful forms of torture filled his mind before he pushed them away. First things, first.

"My love, I wish we could be together forever." He crossed his ankles and looked at Mercy perched on the chair across the table from him. "But I don't know how long we have."

She nodded, the inn's wall showing through her translucent body. "I'm very glad you have finally come home to me."

He swallowed, everything he'd learned about haints coursing through his mind as he inspected his wife's ghostly form. How they lingered until they wrapped up their unfinished business. Some sought vengeance for their death. His wife's killers had already been brought to justice, even if he longed to wreak his own kind on them. Technically, they'd done their time or paid with their life. Some ghosts in his experience lingered in order to ensure their loved one would carry on, move on, not grieve overmuch. What unfinished business did his beloved wife have? He could easily see through her which didn't bode well. He'd apparently returned to her side just in time to say goodbye.

"I'm sorry to have delayed my return for so long. If I'd realized...I'd have returned sooner."

"I don't wish to be separated from you ever again, Reggie." Mercy smiled wearily at him, her lips not quite forming an upward curve. "Please, don't leave me."

"I'm not going anywhere. I promise." He had absolutely no desire to travel ever again. If he'd known how difficult trekking across country would be he might have never left. If only he had foresight, then none of this would have happened. His wife would be alive and well, his daughter still safely oblivious to the machinations of other witches. His sons scattered but living their lives without the threats currently hanging over all of them. He firmed his lips, refusing to speak the truth about how glad he was to have his family reunited, despite everything. He'd find a way to put an end to the upheaval in their lives so they could continue to be together. "I see Abram coming."

"I'm feeling a bit peaked, my treasure." Mercy rose to her feet, shimmering in place. "I'll be close but I'll leave you to your conversation. I feel like Abram wishes to speak to you alone."

"Very well. Rest easy, my love." He reached out to her, she doing likewise with her wispy fingers, as she disappeared from sight. The lump in his throat didn't want to recede as he wondered if he'd ever see his wife again. After the months away, he'd only had moments with her. Were they the last? A nagging question. Finally, he managed to dislodge the lump and turn to greet his son.

"Hey, Pa." Abram hesitated at the foot of the steps leading up to the porch. Dressed comfortably in black trousers and a brick-red flannel shirt, the youth peered at him with piercing blue, assessing eyes. He carried a plate mounded with sandwiches and a matching mug to Reggie's own. "I brought some luncheon out if you don't mind some company."

"Sounds fine to me." Reggie bit back his swelling emotion linked to his wife's imminent departure, smothering it under a blanket of forced calm. "What do you have there?"

His son positioned the plate between them on the table and then gracefully settled onto the opposing chair. He moved with such care, as if on stage, and yet his casual attire suggested he'd adapted to the harsher, more rustic clime. As a boy, the lad had been ungainly and awkward, a typical child gallivanting about like a bear cub playing with his brothers. Reggie suppressed a grin at the memory. Somewhere along the way the boy had refined both his appearance and his movements. He'd grown and matured into a fine young man.

"Ham and cheddar on pumpernickel with watercress salad on top." Abram selected a half from the pile and took a bite. Swallowing, he nodded. "Yep, with mustard. Have one. Sheridan will be disappointed if you don't eat his food."

Reggie snared a sandwich and took a bite, his stomach growling as he chewed. "I guess I was hungrier than I realized. That's the best pumpernickel I've ever eaten."

"Hm, same here." Abram popped the last piece of his half sandwich into his mouth, chewing as he slid his gaze out over the foothills. Lifting his mug, he swallowed a mouthful. "I've missed Sheridan's unique touches with the dishes, but Matt has his own finesse. They'd satisfy appetites anywhere in this country with their talents."

"You've been around, is that what you're saying?" With the refined manners Abram demonstrated with such ease and grace, he should have deduced as much earlier. His observations raised other questions. "What did you do after you left home?"

Abram drew air into his nose and let it back out slowly. "After you kicked me out, you mean?"

The truth still stung. Reggie had tried to rationalize his actions, to remind himself of the very solid reasons behind the decision he and Mercy had been forced to make. It hadn't been easy for either of them. Deciding to end contact with their families in order to protect their children from being taken advantage of, possibly forced into subservient roles they'd never break free from. His boys all had such potential, with or without their special gifts. If they'd been coerced by Mercy's father to serve him for life, they'd never realize what they'd lost. Not until it was too late, then they'd resent their parents. But by binding their powers, essentially hiding their true nature from them, they had even more reason to resent their parents. More reasons to question how their lives may have been different, better, or even more rewarding.

"I've second-guessed that decision ever since we made it, son." His comfort in his surroundings failed to ease the tension inside as he pondered his next words. He needed to see his son's eyes when he spoke them. The young man's piercing blue eyes flashed toward him as he paused. "It's eaten me up for years now. But look at you. You've turned out fine after all, which makes our sacrifice worthwhile. I don't know what I'd go back and change knowing how well you've grown and matured."

"I fought and scrabbled my way to be a senator's aide in order to make something of my life." The fine jagged scar on his chin, evidence of his ruffian boyhood, whitened as he firmed his lips. "All the time not knowing of my shape-shifting ability." He huffed a laugh and shook his head, slanting a wry look at Reggie. "Imagine the things I could have done in the senate if I'd known."

"Proving our point that you needed to mature before you were given free rein with your abilities." Reggie smirked at him, relieved they could still joke with each other. But he wanted to be clear on his feelings while they were alone. "I am proud of the man you've become just by seeing how you handle yourself and your commitment to your brothers and sister."

"Family is and always will be important to me, especially knowing what I know now about ours. The fact our family is growing also lends weight to my decisions." Abram turned as footsteps sounded on the wood porch behind him. He held out a hand, a big smile on his face. "Mandy, come join us for a few minutes. Please?"

Reggie skimmed an appraising glance over the petite

woman. Brown hair pulled back from her slender face to hang to her shoulders. A crisp white blouse and dark blue skirt flirted with her ankles. She wore a pair of silver earbobs but no other adornment. A simple, honest young miss, comfortable with herself and her place in the world.

"If you'd like." She glanced over her shoulder with a flip of her hair, then quickly sat sideways on Abram's lap, smoothing her skirt as she grinned at him. "Only for a minute, though. Flint might object."

"What are you doing back here if you're supposed to be working, then?" Abram arched a brow at her, but his lips still curved into a knowing smile. "A quick break, huh?

"Can you blame me? It's been unusually busy for weeks, and now even more so since word has spread of Sheridan's return." She leaned against his chest with a chuckle. "They should throw another cookery competition then we'd really be swamped."

"A competition?" Reggie peered at her, noting the laughter twinkling in her brown eyes. At first glance the girl appeared plain, even dowdy, until she smiled. Then her entire countenance came alive with light and sparkle. No wonder Abram became smitten. "Oh yes, I recall Flint writing to me about holding a competition. It seemed to be a success?"

Witnessing the rivalry between father and son must have been highly entertaining. Especially when they vied to prove who created better meals and treats. Sheridan had impressed Reggie upon first acquaintance as a man of honor and integrity, but then when his talents in the kitchen came to light he really dazzled everyone. Reggie had scooped him up to work for him at the inn, saving the former slave from a life of forced servitude so he could express his true, hidden talents for everyone's benefit. As a free man and respected member of the Fury Falls Inn staff. How Reggie would have liked to have seen him in competition. Another regret to add to the list.

"Indeed it was. We added some delicious items to our menu as a result." Mandy lifted Abram's mug of ale and sipped, setting it back down as she swallowed.

The two must be closer than he'd realized if she felt so comfortable around Abram. Enough to sit on his lap in front of the man's father. Even drinking from the young man's glass. He inspected their silent exchange of glances and the casual yet telling drape of her hand on his arm. Now Abram's comment about the family growing made sense.

"Is there something you'd like to share, Abram?" Reggie lifted one brow to encourage his honest response.

"I'm not the first and probably not the last to tell you this." Abram grinned, his teeth shining in the midday sunlight. "We're betrothed, Father, and intend to marry before too much longer. Once things around here are settled, I mean."

"I see. Nice of you to wait." Reggie smiled at them, aware beyond his son's words of the deep-seated love he carried inside for the woman perched on his lap. He reached out to Mandy's emotions, tapping in to confirm her own intense feelings.

She frowned slightly and pressed two fingers to her temple.

Too much. Reggie abruptly ended his probe and backed out. No point risking harming her mind and core of emotions. The hint of discomfort on her face cleared after a moment passed. Relieved, Reggie inclined his head toward them. "I hope you'll both be as happy in marriage as your mother and I have been."

"Thank you, sir. I'm very happy to become part of a large family for the first time in my life." Mandy glanced at Abram and then back to Reggie. "I'm an orphan, moved here from Nashville after I reached the age of eighteen to see what more I could do with my life. I never dreamed of meeting and falling in love with a man like Abram. But I swear I will do all in my mortal power to protect him and his family. I understand the risks and am prepared to do my part." She pressed a light kiss to his lips and then stood. "Now, I need to get back to work. Nice to officially meet you, sir. If you'll excuse me?"

"Welcome to the family, my dear." Reggie tipped his head to her, acknowledging her commitment to her future family. "I'm pleased to meet you as well."

She waved a hand and hurried back inside. Reggie watched her sashay away and then met his son's lingering smile with one of his own. "She's quite a find. But she won't need to put her mortal talents to use to protect you. That's what I'm here for."

"No, not like that."

Cassie sat quietly in her chair by the snapping fireplace, keeping tabs on the level of frustration simmering in her oldest brother while Aunt Scarlet tried to instruct him on improving his powers.

Giles focused on a distant spot. "I can feel his concern but not read the cause." He squinted and then squeezed his eyes closed. "Maybe...yes, he's worried about what comes next." He popped open his eyes to grin at Scarlet. "I did it!"

"Which brother did you sense?" Scarlet paced back and forth by the doll's house situated between the front windows of the immense room. "Abram? Silas? Where are they?"

The smile on his face disappeared. "I don't know which one. Damnation."

"We'll try again, but this time picture one of your brothers in your mind's eye. Go on. Which one are you picturing?" Scarlet pivoted at the apex of her path and returned across the floor, her gaze steady on Giles as he stood in the center of the room.

"Silas."

"Bring details of his face to the forefront of your mind." She sauntered back across the room, passing the two-story miniature house in three measured strides. "Got it? Good. Now focus on him, his entirety. Reach out with your inner eye to tap into his emotions, home in on where he is. Now, tell me."

Cassie shifted in her seat, anxious for her brother to succeed in strengthening his inherent abilities, his powers. Aunt Scarlet understood how her other brother Wesley, who served as Guardian for the South Carolina Fairhope nuclear family, could pinpoint where he might be needed. Uncle Wesley apparently could tell when one of the family needed his support and go to them instantly. While Giles had the strength and the gift of talking with her through the connection of their minds, Scarlet pushed him to expand and refine his talents. She intended to train him to be as powerful as his uncle. But Giles struggled to follow her direction and his frustration level increased with each failed attempt.

Giles stared at Scarlet but his sight turned inward, elsewhere. "Silas is sitting in the gazebo. He's quickly jotting down his thoughts in a notebook but his emotions are in turmoil. Torn between leaving and staying."

Anticipatory hope floated into Cassie's heart. She liked the idea of having all of her brothers close by. Of having her entire family, whether by blood or marriage, near. If only Silas might suppress his wanderlust.

"Now go to him, Giles." Scarlet halted in her circuit to sweep her arm outward. "He needs you."

Cassie saw her brother's flash of confusion before he nodded and then closed his eyes. Then Giles no longer stood in the parlor. She blinked and scanned the room, a smile spreading on her lips.

"He did it." Scarlet clapped her hands together once. "I hope he went to the right place."

Cassie grinned, happy for his success, as she tapped into his emotional state and discovered his satisfaction. "I believe he did."

"He has a good grasp of his abilities, but there is more for him to know if he's going to expand his strength to be able to thwart the powers of other witches. He possesses the immense capabilities that go along with being the Guardian, now he needs to learn how to use them most effectively."

"Are there other Guardians besides him and my uncle?" Cassie stood and strolled across the painted floorboards to stand in front of her aunt. "You seem to know a lot about them."

"I only know your Uncle Wesley and we've talked a good deal about it. Your father is a very powerful warlock, you understand. But Wesley looks after him despite that."

"Even from this distance?" Could one warlock protect another across so many miles of valleys and mountains? Such an ability would be incredible. "He must have amazing powers."

"No, unfortunately. That is why he taught me what I need to teach Giles. As Guardian he'll need to move at will not only when summoned." Scarlet twirled away, her long, black skirts eddying about her ankles. She tossed her head, sending her black hair dancing, and then spun to face Cassie. "Giles will need to be Guardian for everyone here so he must know how to sense where he's needed and then go there."

"I wish my pa would have been able to sense how much I needed him all this time." Cassie folded her arms, hugging herself as she relived the worry and fear she'd endured over the past several months. "I wrote to him, begging him to come home, but he refused."

"He wanted to, Cassie. Believe me. If it hadn't been for Beck's stubborn pride your father would have been here far sooner." Scarlet gripped her skirts in both hands, swishing them side to side as she studied Cassie. "Beck had his own ideas about the design and enchanted qualities of the furniture Reggie ordered. Gracious, I wish you could have seen the dismay on Reggie's face when he realized the company he'd been corresponding with was his own obstinate and opinionated brother's." She flagged a hand in the air, sparkles of rainbow colors discharging from her fingertips. "The sparks really did fly between them when Reggie arrived and discovered what Beck intended to create for him."

"What do you mean by 'enchanted'?" Her aunt's humor flowed into Cassie, revealing her opinion of her brothers' relationship.

"Ah, well, Beck had glamoured the already beautiful wood to make those who saw it desire their own. In effect, drumming up business for himself." Scarlet flared her skirts as she spun in place, completing a full circle before her grin aimed at Cassie again. "Reggie was livid and threatened his own spell on Beck if he didn't remove the enchantment. The two nearly came to a warlock's duel over it, but Wesley intervened to calm them down. A close call indeed."

"I'm glad my uncle stopped them." She peered at her aunt, her senses tingling with curiosity. "Though I can't imagine what a warlock's duel might look like."

"Indeed, you don't want to find out. Whether between two warlocks or two witches, or any combination for that matter." Scarlet slowly shook her head as she dropped her skirts and nodded at Cassie. "When two magical beings battle, someone usually dies a horrible, painful death."

"At least they worked things out and now you're all here even if it took much longer than Pa had expected."

"Once he and Beck resolved their...differences, which was about the same time that Zander and Sheridan appeared out of the blue, finishing the furniture was a matter of days and a few waves of his wand. And here we are."

"I'm very glad to have you all home." Cassie crossed the space between them and briefly hugged her aunt. "Now we only need to find and stop a killer and convince my other aunts to leave me alone."

"We can do that, do not worry." Scarlet shrugged and swished her skirts about her. "Or at least I believe my brother has matters well in hand."

Stomping on the front porch halted their conversation and made them turn as the front door swung inward. Flint staggered backward into the room, lugging one end of a rolled up carpet in his hands. Zander gripped the other end as they noisily carried the rug into the parlor.

"Cassie, my love, can you move over by the doll's house, please?" Flint indicated the empty space by the miniature house with a lift of his chin. "Thanks."

The happiness and contentment mixed with excitement tornadoing in Flint's chest brought a measure of the same inside of her. "What have you there?"

Zander and Flint aligned the carpet along the floorboards and then rolled it out. Subdued but vibrant red, yellow, and blue intertwined flowers, vines, birds, and butterflies graced the wool floor covering. The boost of color made the entire room feel warmer and more welcoming. Cassie met her beau's twinkling eyes with a smile.

"Thank you so much, Flint. It's beautiful." Cassie strode to him then, lifting up on her tiptoes to plant a gentle kiss on his lips. Then another. He'd talked about covering up the painted floorboards for some time and now his vision lived up to his promise of improving the appearance and atmosphere of the room. "You were right that the parlor needed one."

"I'm very glad you like it, my love." Flint returned her kiss and then took her hand in his. "What have you two been up to in here by yourselves?"

"We're waiting for Giles to come back." Cassie called out silently to her oldest brother. "He'll be here in a moment."

"Where did he go?" Flint cast his gaze about the room and then back to Cassie. "Should I go after him?"

"I've sent for him." Cassie nodded once. "There he is."

Giles popped into sight at the front door. "You called?"

Flint blinked rapidly but didn't react otherwise. "I'll

eventually grow accustomed to the ways in which you all come and go. I hope."

"Giles, let's you and I spend some more time working on your skills, shall we?" Scarlet ambled closer to her nephew. "You never know when you may be called upon to use them, especially right now with everything up in the air like it is."

"I have a bit more time but I promised Pa I'd meet him in the dining room for dinner in an hour or so." Giles crossed his arms over his chest and perused the others in the room. "But I'm all yours for now."

Flint drifted his gaze over the decorative rug, his pride and satisfaction evident in his expression. Then he cleared his throat. "I must see to preparations for dinner. If you'll all excuse me?"

Cassie felt his contentment like a snuggly blanket on a chilly morning. Then she peered into his eyes and a red haze replaced the comforting feeling with a vision of him aiming a gun with anger and dread shining in his eyes. Sensed his determination to protect even if someone died. She blinked and it vanished, leaving behind disquiet and fear for his safety.

Chapter Five

The dining room hummed like a beehive later that afternoon. Reggie stood at the elegantly arched doorway observing the efficient operation of the inn's dining service. Mandy welcomed and seated customers, ensuring either Larry or Isaac noticed their arrival and saw to their needs. Flint worked calmly and efficiently behind the beautiful mahogany bar, pouring a variety of beverages as the two waiters took orders from the steady flow of customers. Flint had replaced the yellow pine counter with a rich red wood, gleaming beneath the array of glasses and tankards. A young woman who fairly sparkled with life carried a stack of fresh napkins over to a table behind the bar. She worked in the kitchen; what was her name? Mary? No. Myrtle. That was it. Reggie didn't recall her looking so...alive. He'd need to ask about what transformation she'd undergone. Flint had indeed performed miracles with his efforts to improve the establishment in preparation for the esteemed senator's visit the following week. Once the lingering, hovering threats were dealt with, then everything would be in readiness. One thing at a time.

Giles appeared at his elbow. "Here for dinner or something else?"

"I have difficulty recognizing my own business." Reggie shot a wry smirk at his son. "I suppose I should be grateful but somehow I feel like I was holding back my own endeavors from success. Look at this." He swept his arm to encompass the dozens of men and smattering of women engaged in lively conversation and a hearty, delicious repast.

"Flint has done well by you. You made a wise choice in hiring him to oversee things in your absence." Giles gestured to an empty table near the bar. "Want to sit and catch up? I'm sure we have much to say to each other about what has transpired over the past few years."

Reggie gave a sharp nod as his gut clenched. The dreaded moment had arrived. What questions would he demand answers for? Panic flashed through him before he grappled the reaction into a calm he barely felt.

After settling onto the empty chairs, Reggie regarded his son behind his lashes. The lad had grown into a strapping, muscular, powerful specimen of a man. Neatly turned out in a tan hunting shirt and dark pants, with his black hair trimmed and the beginnings of a beard adding to the mystique surrounding him, he seemed ready to tackle anything and anyone. It had been years since Reggie had the opportunity to speak with him. Years in which Giles had learned to be a man without the benefit of his own father's guidance and example. Guilt swamped Reggie. He'd pushed his sons out of the house to fend for themselves. Was it a misguided attempt to protect them? Or necessary? Giles had turned out all right. But would Reggie ever put the repercussions of his and Mercy's decision behind him?

Not possible. They all had to live with the consequences, good and bad.

Mercy shimmered into view, hovering for a moment. Just long enough to let Reggie notice, to know she lingered nearby, then dissolved into nothing.

Something else he'd never move beyond—seeing her vanish and wondering if it was the last time he'd see her.

At the moment, he stood at a crossroads, in the middle of two conditions. Technically, he was a widower and yet his wife's ghost lingered. No clean break upon her death, a chance to catch his breath and then move on without her. He'd never forgive himself, what with her dying all alone while he was far away and unable to protect her. If only she hadn't died a senseless death perhaps he could accept it more easily.

His son motioned to Larry to gain his attention and then rested his hand on the table. "I'm parched. Whiskey or something milder?"

Reggie wrestled his demons, internal ones as opposed to literal physical adversaries. He'd come home to a veritable hornet's nest. Hope and Faith occupied seats at the table near the piano where Cassie played a tune. He didn't recognize the melody, but he did recognize the animosity in the witches as they glared at his daughter. He also sensed the hatred and fear simmering in the group of men his sons referred to as The Gang gathered at the back of the room. No need to turn to observe their shrewd and critical gazes aimed at all of them but most pointedly at Cassie. Having Mercy's ghost pop in couldn't help the situation. A fact she must be aware of since she only stayed long enough to make him miss her all the more.

Reggie sighed as he caught Giles peering at him with

understanding in his eyes. "Whiskey." Maybe the liquor would help assuage his angst.

Giles nodded once in acknowledgement as Larry stopped at the table, a white towel draped over his left arm. "Yes, sir?"

While Giles gave the waiter the order, Reggie strove to ward off the negative energy streaming from the lanky man. He peered more closely at him only to raise his inner defense against the emotional conflict warring inside of him. Larry was in cahoots with the gang. That much was certain, and from what Reggie could determine quickly, he'd attacked Cassie and failed. Leaving him in disgrace with the others. So he harbored not only a desire to kill witches but a personal vendetta against her, merely for thwarting his attempt and surviving.

"Very good." Larry nodded and spun on one heel, marching across the floor to put in the request with Flint.

Giles sighed as he relaxed back in his chair, his gaze traversing the busy room. Then he stiffened, sitting up to grasp his hands together on the table. "The attacking owl is back. Right over the gang."

Reggie blinked at him as he leaned forward to hold a more confidential conversation. "You can see it? That's both good and bad."

"Good that it says I really am The Guardian." Giles flickered a half grin. "Bad that it means trouble."

"Precisely. Larry is part of that trouble. He's working with them." Reggie shook his head slowly. "This is worse than I thought."

"Which is why we're all relieved to have you home." Giles glanced around the room, then back to his father. "The family is finally together again."

"I don't blame your tone, son. I know your life, like your brothers, couldn't have been easy after your mother and I sent you away. I wish things could have been different, but I do think they've turned out for the best."

"Ma said you did it to protect us, but I still can't grasp parents pushing their children out of the nest before their time."

"We had to. It's that simple. My family are good witches and warlocks, using their abilities to benefit the communities we live in. But your mother's side of the family had more ambitious goals. Your grandfather most of all."

"You feared him?"

"Yes. That's why we moved here, so we were outside his territory and hopefully his reach. Though that was always a worry, too." Reggie motioned to cut off the discourse as Larry approached with a small tray held aloft with two glasses of dark amber liquid. After the waiter had deposited the glasses on the table and left, casting a suspicious glance over his shoulder, Reggie lifted his glass and sipped, swallowed. "Living out in the wilderness afforded us some measure of anonymity, especially if any magical happenings started up. Since the people at the inn would change frequently, I mean."

"I don't think that's working very well at the moment." Giles inclined his head toward where Hope and Faith marched toward them. "They seem to have other ideas."

The two tense witches approached, so different from when he'd first met them. Back then, the summer gathering had brought out their happy personalities. The three sisters enchanted everyone with their lighthearted banter as much as their magical prowess. Then their father set his sights on the stars but without the means of reaching them. Unless his daughters formed a trinity to join their significant powers. But the dark magic he proposed turned Mercy against him and toward Reggie. A move which divided her family and set the rest of the events in motion.

"Reginald." Hope halted beside him, sparks glittering in her eyes. "I heard what you said and you should know better than to think any of us would harm you or your children."

Faith smirked as her familiar leapt into her arms, the black cat eyeing Reggie with unblinking malice. "We only wanted to unite our families."

For their evil purposes. Reggie bit his tongue with an immense effort. "It wasn't what we wanted for our children. They have far more to offer the world than merely following the dictates of their grandfather."

Faith glared at him at the mention of the powerful children of Mercy and Reginald Fairhope. He recalled how she'd always envied them having offspring with such varied and powerful abilities. The witch had her own hidden agenda, one he suspected involved the death of her nephew. But how? And why precisely?

Faith angled her chin upward as she stroked the cat cradled in her embrace. "You made sure only you had children to gloat over. It's your fault my nephew met his death. As I've always said. You did nothing to save him, despite all your claims of being a powerful warlock."

He shot to his feet, her prodding hitting an inflamed boil in his past. "I did not kill George and you know it. You both need to vacate these premises at once. I will no longer tolerate you and your insinuations on my property." He dove into his inner coat pocket and flicked his favorite ebony wand. The fine, polished wood he'd carefully burnished vibrated with anticipation in his hand. "Be gone."

Hope arched one sardonic brow at him as she whipped her own wand into view. "Or what? We don't answer to you."

Malachi leapt from Faith's arms onto the table while she aimed her wand at Giles. "He's also to blame, following your orders to let the boy die rather than share any of the praise from Father."

Mercy shimmered into view, darting closer to Giles. "You don't know anything, Faith."

"She knows more than she's willing to admit. Let's see." Reggie swirled the tip of his wand at her as he chanted an old incantation. She went rigid, her eyes casting side to side although her limbs remained immobile. He glared at her, narrowing his eyes. "What really happened that day?"

Hope slashed the air with her wand, blasting Reggie's wand out of his hand. "Leave my sister alone, you wretched man."

Mercy gasped and solidified for an instant before turning translucent again. "Sisters, stop!"

Reggie recognized the signs of his wife's increasing weakness but didn't have time to think more on it. He didn't require a wand to conjure his powers although he did enjoy the showmanship it afforded. No matter. He braced one hand in the air as he snapped the fingers of the other hand, the sound a blast in the suddenly quiet room, as he glared at the pair of witches standing up to his challenge. Hope went rigid beside Faith, her eyes wild with fright, her body frozen in place and unable to defend herself. "You dare defy me? If I could have helped your son, Hope, I would have. He was dead when Giles tried to reach him, beyond help. But there was something more going on. I'm not sure exactly what, but something."

He slid his gaze to Faith's wide-eyed terror. A flicker in those orbs gave him pause, recalling the events of the tragic day when he'd had to make the terrible choice to save his son from the clutches of his own grandfather. The day his son's cousin died in front of him. Giles had let slip the beginnings of his immense strength, his desire to use that power to rescue his cousin, his friend. But nobody could save the boy who had been killed. It wasn't any kind of accident. He bore the marks of witchcraft but Reggie only had his suspicions, no evidence, as to who had used magic to bring about the boy's demise. He hadn't witnessed the moment of George's death, only saw the body floating in the lake, Giles struggling to splash in to attempt to revive him. Somebody knew more about the events of that day, and he'd eventually find out who.

"Not here." Giles leapt up to intervene, holding up a hand at Reggie as he indicated the guests in the room watching their exchange. Cassie stared at Reggie from her seat on the piano bench but continued to play, switching to the calming spellsong she'd composed. Giles drew his attention with a shift of his weight closer to him. "Pa."

Reggie felt Giles' mental push to stop the wizards' duel unfolding in the very public arena of the inn's dining room. Scarlet's teaching already being put to good use. He sensed the urgency behind his son's demand, the concern as to the effect of such a display, and relented only so far as to allow his wife's sisters to move again. "Leave now or I'll finish this...discussion once and for all."

Hope flashed hate-filled eyes at him, grabbed Faith's tense arm, and ushered her and the feline out of the dining room without another word. Reggie didn't need to hear her thoughts, well aware of the underlying mix of anger, humiliation, and curiosity seething inside the woman.

Mercy sighed wearily, shimmered, and vanished.

Reggie resumed his seat, tense and angry himself. Angry with Giles for stopping the confrontation put off for so long. Angry with himself for starting it in the wrong place. He grabbed his whiskey and swallowed half of it, slamming the glass down. One day he'd settle the matter but not yet. He motioned to Giles to sit and then drew in a slow breath. "Now that's over, son, let's try to get back to where we left off."

The hushed crowd slowly relaxed and resumed their conversations, though Reggie felt their concern and curiosity flowing around him. He kept his attention on his son, willing the room to return to their own business and ignore the unfortunate incident.

Giles slowly sat down again, keeping his eyes on his father. "Where were we?"

"Tell me...how did you support yourself once you..." He couldn't even bring himself to say it. He'd felt guilty for so long about having forced his sons away when all he'd ever wanted was to be a good father. To teach them how to be men. To be warlocks. To provide and protect. He had so many questions in need of answers. "Where did you go?"

Sipping from his whiskey, Giles assessed him for a moment. "I foundered for a time, drifting from one town to the next. I met a man outside of Mobile who had his own importation business who needed some help. He hired me, taught me about the buying and selling of goods, inventories, billing, and all that goes along with it." He shrugged and took another sip. "I have a knack for business and eventually had my own importation/exportation business with my own employees. Including Zander and Matt after I came across them on that horrible plantation."

"That's impressive. I'm proud of you, son, for taking a bad situation and turning it into a sound and prosperous life." Reggie studied him for several seconds, pride swelling inside his chest. "You've become quite a fine man all around."

"Thank you, Pa. I appreciate that more than I can say." Giles angled his glass side to side, staring at the reflection on the liquid. Then met Reggie's patient gaze. "I forgive you and Ma for sending me away because without that push I wouldn't be who I am today. I wouldn't be here and have met Haley and have a clear path ahead. So thank you for that."

"With all that is happening, you might consider marrying as soon as possible rather than waiting for a time when things are quieter." Reggie hadn't really contemplated suggesting planning the event now but the more he considered the idea the more he liked it. "Maybe even all three of you loving couples at once."

"A triple wedding." Giles rotated his glass between his hands while mulling over the idea. "Haley said her minister might officiate. Could we marry here?"

"Of course you can." The three young couples had their whole lives ahead, assuming he succeeded in putting to bed the threats against his family. Which of course he would. "Talk to the others, see what they think."

"I'll call a family meeting, and send for Haley and her parents." Giles tossed back the rest of his beverage. "I will let you know when things are arranged."

Reggie watched his son saunter away, with a friendly wave to Flint as he passed the bar and left the room. He'd make a good husband to Haley. Reggie had watched her grow up over the last few years, her magic developing along with her maturing into a lovely young woman. He smiled to himself, glad his friend had finally confessed to knowing his women's witchy secrets. John had enjoyed keeping them in the dark on that score, aware he'd have to come clean eventually. With everything going on around the inn, the dangers surrounding everyone, it was time they all followed suit. No more secrets.

I tried to mask my glare but I doubt I succeeded. The nerve! The two of them sat there like nothing untoward had just happened right in front of everybody. The necromancers nearly fought to settle a dispute in the middle of the dining room. What really grinds my grits is nobody else seemed to realize the immensity, or rather the danger of witches and warlocks fighting with their magic. Anything might happen. They could kill everyone with a wave of their blasted bits of wood. My aim to end this threat must be brought to fruition.

I motioned to Larry and when he crossed the room to see what I wanted, I whispered in his ear that it's time. Time to rile up the rest of the men, to convince them of the critical need to act. To follow my lead. They must do as I command in order to save everyone from the witches. I have no other option but to rid the region of these creatures.

The clan of Fairhopes stuffed the family parlor. Flint imagined a time when only Reggie, Mercy, and Cassie occupied the many rooms on the family side. The smaller family group must have seemed quiet by comparison. Then Cassie summoned her brothers to her, slowly changing the dynamics of the entire place.

In response to Giles calling a family meeting, the sparsity in the parlor was no longer the case. Everywhere he looked he saw either a Fairhope family member or their special someone. Her brothers and their women, as well as Scarlet and Beck, occupied the chairs surrounding the large dining table. Reggie took his place at the head of the table, Giles at the side in the second place of honor. Hope, Faith, John, and Tabitha took the chairs grouped around the crackling fireplace. The Bakers had tagged along with Haley at Giles' insistence. Sheridan, Pansy, Zander, and Matt had all gathered in chairs grouped off to one side of the room. They obviously wanted to spend as much time as possible together as a family.

All told, eighteen people crowded into the parlor, not counting the hovering ghost of Mercy drifting around the room, unsettled and shimmering. He folded his arms as he stood by the fireplace, preferring to stand on the perimeter of the room to sitting at the table. Being in the midst of so many Fairhopes proved daunting.

"Settle down, now." Giles stood at the far side of the table, waiting until the chatter died away. "I'll make this quick since I know several of us have to get back out there before the supper rush begins."

"Is this really necessary?" Beck chimed in from his seat at the end of the table. "I've just become acquainted with all of you so I'm sure my opinion doesn't matter in whatever family emergency this is about."

"Be quiet, Beck. Let our nephew have his say." Scarlet

shook her head and pursed her lips at her brother. "If you'll behave, then this won't take long at all. All right, Giles, proceed."

"If you'll both stay quiet, I'd like to hear what my nephew desires to discuss." Hope stared haughtily at Scarlet, her open dislike for the other woman plain on her face.

Scarlet sniffed and turned to face Giles but refrained from saying more.

Flint smirked to himself at the friendly infighting between the family factions. He shot a look at his own sister sitting at the table beside Daniel. She seemed perfectly at ease with the entire clan surrounding her. Unlike him. Why did he always feel like an outsider? Like he wasn't measuring up to the yardstick of the Fairhope expectations.

"Right. The reason I asked you all here is to ask a question. Our father suggested that we—that is, me, Cassie, and Abram—not put off our marriages. I have to agree. With everything in turmoil, why wait? Pa came up with the idea of having a triple wedding here at the inn." Giles scanned the reactions on the faces gazing up at him. "Perhaps out at the gazebo where we could invite the entire family as well as the guests to join in witnessing the happy unions."

Hope and Faith both shifted in their chairs, Faith's familiar curled in her lap. They struggled to hide their pleasure behind carefully controlled facades of disinterest. Flint huffed to himself at the thinly disguised anticipation of a wedding. Women. Even if they were powerful, angry witches most of the time, they still craved the romantic nature of a wedding ceremony and all that went with it.

Haley sat up straighter in her chair by the fire,

addressing her betrothed. "When?"

"Soon. The sooner the better." Giles cast a loving smile on her.

Silas pulled his notebook out from his vest pocket and opened it, jotting notes with a pencil stub. Then he frowned and pierced Giles with a sharp look. "Will you be sending invitations? What about gifts for those who attend? We'll need time for both of those."

"Is it necessary?" Matt spoke up from his seat. "I mean, we can give them a feast afterward, and the only people we'd want to invite are already here. And you're not required to give gifts, are you?"

"A fine point, Matt." Giles nodded at him. "Then when?"

"I agree with the sooner the better." Reggie pushed to his feet and surveyed the others. "Life is too uncertain to wait. How quickly can you gals put together your wedding outfits?"

Flint didn't have empathic abilities but he could sense his boss felt some kind of urgency about seeing his children wed. Reggie flashed a glance at Mercy, lingering for a moment, then let his gaze drift over the other countenances around the room. Mercy seemed more translucent than earlier. Perhaps her time to linger approached an end and thus motivated the concept of a triple wedding. Then again, Reggie looked rather tired and wan after his journey home. Or after confronting the challenges upon arriving at the inn. Something more motivated his desire to see the three marriages happen soon.

"I have some ideas on attire, after all I once was called a dandy by my soon-to-be brother by marriage." Abram smirked at Flint and then jumped to his feet, mischief in his grin. "Let's see now... How about this one?"

Abram shifted into Cassie's form with a flowing, aqua gown, sequins dotting the bodice, filmy sleeves gathered at the elbow. He twirled slowly around and then strolled into the center of the floor to a smattering of applause and chuckles. Pansy pressed her fingertips to her open mouth while Sheridan tried to calm her with a hand on her upper arm.

Flint studied the aged couple, aware that Pansy needed to become accustomed to the magic and enchantments everyone else took for granted. She didn't seem overly upset, though, which showed her resolve to fit in to her new home and extended family. How admirable. The more he discovered about Pansy, the more he appreciated her. No wonder Sheridan loved her so much.

As he loved Cassie. His heart soared with delight at the clear path ahead to their union. Contemplating their marriage lightened his mood and his step. Finally, they had her father's blessing which enabled them to see their future together. After months of indecision and doubt, his confidence in their pending nuptials now flew as high and strong as Allegro on an updraft. The tension in his shoulders eased as he observed her brother's attempt to bring a touch of levity to the occasion.

"I'm glad you liked Cassie's." Abram chuckled as he curtseyed, flouncing the long skirts, and then quirked one brow. "Or perhaps this one for my girl."

Again he shifted, this time into Mandy's form wearing an ankle-length cream and white gown arrayed with rhinestones and ribbons, a lacy hat perched on his head. Applause erupted from the group as he exaggeratedly curtseyed. Pansy joined in alongside Sheridan this time, readily accepting Abram's comical antics.

"Enough, Abram." Giles grinned in spite of the harsh tone of his command. "We don't have much time."

"Just trying to help." With a wink, Abram shifted back into himself, his dark green trousers and cream shirt a far cry from the colorful gowns he'd just donned, and resumed his seat. "I'm sure the ladies can pull together something appropriate no matter what date we settle on."

"I don't know about that." Cassie worried her bottom lip for a second. "When I went to Haley's we'd meant to look at options but I was too distracted to focus on such frippery then. And I had no idea we'd be having the ceremony so soon."

"We'll work together to make sure we have a respectable event." Flint dropped his arms to his sides as he stepped toward Cassie. "I can go pick up fabrics in town if that will help."

Haley poked a finger at the ceiling to draw their attention. "That will take too long, I believe. But I have many gowns tucked away in trunks. I'll bring some dresses here and we can all look through and decide what might be remade or refreshed to be suitable."

"That would save time, indeed." Wilma tapped her hand on the armrest. "I only wish Daniel and I could join in, make it a foursome, but that would be unfair to my sister."

Flint regarded Wilma with a tender spot in his soul for how caring she'd become as she matured. She always considered others' feelings and preferences. Yet she had a core of steel she didn't often reveal to others. Having grown up with her, he could recognize the signs. Her raised chin. The sheen in her eyes. A humming tension in the set of her shoulders. But most concerning, the near whisper she dropped her voice to when she really wanted your attention. One had better pay close attention when that happened. At the moment, she acted serene and comfortable. A very good sign indeed.

"So when do we want to tie this knot?" Cassie peered around the room, her usually sparkling eyes dimmed with concern. "How much time do we have to plan the festivities?"

Flint considered the options, the upcoming events and plans already laid. Then he stepped forward to gain everyone's attention. "What about two days? We're already planning a party for Allhallows the day after, so the property is prepared. The food is already purchased in abundance. You'll just need to fix your dress and fashion your hair, the grooms can wear their best suits, and we can be wed."

"A very good idea." Scarlet sauntered about the parlor, her long, green skirts swishing and rustling as she moved around. "Most everything is prepared and ready, so why not?"

"One obstacle I can see. We'll need a minister." Zander darted his gaze from face to face. "Do we know one who can officiate on such short notice?"

"I do and he will." John flitted a smile about the group. "Let me take care of that."

"Then that's it. In two days you get married." Tabitha grinned, delight in her twinkling eyes and rosy cheeks.

Stunned silence settled on the room as each person pondered the many tasks necessary to throw an elegant if hurried affair. An amused grin slowly pulled on Flint's face as mouths fell open and eyes widened at the enormity of the happy decision. Then Cassie stood up and walked closer to him.

"Are you sure? We have much to do, if so." She peered at him, the slight frown very slowly changing to a gentle smile. "Two days, is it?"

Pansy coughed delicately, causing every head to swivel her direction. "If I may be of assistance, I was a seamstress back in Georgia. I'm fast with a needle."

Haley glanced at the older woman with a growing smile. Then she surveyed the other reactions around her. "If there's no objections?"

"I wouldn't think so." Flint pulled Cassie close to him, joy blossoming inside his chest. Cassie would soon be his forever. His wife. And he would be her husband until death parted them. Marriage to her was the kind of life sentence he'd give anything to have. His smile grew at the quizzical glances between the others in the room, checking for any possible negative responses. "Then let's get busy."

Chapter Six

*L*ater that evening, Reggie settled into a comfortable chair for a few private minutes to watch the night shadows come down over the foothills. He stretched his legs out in front of him, resting his interlocked fingers on his belly. Somewhere in the distance, an owl called out to its mate, the soft hooting captivating in the twilight. The day had been eventful with a mix of good and bad moments flickering through his thoughts. However, soon he would welcome new members into his family.

"Mr. Fairhope, might I sit with you for a moment?" Sheridan edged closer on the porch, a hesitant expression on his face.

"Call me Reggie, please. I thought we'd agreed to that already." He waved the older man into the seat across the table. "We're friends and colleagues after all."

Sheridan sat down and slowly relaxed back in the chair. "It's a mighty hard habit to break but I'll try."

Unsure how to respond to the reference to Sheridan's former condition as a slave, Reggie pondered the darkening mountain as if seeking answers to age-old questions. Trying to imagine Sheridan's prior life left him floundering and angry in turns. Imagine having no say in the direction of your life. Of living solely to serve another person with little opportunity to grow as a man. The opportunities Reggie could take advantage of were not available to enslaved men. While not every slave suffered at their master's hands, enough had been beaten and tortured in one form or another to endorse the image of a present-day master similar to the Biblical version of a slave driver, bull whip in hand, refusing other men even a sip of water to slake their thirst.

Reggie pivoted his head to assess his friend's state of mind, probing his jumbled emotions with a gentle nudge. As he surmised. "Sheridan, I am glad to call you friend."

Sheridan stared off into the distance. "If it weren't for your kindness, I wouldn't be sitting here nor have found my family again."

"We were brought together due to a horrible accident, but I believe Fate had a hand in our meeting as well."

A carriage had tumbled down the side of a hill, almost hidden among brush and trees edging the dirt lane. Reggie nearly rode past without even a second glance but something made him rein in and inspect the damage more closely. He'd found Sheridan unconscious along with another couple, the vehicle shattered and the horses injured and trapped in their traces. Untangling everyone and everything took many agonizing minutes. The couple turned out to be the plantation owners, and Sheridan their driver. The master had threatened to flay him alive for wrecking the carriage and injuring his fine horseflesh, but Reggie had stepped in. He'd essentially flung money at the man and then took Sheridan with him, his papers signed to confirm his new status as a freeman. When Sheridan demonstrated how skilled a cook he was, as opposed to a horseman, Reggie had suggested a switch in his roles and the rest fell into place without any more accidents.

"You were never much good with handling horses." Reggie stared at the darkening mountain, reliving the past years of working with Sheridan. "I hope now you'll have a fresh start with Pansy and the boys."

Clearing his throat, Sheridan shifted in his seat. "Thank you for everything you've done for me... Reggie."

"My great pleasure. I am pleased Giles brought Matt and Zander along with him, or you wouldn't have reunited with your sons."

"And you freed Pansy so she could come home to us all." The older man paused, his gaze sweeping the row of outbuildings in the rear of the inn. "She's the greatest gift you could give me."

"Thank goodness Cassie thought to ask me to look for her. Pansy was not in a good situation. But now she's free and safe." He glanced at the man, aware of his deep gratitude and hope inside. "Like Mercy always said, a family is stronger together. Now you'll have the chance to witness the coming together of your family once again. Will you stay on or start anew?"

"I don't have any plan to leave. I've been content with my work here." Sheridan contemplated Reggie for several hoots of the owl. "Unless you're wanting us to move on?"

"Not at all." The customers would revolt if they discovered Sheridan no longer worked at the inn. "You're welcome to remain in your position for as long as you want it."

Sheridan nodded and then laid his head on the back of

the chair. "Pansy told me she thinks this place is a fine place to live and I have to agree with her. I suspect the boys will find their own way, their own women, too."

"More than likely." Reggie pushed to his feet, striding to the edge of the porch to survey the yard. Why did a new well need to be dug? Although the location seemed more convenient, when he'd left the original well still functioned and provided ample water. He pointed to the freshly dug earth surrounding the new well. "Why did Flint have a new well put in?"

"The old one was tampered with by that young boy's no-good pa." Sheridan also stood and ambled over to stand next to Reggie, peering into the growing darkness. "Mr. Baker leant him some slaves to do the work. Cassie wasn't too happy about that, neither."

"Humph." With good fortune, slavery would be abolished during his lifetime. Why did any man believe he had the right to own another? To dictate every action of another person? Reggie would free them all if he had the funds to pay off the owners. Would doing so make him as bad a person by confirming the supposed monetary value of a human being? Bah! He drew in a deep breath and let it out slowly. An answer lay somewhere but he didn't know what might happen to end the dastardly practice of slavery. "I'm not surprised to hear my daughter is against slavery as well."

"Your daughter is a right fine young woman." Sheridan leaned against a column as he slowly turned his head to regard Reggie. "She'll make a fine wife and mother."

"She values your friendship. I think she'll be happy to hear you're planning to stay. As long as you and Pansy are content here, she'll be satisfied with your company."

"What about you? Are you content now you're home?" Sheridan peered at him, his intense gaze making Reggie squirm.

He'd longed for home the entire time he'd been away. Guilt had consumed him after his wife was murdered. Cassie, his only daughter, remained on her own and vulnerable. When she'd conveyed she'd written invitations to her brothers in a letter to him, relief replaced the guilt. But only for a short while. Knowing his sons might respond by attending her, he could delay his return until the requisite furniture suited his vision. Others might disagree with his decision to remain in Georgia despite the risk to his daughter, but he'd faced opposing goals and choices. With Mercy dead and buried, what could he actually do if he returned before his mission was completed? John had reassured him that Flint had matters under control, and then with each of her brothers showing up he knew they'd have the necessary powers and means of defending her. So he'd pushed the guilt aside and focused on finishing what he went there to accomplish. He'd vowed to make amends to his family for his selfish decision, and so far they'd accepted his apology. Now he just had to live with the ongoing emotional ramifications of his decision.

"I can't answer your question at the moment, Sheridan, because things are still so up in the air." He sighed again, aware of the turmoil surrounding him. "I'm still sorting through my options."

Sheridan pivoted to face him, exploring his countenance with wide eyes before nodding once.

His look told Reggie of his growing understanding as to what those options actually entailed. In truth, Reggie could only see one path forward. Despite having come home, he still felt adrift. His beloved wife's ghost had waited for his return but how long did he have with her? His daughter and sons each verged on beginning new married lives of their own, heading toward their own homesteads and children. Leaving him ultimately alone even though he'd probably have grandchildren one day. Could he ever truly be happy without Mercy at his side? Especially in the building they'd designed and lived in for so many years. He'd have to find another place to live. But where remained elusive. He didn't want to live without Mercy. Nor did he plan to remarry.

He returned Sheridan's level gaze and then returned the nod. "I'm not exactly sure what will happen next, but I am glad you're here and intend to stay. Thank you."

"I'm honored to continue to look out for Cassandra and the rest of your family as best I can." Sheridan gazed at him and then a slow smile crept onto his lips. "I don't have the magical finesse you and they do, of course. So hopefully they won't get into too much trouble."

Lightning flashed over the mountain, followed a few seconds later by a thunderous rumble. A storm brewed nearby and the air crackled with electricity, presaging a change in the atmosphere around the inn. Fall thunderstorms were not common so his instincts warned of an impending danger. But of what kind?

"It's a relief to know that if something happened to me, they'll have a strong group of people to support them." If only they could stay out of trouble, then the rest of his worries would dissipate. "Now if you'll excuse me, I have a private tea to get to."

Thunder rumbled outside, vibrating the tray of chocolate and tea Cassie carried into the parlor. Giles held the door open for her before following her to the group of chairs around the fireplace. Over the past few months, the number of seats had increased to match her growing family and their associated friends. The murmur of conversation stopped as she sauntered closer. John and Tabitha sat farthest from the fire, Haley and an empty chair to their right. Giles crossed to sit in the seat beside his betrothed while Cassie placed the tray on the low table in the center of the group. Reggie and Flint sat opposite Haley and Giles, a chair closest to the fire waiting for her.

"My apologies for taking so long in the kitchen. Matt and Sheridan were having a discussion about what to serve tomorrow and the maids had differing opinions." Cassie perched on the edge of the chair then pulled a cup and saucer closer to her. "I think it is all settled now though. Chocolate or tea?"

"Chocolate, please." Tabitha accepted the beverage and then took a sip. A thud sounded outside, as if up on the roof, briefly drawing her gaze to the ceiling. She nestled the cup on the saucer. "I wonder if the rumors are true given the bump on the roof. Reggie, you do know the history of this property, don't you? Did the previous owner tell you about the rumors?"

Cassie handed round tea and chocolate, finally giving herself a cup of chocolate. She faced Tabitha, anticipating a good tale for such a stormy evening.

Reggie drained his chocolate and set down the cup and saucer on the table. He shook his head. "What rumors?"

"Oh, dear, I thought you knew." Tabitha glanced at her husband, exchanging a rueful expression. "Well, you should know even at this late date."

Holding her breath, Cassie watched the play of emotions on her father's face, felt the conflict simmering in his chest. Until he shifted his gaze to hers and raised his inner barrier. Whatever he truly felt, he wanted to keep private. She raised her own protection as she waited for Tabitha to continue.

"John, why don't you begin this story. I believe you know more about it than I do." Tabitha deposited her saucer on the table and sat back in her seat.

Cassie gripped her saucer with one hand, the fingers of the other wrapped into the porcelain handle of her cup. No rumors had circulated in her presence. What kind of legend or myth might they involve? Surely, people didn't make up tales about the property. Or at least not based on factual encounters. She trembled as her imagination filled her head with dreadful possibilities. When the cup chinked against the saucer, she set it down. John seemed very serious as he prepared to tell the story.

"Long before either of us moved here, Reggie, this area was known for being haunted. Or at least suspected of such. People reported hearing wolves howling but never seeing any roaming about."

"Don't forget the lights, dear." Tabitha gestured with a limp wrist. "They're most difficult to comprehend. Some thought they were Stingy Jack's lights."

John nodded as he quirked his brows. "Indeed. Some men claim they saw flashes of lights, all different colors too, winking and blinking among the trees, across the fields, but they could never determine their source."

"Probably fireflies." Giles shrugged as he looked uneasily around the small group. "Nothing to worry about."

"No, not fireflies. Not anything anyone could explain." John regarded Giles for a couple of beats and then skimmed his gaze around the others. "In addition, there have been reports of ghosts walking the hills, even relaxing in the springs up there."

Cassie blinked at the concept of more haints lingering about the property. "Ghosts. Are you certain?"

"I haven't heard any of this. The seller should have told me." Reggie's inner agitation shook his protective barrier, letting Cassie experience moments of his concern. He didn't reject the notion out of hand but seemed resigned to their presence. As if he'd sensed the spirits for himself. "Are you certain?"

Mercy shimmered into view and glided closer to Reggie. "Yes, there are many spirits around here. I can sense them all about just like you can. There's no doubt of their presence." She glanced at Flint, Cassie suddenly aware that Flint was uncomfortable. "Right, son?"

Flint firmed his lips as he gazed back at Mercy's ghost. "I know of one that arrived before your death, Mrs. Fairhope. A Revolutionary soldier I spoke with and sent on his way. And of course, the crone whose haint visited us."

Since there were ghosts around, how might they be affected by Allhallows Eve? After all, it was the time of year when the boundary between the everyday world and the afterlife thinned so much the living could reconnect with the dearly departed. Or even the not-so-dearly departed. What unfinished business might the spirits have that they might need help with? She swallowed back bitter bile, thinking of how ghosts might want to seek revenge instead of assistance.

"Indeed." Reggie stared at him. "You didn't say anything about such apparitions before."

"I didn't want to confirm the rumors of my ability to speak with ghosts." Flint slowly shook his head. "Not that it's a special ability since all of you can do so."

His unease grew along with his insecurity. Hadn't he already come to grips with his lack of confidence? Cassie took his hand in hers and squeezed gently. He had to know he, as himself, was the man she loved. He didn't need to try to be something more or greater than himself for her to want to marry him, to be with him forever.

Tabitha leveled her eyes at him, perusing him head to toe until even Cassie grew uneasy with the inspection. What was she looking for? What did she find? Cassie clutched her beau's hand, willing him to be steady and strong under her intense scrutiny.

"As I thought, Mr. Hamilton." Tabitha pointed a finger at him. "You *do* have a very special ability."

Shock and surprise reverberated through Flint at the woman's proclamation. Cassie squeezed his hand to help calm him, refraining from employing her calming spellsong with an effort. A song didn't feel appropriate.

"What kind of special ability do you believe I have?" Flint's carefully measured words floated softly on the electric air.

Lightning flashed, illuminating the room. She closed her eyes, focusing all her senses on her surroundings. After another flash of lightning she sensed several spirits hovering around the inn. Reaching out farther, the number multiplied. Each seeking their own kind of respite from eternal wanderings. So many souls she could sense now. More than when she'd returned from the Bakers' a day ago. How could she detect so many more? What had changed?

"Cassie?"

She opened her eyes, blinking to try to clear the worrisome findings.

Giles leaned toward her, worry in his expression. "Are you all right?"

"Yes, of course." Not really, but she didn't need him worrying over nothing. "I'm just sensing more and more spirits. How?"

Mercy drifted closer to her. "I told you, sweetheart. As your brothers and father have come home, your powers have grown and expanded. You're all stronger and more powerful together."

"And Flint?" She stared at her mother, willing her to confirm her fondest hope. That he'd finally have a unique gift to bolster his confidence, his self-respect.

Allegro darted through the open door and swooped around the parlor before landing on the hearth near Cassie. She sent him a silent thank you for coming while they discovered what Flint could do. The falcon's mere presence calmed her agitation. Was Flint about to have his own supernatural power revealed? She crossed her fingers in her lap.

"Tabitha, go ahead." Mercy gestured to Tabitha to continue and then sank to stand on the carpeted floor.

Cassie glanced sharply at her mother's ghost, sensing her weariness, seeing how vaporous she'd become. What was happening to her? She probed her mother's emotions and then withdrew from the truth. Her ma's spirit seemed fragile in a way Cassie couldn't fathom.

"You can host another's spirit so they can interact with the living, perhaps to resolve unfinished business of one kind or another." Tabitha smiled gently at him. "It's an amazing ability, Flint. Not many have such talents."

"Host them?" Flint stiffened. "What does that mean?"

"You can accept them into your body so they can speak directly with another person. You should be proud to have the capacity to help them thus. Congratulations, Flint. I know how much you wanted to have a special ability."

He didn't move for several seconds and then grimaced. "Thanks?"

Flint's consternation mirrored her own. If ghosts could occupy him, possess him, how wonderful for them. They'd be empowered to solve problems, or reveal their cause of death, or at least how they died. On the other hand...how long would such a possession last? How would it impact Flint to have someone else invade his body. But more concerning... On the upcoming Allhallows Eve, what might an evil ghost do if given human form?

Chapter Seven

*L*ightning flashed behind the drawn curtains while rain pummeled the window panes. Reggie finished undressing and slipped under the bedcovers, sitting up while the lamp cast its glow on the room. He didn't want to lay down to try to sleep alone in the bed he'd shared with Mercy their entire married life. Doing so meant he'd accepted her death, something he hadn't yet managed to do. Sure, his mind recognized her ghost haunted the inn. In order for her to be a ghost, she must have died. But maybe he was having a bad dream, a nightmare. A rumble sounded outside, echoing the rumble of protest in his heart.

He yawned so wide his jaw popped. Rubbing it until the jolt of pain subsided, he sighed. Nothing for it but to attempt to sleep. His tired body demanded rest. Flopping back, he pulled the pillow around until his head rested comfortably on the stuffed linen. A flare of white light briefly illuminated the knot holes in the ceiling. When he reached out a hand to where Mercy used to sleep, the cool sheet emphasizing her absence, a tear erupted onto his cheek. He brushed it away and forced his eyes closed. His life could never be the same without her but he must push on.

Daniel possessed the ability to skip back in time and change the past. To stop Mercy's death. But that would undo all the good that resulted from the mournful event. He wouldn't even broach the subject, to ask his son to defy the past. He had no other choice in the matter despite his desperate desire to change what happened.

Indistinct murmurings on the stairs told him the others were heading to their respective bedchambers. Footsteps on the wooden floor boards in the hall outside his room echoed in the quiet between rounds of thunder. One by one, doors softly thudded closed. He fought with himself to keep his lids down, to not stare at the light playing outside his window. Even with his eyes shut, he sensed the lightning signaling the thunder, beckoning the rolling pounding of sound closer with each passing minute. He listened for the next rumble, and then the next, until he drifted off to sleep.

He found himself wandering down a dirt lane and realized he neared the swimming hole the boys retreated to on hot summer days. The place where his nephew drowned. He could hear them now, calling to each other, banshee yelling as they swung on a rope to drop into the shallow lake. Quickening his pace, he saw George racing toward the rope swing. His sons splashed about in the lake, playing and dousing each other with the cool water. George yelled as he dove into the water and Reggie stopped walking as horror filled him. They'd been warned not to dive in as the water was not deep enough on that side of the lake. He started running toward the rough water and saw himself sitting beside the lake, watching the horrific scene.

Giles started toward the water but Reggie's other self ran after him and held him back. He kept looking toward an old maple tree near the edge of the lake, its wide trunk and expanse of leaves providing protection from the blazing sun. But why did his other self continue to look at the tree and not the body floating in the water, face down and motionless? In his dream, he stared at the tree until he spotted movement on the far side, black boots peeking out from under dark skirts, a hand moving a wand, the flick of a black cat's tail nearby.

Reggie awoke with a start as the memory crashed into his foggy, sleep-deprived brain. His heart thudded in his ears as he dried his damp palms on the quilt. Was it a memory? Or had his brain invented the fiction of another witch's interference on that dreadful day? The pounding in his ears blocked out every other sound but not the vision of that menacing hand wielding the wand as George had changed his position from a standing jump to a dive from the swing. The witch either cast a spell of suggestion or of manipulation to force the boy into the dangerous and deadly dive.

He pushed back his hair with a shaky hand as he stared unseeing at the silent room. Was it real? Or did he imagine a witch interfering? Which witch though? If he were a gambler, he'd lay odds he knew exactly who. He stretched out again, pondering what his next steps should be in order to reveal and act upon the shocking truth crouching within his dream.

He didn't like it. Flint hadn't been able to sleep despite lying on his bed for the past thirty minutes. The storm had passed and left the air oppressively chill, damp, expectant.

The last time he experienced such an unsettled feeling, the ghost of a murdered crone made an appearance. What would tonight bring? With luck, no additional ghosts to contend with. A shiver raced through him. Perhaps a toddy would help ease his inner tumult. He rolled out from under the quilt, shoved his feet into slippers, and pulled on a robe.

Ever since Reggie and the others had returned to the inn, a certain sense of disruption pervaded the air. As if unknown forces lurked, waiting for the opportune moment to pounce. As undefined as those forces were in his mind, he'd not share with the others the feeling of anticipation. Perhaps his imagination had taken a run with possible deadly outcomes. Whatever the feeling portended, best to keep it to himself for the present.

He pulled open the bedchamber door and padded into the hall. Something made him pause outside Cassie and Mandy's room. What? He didn't hear or see anything out of the ordinary but something was off. The hair on his nape tingled, lifted. He stilled, listening. No sound interrupted the quiet shrouding the inn. Shrugging off the sensation, he continued toward the steps.

Cassie's scream stopped him cold.

Giles burst out of his room behind Flint, hair wild and eyes hard. "Get in there!"

Startled by the big man's surging presence, Flint raced to open the door to Cassie's room. "Cassie?"

A rush of wind coursed over him as he scanned the bedchamber for Cassie. At first he didn't see her, but then she sidled closer to him as if seeking his protection. He ignored the thrill the act sent through him, focusing instead on the cause of her wide-eyed terror and trembling body.

"Over there." Cassie hunkered near the door, facing the

fluttering curtains at the window. "It's—it's Greg."

Giles pushed into the room, shoving Flint sideways. "I'm here."

Recovering his balance, Flint grimaced at Giles before turning to stare at the ghost glowering at them from where he hovered between the bed and the window. The man looked terrible. Or rather the haint did. Long, greasy blond hair swayed side to side as if in a strong wind. His once bright green eyes had dimmed to the color of a moss-covered pool. His clothes, torn and dirty, hung on his gaunt frame. The time he'd spent in jail prior to paying the price for his crimes had left its mark. He surged forward several feet, shifting from one foot to the other.

"You witch! You're why I'm left hanging between worlds. You must pay for doing this to me." Greg shuffled slowly toward Cassie.

She backed away until her back was against the door but ire flashed in her eyes. Despite her apparent fear of the hateful ghost, she intended to stand up to him. He could see her resolve hardening as she straightened her spine and glanced meaningfully at him. She had some form of a plan. But she wouldn't fight this ghost on her own.

"Stop right there." Flint strode quickly in front of her. "You have no business here."

He stared at the ghost, very much aware of his lack of ability in making a spirit depart. Still, his hand gravitated to his pistol. Not that it would do any good against a ghost but nonetheless it made him feel better.

Greg chortled. "I have more business here than you think, Flint Hamilton." He jabbed a finger at Cassie. "She tricked me into thinking her mother hoarded valuables, not trinkets. Set me up, she did, so I'd end up hanged for stealing and murder. But I took something the wench will want back." His cackle of delight echoed across the fraught space.

Cassie stiffened beside Flint but her attention remained fixed on the ghost. She took a slow step forward, splaying her hands to invite his trust. "What exactly did you steal?"

Greg's ghostly eyes glowed in the soft lamplight. "Something mighty precious, I'd guess."

"You had no right." Cassie took another step, her body vibrating with growing anger.

"Cassie, stay back." Flint put a hand out in front of her, attempting to keep her behind him even as she sidestepped into full view. "You can't..."

"He's right, Cassie." Giles eased closer to Cassie, flanking her other side.

Flint glared at the burly man, very much aware they were both defenseless against a ghost. Even with all of the other man's strength and magic he couldn't protect Cassie from a spirit. Someone with greater powers than either of them possessed needed to deal with the intruder. Bullets and muscles were no defense at all. A chill swept through him, not only from the lingering cold in the air but also from the stark reality facing them. What defense did they have against an angry phantasm?

Greg huffed as he marched closer to Cassie, his slime-green eyes glowing in the dim light. "The witch is the reason I'm dead. If she hadn't said about the supposed treasure me and my boys would never have been in such a sticky situation. But I hid something precious, all right, at least to the woman. I was going to come back for it, but I got hanged instead. So now you'll just have to do without."

"What did you take?" Cassie stared at the haggard spirit

with wide eyes. "Please, Ma didn't deserve to die either."

"Makes no matter now, does it?" Greg's ghost pulsed in the air, shimmering with agitation. "Why? You want it back, do ya?"

The spirit dared to taunt Cassie, egging her on to beg for information. Flint bristled but what could he do? He stayed close to her, using his body to protect her from whatever the ghost intended to do to harm his girl. He glanced at Giles, both acknowledging their limited ability to fight off the haint.

"Please." Cassie lowered her arms to her sides, then slowly crossed them at the wrists. "Won't you tell me where you hid it, whatever it might be?"

Greg cackled, hate and malice dripping from the sound. He shook his head at her as he flowed steadily toward her. "What if I want it back for myself?"

"You have no use of it now." Cassie stiffened, bracing for action.

Flint darted his gaze between the two, preparing to put himself between them to protect his girl. He didn't have a clue what Cassie planned but he hoped it would work. Something had to stop the ghost from doing more damage and definitely before anyone was hurt.

"Maybe not, but you do. I ain't saying where it is though. You'll have to find it without my help." Greg sneered at her. "Or do without."

Heat flowed from Cassie standing beside Flint, her frame trembling in anticipation. Of what? He glanced at Giles who shook his head once with a one-shoulder shrug. They were both clueless as to what Cassie intended doing.

"Then go!" Cassie waved her arms outward in an abrupt motion.

A blast of wind and light radiated from her, sweeping through the room. Flint grabbed for anything solid in the face of the onslaught while Giles anchored himself by grabbing hold of the footboard of the bed. Finally snaring hold of the door frame, Flint watched in awe as Cassie lowered her arms and the wind died down. Her powers were indeed growing stronger. Even so, Greg's ghost remained.

The haint wavered and then solidified. "You can't make me go that easily. You must pay!" Greg picked up the chair by the writing desk and hurled it at them, the wooden legs splintering off as it crashed to the floor beside them. He hefted the lantern with some effort, aiming it toward Cassie.

Shocked by the turn of events, Flint grabbed Cassie by the shoulders. "We need to go."

"Now!" Giles shielded Cassie as Flint pushed her through the open door. He slammed the door shut behind them as glass shattered against it. "We need help."

Cassie stumbled to a halt when the three of them stood in the hall. They needed someone who knew how to banish ghosts. "I'll wake Pa."

Flint reflexively ducked when something heavy crashed to the floor in the closed off room. "Hurry!"

Cassie marched toward her pa's room, then hesitated at the top of the stairs to turn around and aim troubled eyes at Flint. "Greg is right, you know. It's all because of my slip of the tongue that all of this happened."

"Stop blaming yourself." Flint gripped her shoulder, trying to quell her guilt. Ever since her mother had been killed, she'd shouldered the blame like a mantle of shame. Yet no one else thought any of the evil acts her fault. "Right now, we need to expel a ghost and then figure out what he stole and hid."

Giles kept a close eye on the door to Cassie's room, watching as the light flickered under the door. "It never occurred to me I'd need to protect my sister from a ghost."

Growling preceded another thud inside Cassie's room. Flint stared at Giles, feeling helpless yet again. Another ghost to contend with, and not a friendly one like the soldier he'd helped on his way. If only he had some kind of special talent that could aid them. But one thing remained certain. "It's always something with you Fairhopes."

"What is all the ruckus about at this time of night?" Aunt Hope's strident voice sounded from the stairwell as she climbed the last few steps to the landing, emerging into view dressed in her nightgown and slippers.

Faith reached the landing a moment later, her eyes wary, Malachi at her side. "We could sense turmoil in the fabric of this place from our chamber. What is going on?"

"I'm sorry for the disruption." Flint had never been so glad to see them as at that moment. "But we could use your help with an uninvited guest."

Chapter Eight

"What are you about this time of night?"

Aunt Faith cast a sidelong look at Cassie, assessing and judging her. Granted it was near midnight, but why did Faith appear disdainful? But she had to ask. She stifled a reluctant sigh. "We need your help. A killer's ghost is ransacking my bedchamber."

"Oh, dear." Faith straightened her shoulders and wiped the agitation from her countenance.

"Always at midnight." Hope's grumbling elicited a grim nod and slight smile from the group.

"Please hurry." Cassie didn't know what would be left of her furniture and clothing by the time Greg's ghost departed, willingly or not.

"I know a spell that will help him on his way." Hope whipped her wand from her skirt pocket. "Let's make this ghost leave so I can go back to sleep, shall we?"

Giles eased out of the way as Hope and Faith started toward Cassie's bedchamber door. The sound of shattering glass confirmed the violent ghost continued to destroy her belongings. Anger surged inside, her fingers aching with the need to strangle him—if only she could.

"Cassie, where is Mandy? I didn't see her." Flint frowned at the closed door. "If she's in there, she'll be hurt."

"No, she's…" Honestly, it wasn't anyone's business where the girl was, but they had a right to know she wasn't in danger. "She's with Abram out in the barn." The hayloft to be exact, or so she believed. The young couple snuck away as frequently as they could. Aunt Hope raised a sagacious brow at her but said nothing. "What do you need us to do?"

"Just follow my lead." Hope laid a hand on the door latch and then released it to regard Cassie and Faith. "You two repeat after me without pause until the ghost is gone, understand?"

"Klee! Klee!"

The Merlin swooped into the hall and darted around for a moment before settling on Cassie's shoulder, its yellow and black claws steady against the quilted fabric of her robe. "Thank you, Allegro. I'm glad you're here. Ready to help us rid the house of a ghost?"

"Klee!" The bird tilted its blue-gray head and aimed its intelligent eye at Aunt Hope.

"Yes, she's going to help." Cassie stroked Allegro's feathered head. "We all are."

Together, the three witches would work to banish the ghost. If they were powerful enough. Maintaining the image of calm became ever more difficult as she sensed the anger in the ghost in her bedroom. Sensed his all-consuming rage as he continued to throw things across the room, demolishing everything he could. How was he so powerful? Could his anger fuel his strength? His ability to move solid objects? Her mother had only realized that capability after she'd grown furious with her sisters and launched herself at

Hope. His anger, then, increased the threat he posed. Confronting Greg's ghost may well be more dangerous than they'd anticipated. Beyond their combined power.

"Aunt Hope, there's something—" Dread and certainty filled her core.

"Not now, dear. Tell me after." Hope shook her head sharply as she hushed her with a severe look.

Cassie swallowed the rising fear in her throat. She couldn't succumb to her increasing terror. She had her familiar at hand. She had Giles' strength and Flint's calm to steady her. What did her aunts offer? She regarded her aunts and reached out to them mentally. A wavering concern flowed from Faith but Hope exuded confidence and determination. Between them, surely they could defeat and banish the furious haint.

Flint eased closer to her with a question in his eyes. "I'm here for you, Cassie. You needn't worry. Just do what you must."

"We don't have time to chatter." Hope gripped her wand between her hands, tip to handle. "Together we can deal with this threat."

Doubt simmered in Faith as she studied her sister. "I don't know that this angry spirit will respond to a spell."

"We chant the spell at least three times." Hope glanced at Faith and then Cassie, her expression tense. "After the third round of the chant, he'll be forced from the property. Ready?"

It sounded easy. Perhaps too easy. Greg's furious spirit flew about her room. Harboring all forms of ill will and bitterness toward her and her family. Could the power of their words force the ghost from the dwelling? Her aunt seemed to believe so. She squared her shoulders and swallowed. She must trust her aunt.

Flint squeezed her hand as Allegro shifted on her shoulder, both offering their reassurance in their own ways. Cassie briefly closed her eyes, centering herself as quickly as possible, and then nodded to her aunt. "Ready."

Hope motioned to Giles. "Open the door."

The Guardian squared his shoulders and quickly pushed the door open before stepping out of the way.

"Witches! You can't touch me!" Greg rampaged around the room, sending one object after another flying. Smashing into the opposite wall. A mass of glass and wood splinters littered the floor. "I'm not the only vengeful spirit waiting to wreak havoc here at this doomed inn." He flew toward Cassie as Giles rushed in with Flint right behind him, but Faith waved a hand and barred him from coming closer.

"Stay out of this, you two." She waved her other hand and the door slammed in the men's faces.

"Let me in!" Giles yelled and rattled the latch but the door remained closed. "Damnation. We'll get help."

Footfalls faded as the men went for backup. Cassie reached out to Allegro for comfort, realizing her banished Guardian and fiancé couldn't help her, couldn't steady her. But knowing Flint hovered nearby did help stabilize her emotions. She concentrated on the spirit dashing about the room, jerking from place to place, his rage palpable.

"The others come to seek their vengeance for their untimely deaths. They're going to make you all pay!"

His words made no sense. Nobody at the inn had caused the death of others. What was he referring to, then? Who might think someone living or working at the Fury Falls Inn had caused someone to die?

"And I'm going to laugh while you all try to figure out

what I've hidden and where." Greg paused in his demolition of the room's contents to gloat at the three witches. "You'll search forever without finding it. You'll go mad trying!"

"Don't listen to him. Follow my lead." Hope moved into the center of the room, forcing the haint to jerk backward a couple of feet. She began chanting, repeating the same words over and over, Cassie and Faith joining in.

"Light and life reject night and death, be gone and never return!"

Hope glared at the spirit as if her look alone would banish his presence. Then her eyes widened when the ghost merely smirked at her.

"How pathetic." Greg laughed at the three witches gaping at him. "You don't expect I'd leave that easily, now do you? That witch must pay for my death. It's all her fault!" He grabbed a vase of flowers and threw it at Cassie. Glass shattered at her feet, stems and water scattering around her.

Cassie gasped and dodged, Allegro flapping his wings as she jumped backward from the livid haint glaring at her. "What now?"

The bedroom door blasted open with a flash of light, the wooden barricade clattering to the floor. She spun around to see her pa stride inside, raising his arms up and out from his shoulders as he aimed a crystal-topped ebony staff at the ghost. He had grown larger than life, almost as if he'd become a living crucifix overshadowing all before him. Cassie trembled at the vibration of power and energy filling the air around her. He motioned her out of the way with a swipe of the staff and then concentrated on the ghost, an aura of red and black emanating from his body.

"Go where you belong, ghost. Vanish! I banish you now and forever!" Reggie brandished the staff in a flourish of defiance, a severe and stern look thrown at the spirit.

"Nooo!" The ghost swirled into a black tornado of smoke, its human form disintegrating into the darkness.

A boom of thunder and a yellow blaze rocked the building, knocking Cassie sideways. She barely maintained her balance, with Allegro's help and support. Crimson fog filled the room, forcing her to cough and her eyes to tear. When the air cleared, the room was silent. Hope helped Faith to her feet. Giles and Flint rushed into the room, Flint soon wrapping an arm around her shoulders to help steady her.

But most importantly, Greg's ghost was gone.

Reggie lowered his arms and glared at each of the others in the room. "Why didn't you send for me sooner?"

"I thought they could handle a simple ghost." She glanced at her aunt and shook her head. "I guess I was wrong."

Hope huffed as she regarded her niece. "Then why did you ask?"

"I appreciate your attempt, both of you." Cassie drew in a steadying breath. "Working together felt really good. I think we weakened the ghost some but his fury increased his strength. Like with Ma's when she first knocked you down, Aunt Hope. We hadn't counted on that. But we did work together, and for that I'm grateful. Thank you, Aunt Hope and Aunt Faith."

Faith regarded her silently, her expression morphing from one of utter contempt to surprise. "You're welcome."

Hope propped her fists on her hips and stared at her, the harsh glare softening to something resembling a smile.

"Indeed."

"I'm thankful you were both here." Cassie blinked away the lingering fog from her eyes and then addressed Flint's concerned frown. "I'm glad you're here. Knowing your quiet strength stood nearby gave me strength, too." She pushed up on her toes to give him a kiss. "I wouldn't have managed as well without you."

"Now that the mutual gratification is over," Reggie said as he strode closer to her, "would you please tell me what in the world has been going on around here?"

A man couldn't let emotion stand in the way of what needed to be done. Yet he had hesitated before reentering their—or rather, his—bedchamber. Reggie stood with Mercy in the middle of the room he'd shared with her for so many years, denying the feelings tapping against his heart. Yet everywhere he looked another memory battered his mind, attached to everything from the wardrobe at the base of the circular staircase to the small box on the dressing table with the dove carved in the lid. He'd shaped the symbol specially for his cherished wife. A desire for their life together, to share a world filled with both peace and love. Only to have her die at the hands of a violent man. As a result, he had yet to succeed at sleeping in the room. First, the dream which felt like an unearthed memory of his nephew's demise. Then the violent interruption earlier that night by the ghost attacking his daughter. Now his ghostly wife hovered nearby, calling to mind even more memories of their past together.

After the hanged man's ghost had been vanquished, they needed to identify what the man had stolen. He'd sent the children to bed and summoned Mercy to help him search their room. She would know what had been taken far better than he could recall. Having her sweet presence at his side while he rummaged through their shared life also enabled them to spend more time together. A clock in his mind ticked away the seconds they had to share before her spirit crossed over. If only he could stop the sweep hand.

"Nothing seems to be missing." Mercy shimmered beside him, translucent and yet present in the room. "Maybe that oaf lied, toying with Cassie."

"And us, then." Reggie stifled the onslaught of memories while surveying the sentimental contents of the room. All around him small gifts and purchases evoked loving moments along with their associated hopes and dreams. "I don't see where anything is missing."

She drifted to the dressing table and reached out toward the looking glass with her wraithlike fingers. "Abram sent this, intending for me to see myself clearly. I didn't understand at the time but since he's returned his real meaning is apparent."

The pale blue dress he'd selected for her graced her lovely frame as she turned to look at him. The dress had called to him at the tailor's shop when he'd gone to pick up his new trousers. Apparently forgotten by another client, it only needed minor alterations to fit her perfectly. The color emphasized her unique eyes when she smiled her gratitude upon receiving the dress. He cherished her smile, her sweet expression, her heart. He stayed near the door to the room, hesitant to move farther into the mire of memories entombed in each object. "What do you mean, my heart?"

Mercy traced the outer edge of the elaborately carved mahogany frame nestled on a four-footed stand of matching wood. Casting a brief, rueful peek at him, she stared at the mirror. "He felt I didn't understand him well enough and only through deeper self-reflection would I see what he wanted me to see. As in, who he really was instead of who I wanted him to be."

Despite his reluctance, Reggie took a few steps toward his wife as her agitation became apparent. Changing the subject might ease her angst. "Do you remember when I made you that box? The one with the dove."

She rested her fingers on the rectangular wooden box. "A place to hold the letters you wrote to me, to keep them safe."

Letters he'd penned since before they married in 1798, twenty-three years ago. Time had certainly passed rapidly. They'd experienced many changes over the course of their marriage. They'd begun with such happy expectations for their life together. Safe in the knowledge their families supported the union. Only to discover the dubious reasons behind Mercy's father giving them his blessing. After Giles was born, and then with each subsequent child, everything transformed. Especially after Cassandra's birth. Reggie saw hidden motives in Robert Covington's every action, every statement, and every gift. What did he want in exchange? The doubt behind the unspoken question riddled Reggie with guilt even as he couldn't shake the feeling the man obscured his own agenda.

"I didn't write often but I meant every word of my love for you." He couldn't help closing the gap between them. Mercy was his world. Would always be his world. "I love you, Mercy."

She pivoted in place, hovering a few inches above the floor. "And I you." She drifted close to him, extending a hand. "I long for you, my dear."

His fingertips sensed the coolness of her insubstantial being but naturally he couldn't touch her the way he desired. Hand in hand, lips to lips, body to body. Being with her as they once shared their marriage bed together. "You'll always dwell in my heart."

If only he knew then—back in June before he cavalierly mounted up and rode away without even saying goodbye—how events would alter everything in his absence. Looking back, the way things unfolded could almost have been predicted. At the time, he'd based his decisions on his dreams for his business. He'd left his daughter and wife to fend for themselves. Sure, Flint was there to run the business. But nobody had been there to protect them from the real threats: robbers, Mercy's sisters, and a witch-hunting gang of men. He'd gone in an effort to bolster the inn. But he hadn't taken into consideration the ramifications to the rest of his life. To his family.

Mercy smiled sadly at him before turning back to the dressing table, scanning the surface. "The beautiful filigree bowl is there as is the fairy figurine I bought in Nashville. Isn't she graceful?"

Reggie dismissed his melancholy thoughts and peered at the lacy-winged fairy, seated on a cream-colored toadstool covered with red dots, a book open on her crossed legs. "A fine memento of your trip, my love."

The trip she took with Cassie to refresh their wardrobes with new dresses and bonnets and other feminine necessities. He'd anticipated their return when his daughter would model her finds for him as she'd done years before. He'd missed out on all of the frivolity, the laughter, the ooh's and ah's that accompanied each new frock and hat.

What a fool he'd been.

"Please, dear, don't frown so." Mercy angled her head as she studied him. "We're all fine. But...do you regret moving here to north Alabama?"

He eyed her, considering her question before responding. They'd left behind everything they'd worked so hard to build. The home and family ties as well as the community's respect and support. Moving away from the southern part of the state meant starting over. It meant parting ways with his sons, a very painful part of the decision. It also meant protecting his family from the real threat posed toward each of them. So, no, he had no regret on that score. But still, if he could have changed things he might have.

"I don't regret protecting our children. But I do regret not being here to defend you from that awful man." He raked his hand through his hair and clutched his nape. "I'm sorry I wasn't here to safeguard you. I should have come home sooner. Or perhaps not have left in the first place. I was so selfish, so intent on impressing the senator every way possible, to build my reputation as an innkeeper. Denying my own warlock heritage in order to justify my choices. What was I trying to prove though? I don't know any longer. I'm so sorry, my love."

"No, don't." She held out her hand, the wafting curtains at the windows a faint background through her palm. "Yes, I was very upset you'd left and made Flint innkeeper instead of me. I could have handled the management of the inn for you. But I understand now. You did so for my benefit, and I appreciate your consideration. The rest..." She waggled her hand in the air. "The reality is that if I hadn't died and Cassie written to her brothers, our family wouldn't be together again. They'd have had no reason to come, to reunite our family. And look how Cassie has matured into such a fine young woman about to begin her own family. Our sons, as well, are finding their life companions and forging their futures."

"Yes, but..."

She shook her head at him. "It's all right. It's worked out the way it was supposed to." She shimmered, fading for a moment and then steadying her presence.

Her stance, her view of the events and the results of them, gladdened his heart. What could he have changed that would then yield a better result? Nothing. His beautiful, loving wife was correct. "I love you so much, Mercy. You have a way of putting things, of seeing the best in even a seemingly horrible situation. I only wish I could be with you as before."

"I wish for the same even if only for a moment." She smiled as she looked away, perusing the room. Then she stopped, a frown settling on her brows. "I wonder...is it still there? Those men rifled through all my things so I wouldn't put it past them."

In Reggie's mind his wife's recollection played of how the three burglars tore apart her bedroom, pawing through the private and precious knick-knacks and mementos. He closed his eyes but still the scenes unfolded, one horrific sight after another. He forced them to stop before Greg pulled the trigger, opening his eyes to watch his wife's distressed emotions playing across her lovely face. The face he'd held in his hands while he pressed his lips to hers. He'd prefer to remember her that way. He couldn't—would not—relive her last moments through his own eyes. He had no stomach to watch his wife murdered.

"Anyway, check in the box." She moved to the dressing table and pointed to a collection of small boxes. "Look in the middle one. Is my locket safe inside?"

The family heirloom had been handed down for generations. A very special bit of jewelry, the enchanted locket served as a protective talisman. His mother had gifted her the locket upon their union, her way of ensuring her safety and well-being. She would finger the gold case whenever she missed her loving mother. Her friend and confidante.

He hurried to lift the lid on the box in question and rummaged among the satin nest. Then he peered at her, his chest tight as the implications of his discovery reverberated inside. "It's empty."

Chapter Nine

The squeal of delight pierced Cassie's calm, forcing an involuntary humming of her calming spellsong. Granted, the shriek demonstrated how excited Mandy was to find the perfect dress to wear for her marriage to Abram. But the high pitch and volume left her ears ringing. The girls scurried between Cassie and Mandy's bedchamber and her ma's down the hall, creating a festive air to the entire event. Pansy perched on a padded chair by the writing desk, jotting notes regarding each bride's preferences, giving advice on lace and ruffles, reaching for her tape measure to take their sizes, all while beaming with anticipation of the triple wedding the next day. Even the two sister elves glowed with pleasure as they helped rifle through boxes of ribbons to find the perfect one.

Cassie paused in her own search, holding a length of lace in her fingers, as she contemplated the scullery maids. The sisters had worked in the kitchen for years, but only recently discovered their heritage as elven princesses. On Myrtle's birthday in fact. Their appearance had morphed overnight from dowdy, gray-haired young women to sparkling silver-haired beauties. Their skin glowed with life and magic as they went about their work. In spite of their regal family tree, they had elected to continue working in the kitchen. Overseeing the food preparation enabled them to add a sprinkle of good will to the dishes served to the guests. No harm could come from suggesting kindness between each other. Cassie regarded the green lace in her hand with mild distaste and then laid it aside.

"Found it!" Meg, the younger elf, practically shouted as she held a pink satin ribbon in the air.

"You're making enough noise to wake the dead, sister." Myrtle flipped the pages of a fashion magazine featuring pictures of the latest dresses, shoes, and hairstyles.

"Please, no." Cassie chimed in with a quick shake of her head, her pearl dangling earbobs swinging and bumping her cheeks. "We put one to rest last night and he needs to stay so."

Haley sauntered into the bedchamber with a turquoise dress draped over her arm, picking at a loose thread. "Indeed he does. We have much to plan and little time to do it. No time for any ghostly nonsense." She paused to shake out the gown and hold it up to Cassie's shoulders. "What do you think of this one?"

In her mind's eye, she imagined herself standing by Flint before the minister wearing the gown. The dip of the bodice emphasized her cleavage while the flare of the skirts created the illusion of ample hips. Both features designed to underscore her fertility. She swallowed the rising nervousness threatening her composure. Marrying a man typically led to having his children. She wanted a family, so marrying him made perfect sense. But the idea of sleeping with a man still seemed daunting. Many other women had succeeded in wedding and having children. She squared her shoulders with firm resolve. So could she. Now about the dress.

"I love it." She tested the texture of the cloth. "It's beautiful. Thank you."

"Here, let me help you put it on." Haley grabbed Cassie's shoulders and spun her around so she could help her out of her day dress and into the gown.

The shimmery fabric draped smoothly to the floor, its leg of mutton sleeves gathered at the elbows. The bodice sat high and emphasized her silhouette. Cassie peered down at the flowing skirts and then looked to Pansy. "Well? What do you think of the color?"

The older woman angled her head, tapping a forefinger to her lips. "It's a lovely color for you, Miss Cassie."

Light footsteps drew Cassie's attention to the open door. Wilma hesitated at the threshold, an eager if hesitant expression lighting her eyes. "What's going on?"

"Come on in and help me choose my gown for tomorrow." Cassie beckoned to her. "I love this color, but is it the right one for a wedding?"

Wilma flowed into the room, as graceful as a panther. Her time spent with perfecting her archery imbued her entire person with a fluidity of movement and self-awareness enviable by anyone observing her. Her own attire bespoke the care with which she clothed herself, hinting at a refined taste and inherent instinct. Wilma slowed to a halt near Cassie, examining the gown.

"The color...while lovely, seems a touch too effusive for an autumn affair. Don't you think?" Wilma glanced nervously around the room.

Wilma's uncertainty swept through Cassie, catching her

by surprise. Probing gently, she felt her indecision regarding whether she belonged in the room with the other brides. The group of women had come together to choose outfits for the morrow and Wilma, although engaged, would not be wedded with them. As a result, she hesitated to insert herself into the group. Cassie strode over to her and took her hand.

"Come tell me your opinion. Soon we'll be sisters, and I'd appreciate your view."

Wilma flashed a relieved smile at her as she followed Cassie farther into the room.

Haley sauntered over to sit on the bed and study the dress. "I agree with you, Wilma. It does seem too...vibrant. Think of the colors of the trees out yonder, all once lively but now muted and even somewhat dull."

Pansy snapped her fingers. "That's the answer." She jumped up and hurried to the open trunk by the window, rummaging inside for several seconds. "Ah-ha!" She lifted a cream-colored lace overskirt from the depths and shook it out for everyone to see. Then hurried to Cassie in rapid strides. "Let's add this and see if it mutes the color adequately."

Tying the lacy skirt around her waist, open in front to allow a sliver of the pure turquoise to flash with each stride, Cassie modeled the dress. "Well?"

"It's nice, but I still think it needs something." Pansy tapped a foot on the bare floor.

"Oh, I know what it needs. Give me a moment." Meg spun on her heel and left the bedchamber to race to Mercy's bedchamber where other dresses, scarves, and skirts hung in the immense wardrobe. She returned in moments, a cream neckerchief in her hands. She draped it around Cassie's neck, brushing against her nape and bun with her fingertips. "Tuck it in and let's see how it looks."

The silk flowed between Cassie's hands when she did as requested, though it proved uncomfortable with the bunches of fabric in the snug bodice. If the overall effect worked, then she'd layer the fabrics in the correct order so everything lay smoothly. For now, it would have to do to determine its suitability. She slowly spun in place, perusing the reactions of the women around her as she made a complete circle. "Looks like...perhaps?"

"It's lovely, Cassie." Mercy shimmered into view by the open trunk. "You're lovely."

Surprised, Cassie pressed a hand to her waist. Her mother's sudden appearance made her realize what had been missing in the gaiety of the morning's fashion critique. Her mother's input, guidance, and approval. "Thank you, Ma."

Mercy shifted sideways, slowly circling Cassie to inspect her choice from all sides. Cassie held still, but longed to pivot to observe her mother's expression. As her mother crossed in front of the open window, her image nearly disappeared into the brighter background. Her ma's ghost had less presence in the room. She appeared fainter, wispier, as if on the verge of vanishing altogether. A gasp escaped her as she covered her mouth with one hand. No, it couldn't be true.

"What's the matter?" Mandy asked, coming around to look into her eyes.

She had no proof of her suspicion, and didn't want to worry anyone else until she knew more. She'd need to speak to her pa. He'd know. "Nothing to worry you about."

Mandy lifted a brow but held her tongue. "Is this the

outfit you want to wear tomorrow?" She peered closer and frowned. "You're missing one of your earbobs."

Mandy's voice disappeared into Cassie's frantic thoughts. What if her mother vanished and never returned? Cassie steeled herself, well aware she'd been given a gift of her mother's lingering presence for several months. At some point, her spirit would need to rest in peace. But why now? The day before her wedding. If only her ma could be present for her daughter's wedding. If only her ma could actually attend in her corporeal body. If only her ma could give her a hug and a kiss of good fortune as she embarked on her own married life.

"Cassie? Did you hear me?" Mandy clasped her upper arm. "Are you all right? Nervous perhaps?"

She shook her head once. "I'm fine. This dress is fine. I'll be fine, really."

Her ma came closer to stand near but not near enough for Cassie's liking. "My darling, you're about to begin your own marriage, experience all that a loving relationship offers. I know I didn't think Flint good enough by far for you, but he's proven his love, his regard, and his worth. I give you both my blessing for a long and loving life together."

"Oh, Ma, thank you for saying as much. Your blessing means everything to me." Tears burned in her eyes. She reached out to hug her ma, longing to wrap her arms tightly around her, but only grasped cool air. She swallowed her disappointment with an effort, struggled to smile but failed utterly. "I'd hug you if I could."

Mercy smiled wanly and then shimmered. "I must go, my dear. I love you."

"I love you, Ma." Cassie swiped at the wet trails on her

cheeks. "I miss you so."

"I'm still here for now." Mercy shimmered more, wavering until she became gossamer. "I'll see you later." Then she vanished.

"Oh..." Cassie wrapped her arms around her waist as the tears erupted and flowed down her cheeks.

She'd lost her ma all over again. The pain and grief overwhelmed her, shaking her to the core. She gasped for air, bending over under the burden of her mother's death. The loss of her protective love and guidance. No matter she'd been overbearing at times, now Cassie understood, recognized the depth of her love, the sacrifice she'd made, all for her children.

Haley joined Mandy in embracing her as she sobbed uncontrollably. Her mother had grown weaker, less substantive, a wraith. Just when she needed her the most. What did it mean? Would she ever see her mother again?

The rhythmic swish of the broom across the wooden floor in the dining room soothed even as it accomplished the job of readying the room for the luncheon rush. A lull in business also gave Flint the opportunity to reflect on recent events and muse over what else might be prowling about. They'd all been busy putting the final touches to the plans for the wedding ceremony that evening. Only hours separated him from calling Cassie his wife. Calling her his.

A few flicks of the broom ushered the pile of dirt into the dustpan. Carrying it to the front door, he went outside and dumped it in the front garden. Then he perused the quiet lane and carriageway, the dogs sniffing about the yard, the horses in the field behind the barn, and drew in a deep breath. A moment of peace proved hard to come by lately. But it could only last for a moment, as he had much to accomplish in a short amount of time. He spun on his heel and went back inside.

Sheridan fell into step beside him as Flint headed back toward the dining room, the older man carrying a black slate in one hand and a piece of white chalk in the other. "I need your approval on this."

A quick scan of the slate revealed a familiar list of victuals. "I thought we did that already."

He nodded slowly as he stared at the list. "I changed the breads and added a soup. Do you want everything ready for tonight's reception? Or split it between tonight and tomorrow's festivities?"

Flint took the list from the cook and studied it. The wedding feast should be something special but not enough to outshine the big event on the morrow for everyone to enjoy. "I'd say keep it noteworthy but limited for this evening's supper. Say, the roast turkey with cranberry relish, stuffed eggplant, and the pumpkin bread for tonight, along with a special cake of some sort. Oh, and open a few bottles of champagne." He handed back the extensive list. "Matt is helping you prepare everything, isn't he?"

"He is." Sheridan grasped the slate, marking a check beside the items Flint had mentioned. He lifted his gaze to grin at Flint. "I'll make sure everything is ready and waiting after you tie that there knot. Don't you worry about it."

Flint clasped the other man's shoulder for a brief moment. "Thank you for everything, Sheridan. I know this is a lot to ask after you've only just returned to the inn."

"My pleasure. I'm mighty glad to be home and back to work." He leveled his somber gaze at Flint. "Having Pansy at my side for all time made the hardships of that journey worth every bump and jounce and snide remark."

His last comment forced Flint to look sharply into Sheridan's clouded eyes. "I'm sorry to hear you faced criticism."

Sheridan brushed aside Flint's concern. "Never you mind. It's not anything I haven't heard before and probably will hear again some time."

"You're a good and decent man." Anybody could look at him and see as much for themselves. If they would really look at him, talk with him, understand him. Not make assumptions based on first impressions or their own prejudices. "I'm glad to know you."

"Why, thank you, sir." He nodded at Flint, his brown eyes alight with pleasure. "I appreciate your sentiment."

"What sentiment might that be?" Cassie strolled up to where the two men talked at the bar. "It's so good to see you back around the place, Sheridan."

"I'm glad to be home, Miss Cassie." He tapped the slate with a forefinger. "I best begin on preparations for your wedding supper. If you'll excuse me."

"Of course." Cassie nodded to him and he turned to depart. Then she met Flint's eager gaze.

"We're only hours from being husband and wife, Cassie." Flint scrutinized his future wife's happy countenance, the slight blush in her cheeks, the light in her eyes, and the lift to her tempting lips. "Are you ready?"

"I have a few things to take care of first, but I am ready to be your wife, if that's what you're asking." The light in her eyes dimmed. "I need your help with one very important thing."

"I'll help anyway I can, my dear." Resolve glinted in her

eyes. He steeled himself before probing into her reason for seeking him out. "What is it you need?"

"Remember how Aunt Scarlet told you about your special ability?"

Ghost hosting. She didn't need to explain further for him to decipher the gist of her request. "What is it you're asking?"

Pressing her lips together for a second, she regarded him. "Will you host my ma?"

Shock swept through him. "Mercy?" Inside of him? After all the hateful, hurtful words she'd hurled at him? "She barely tolerates me. Why would you ask me to allow her to inhabit my person?"

He could well imagine the kind of chaos or damage she might inflict if permitted inside of him. Or perhaps he didn't fully comprehend the results of hosting any spirit, let alone the spirit of his reluctant mother-in-law. Having another person's spirit residing alongside his own for any length of time could be uncomfortable, unsettling, and unnerving. But Mercy inside might be an entirely different level of an anxiety-inducing event.

Cassie's eyes glistened as she sucked in a shaky breath. "I need her, Flint. I need to feel her arms around me in a motherly hug before we marry. She may disappear and be gone from my life forever. I won't ever have this chance again. Consider it my wedding gift. Please?"

"Is something amiss? What's prompting this sudden, urgent desire?" So much had happened in the last few days it could be anything. Dismissing Greg's angry haint. Her aunts' mere presence could have upturned the apple cart for her. Having her pa and Sheridan back. "Speak to me."

"She's..." Sniffling, Cassie retrieved a lace-edged

handkerchief from a skirt pocket and wiped her nose. "She's fading. I don't think she'll be around much longer."

"Why now?" Mercy *had* seemed rather faint the last time he'd seen her. He hadn't thought much about it, assuming the lighting in the room had caused the effect. "What changed?"

She dabbed at her eyes. "I just need a hug. Will you help me?"

He'd do anything for his girl. He'd do anything to keep her from crying, tears glistening down her cheeks as she waited for his answer. And yet, the idea of hosting Mercy inside, indeed hosting any spirit, seemed both dangerous and scary. He shuddered and then stiffened. How could he satisfy her desire without risk to himself?

"I don't know how to do that." Until he understood more about the process, his best reason to delay such an event remained his lack of knowledge. "I'd need some help with how to host a spirit."

"I couldn't help overhearing, Flint. But I can help you." Scarlet marched into the empty room with a pitcher in her hands. "Where do you want this cider? And then I'll give you some pointers."

He waved vaguely in the direction of the bar as he scrambled to find another valid avenue to avoid agreeing to any venture in haint hosting. "You know how to host?"

Surely this woman didn't know everything about witchcraft. Or did she? His boss seemed to know more than he'd ever suspected, so his sister might be able to do more than he'd bargained for. What if she could teach him how to host a ghost? Then what possible excuse would put off what seemed to be an eventuality by Cassie's determined look? His heart sank as Scarlet nodded vigorously, drying her hands on the apron tied around her waist.

A glint in her eye spoke to her assessment of his reluctance. "I do and it's not that hard. You merely need to open yourself to the spirit, welcome her inside, and let go of controlling your body."

Lose control over his own body? Give command of his corporeal form to Mercy? Or anyone else, for that matter. He shuddered but kept a steady gaze aimed at Scarlet. If he looked at Cassie, all of his resistance would simply fade away. He didn't want to deny her anything, and yet the very idea of turning over his body to anyone, let alone the woman who had espoused such distaste for him, turned his stomach.

"Flint, please? It would only be for a few minutes." Cassie touched his arm, drawing his gaze reluctantly to meet her tearful one. "I'd be forever grateful."

How could he say no? Her eyes pleaded with him to say yes. His heart gravitated toward pleasing her, giving her anything she asked for. But his mind balked at the idea.

"Flint, there you are." Zander strode into the dining room.

Relieved, Flint shrugged an apology to Cassie and faced the new arrival. "What do you need?"

Zander stopped beside Cassie, glancing between her and Scarlet and then back to Flint. "I'm sorry. Did I interrupt?"

"It's all right." Flint swallowed, mightily aware of the lingering, knowing look from Scarlet. "You were saying?"

"I ran into Sheriff Neal on my way in, he's waiting out front to speak to you on a matter of some urgency. He only has a minute or he'd have come in with me." Zander's light brown eyes danced with sudden humor. "I can tell him he'll have to wait until you're finished here—"

"No! I'm sure it's important." Flint took Cassie's hands in his, meeting her wet eyes all the while hoping she wouldn't see the truth in his gaze. "I'll think about it. I promise. But the sheriff wouldn't have ridden all the way out here if it wasn't urgent."

She contemplated him for a long moment and then pursed her lips. "I understand. Go on then. We'll talk later."

"Thank you." He kissed her quickly and then released her hands. "I'll be back in a few minutes."

He turned to Zander and grinned, relief sweet in his chest. "Let's go see what he wants."

Flint hurried out of the dining room, Zander beside him. He had a reprieve but only for a short time. Somehow he needed to come to terms with his beloved's request. Only a few hours remained until the ceremony and she wanted her mother's loving embrace prior to the long-awaited moment. But could he take in her ma's spirit without harm to himself?

Chapter Ten

The aroma of steaming-hot chicken pot pie made his mouth water. Reggie forked a bite into his mouth, inhaling the exclamation of pain as the gravy landed on his tongue. He'd assumed his rightful seat at the head of the table in the family's dining area, Mercy seated to his left, and his sons on his right. He'd invited Daniel and Silas to join him as a way to catch up with them, learn about where they'd gone and what they'd done after they left home. They'd accepted but he sensed their reluctance and resistance. After a moment, he chewed and swallowed the delicious luncheon offering. Sheridan's cooking always delighted, even more so after he'd had to make do with the mediocre fare the steady stream of tavern keepers had on offer across the country. Quality didn't always hold up when quantity reigned supreme. He'd stick to quality and less quantity around his establishment.

Mercy shimmered in her seat, quietly observing as the men enjoyed their luncheon. Reggie peeked at her ghost sitting nearby as if his wife remained at the inn. But in truth, only her spirit lingered, waiting for its final release, its final resting place. Her image hovered at hand but her whole being had already departed. With a silent sigh, he addressed his sons instead of dwelling on a past he couldn't change.

"I'm glad to be home to enjoy Sheridan's cooking once more." He lifted a forkful in salute and then devoured it.

"Sheridan gives Matt some competition, that's certain." Silas held a bite over his bowl to give it time to cool. "I thought Matt a fine cook, but this is superior."

"Don't allow Matt to hear you say as much." Daniel poked at the meat and vegetables steaming in the bowl before him. "Those two would throw another cookery competition tonight instead of making the wedding supper."

"I hired Sheridan because of his culinary excellence." Reggie selected a morsel from the dish. "He's been a real find for the inn."

Silas glanced at him but remained quiet as he stirred the vegetables in his bowl.

Reggie reached out to him, dismayed to feel him actively resisting his probing. Using his inner defenses to shield his true emotions from detection. Discovering his past would need to be done more traditionally. "So, tell me what you did after you left home."

Silas shrugged and kept eating, glancing at his brother.

Daniel laid his fork down and reached for his wine glass. After swallowing, he met Reggie's curious gaze. "I worked at a book shop for a while, then studied under Dr. Paul Jenkins in Philadelphia before I earned my teaching certificate. After I passed my exams, I was hired by the East Tennessee College to teach natural science. I worked hard to earn that position and the respect of my peers. And now I'm here, jobless and a warlock."

His son sounded upset and defensive despite the pleasant expression aimed at Reggie. He sensed Silas wanting to speak so he looked at him. "And what about you?"

He expected a rebuke from his son. Especially knowing how much the lad resented being shunted from the family. Sent out into the big, bad world on his own. As well he might. Reggie hadn't wanted to boot them out the door, but if he hadn't they would not have grown into the self-reliant and resourceful men they'd become. He regretted the necessity which forced his hand, but he'd do it again if it meant saving them from being pawns in someone else's game. His son gazed at him with a glint of anger.

"You know me, always flitting from here to there." Silas shrugged, his expression grim. "I went to Boston and finagled a job as a travel writer, so I could flit from place to place and never be required to settle down. Take advantage of my natural tendency to be flighty and irresponsible."

Sarcasm dripped from every syllable. His son's words recalled the boy's childhood. How Reggie had chided him for not finishing his little projects, always jumping on to the next wagon of interest. Starting something and then letting a new idea interrupt and he'd abandon one project for another. His easy curiosity led him to discover many adventures, true. But he wouldn't be able to hold a position for very long with his interests always changing. But when had Silas become so cynical and hurt?

"You both turned into fine young men despite your hardships, or perhaps because of them."

"What do you mean by that?" Daniel curled his fingers into a fist on the table.

"Daniel, please." Mercy held out her wraithlike hand as

if she'd like to lay it on his arm but hesitated.

"Now, son, don't upset your mother. I'm sorry about how your youth became such a challenge, but it forged you into real men." They had matured over the years, their trials and tribulations shaping and honing their confidence and skills. "You know your mother and I wouldn't have sent you away if—"

"Don't. Please." Silas held up a hand to stop him from continuing. "We can't change the past, Pa. Only look to the future. Or rather to the present mess we're all facing."

"The wedding this evening comes first, of course." Daniel pulled the cloth napkin from his lap and wiped his mouth. "Wilma is anticipating a fine evening and a beautiful ceremony."

Silas smiled at Daniel, a teasing quality twitching his lips. "I know she's anxious to plan her own wedding, but I do think it very kind of her to hold off until after her sister's wedding next month."

Why did they not want to clear the air about being forced from home? Instead, changing the subject to their individual futures. Well, if that was how they wanted to handle things. "Yes, it is. It's also very considerate of both of you to have come at your sister's plea." He glanced at his ghostly wife, a niggling feeling inside of him that time was running out. For who? A compulsion to make amends simmered in his chest as he regarded his sons. "I'm very proud of both of you."

"We don't need to have this conversation now or ever." Daniel tossed his napkin on the table. "In fact..."

"Everything all right in here?" Cassie and Wilma sauntered into the parlor and across to the table. "I could sense some tension so I thought I'd look in."

"Right, we want everyone to be happy on this grand day." Wilma smiled softly as she halted beside Daniel. He stood and pulled out another chair for her to sit down, which she did gracefully. "Thank you. Now, what were you discoursing about?"

"I was trying to apologize to Daniel and Silas for how we were forced to treat them before." Reggie scanned the faces peering at him. "I hope you can all forgive us and try to understand how much we love you and did what we had to in order to safeguard you."

"I accept your apology, Pa, only so you'll let the topic lie." Silas clutched his napkin in his lap and then dropped it on the table. "I've heard the excuses enough. Let's move past it."

Reggie nodded slowly as he regarded his sons. They'd both made good lives for themselves, ones they'd put on hold to come to their sister's aid. His entire family was growing and changing in wonderful ways. Being home again and surrounded by family felt right and good.

"Very well." He lifted his wine glass and the others followed suit. He smiled around the table at each of them. "To the future of our family."

The sheriff galloped away, leaving consternation to settle along with the dust from the horse's hooves. Flint stared after the receding horse, sifting through what he should do in answer to Neal's challenge. Well, not so much a challenge as a demand. One he'd hoped to avoid by going to the sheriff in the first place. Yet it landed right back on his doorstep. Heaving a frustrated sigh, he slowly turned to climb back up the front steps of the inn to the porch.

Giles picked at his guitar, a soft melody floating on the early afternoon air. He peered up at him with a quirked brow. "What did Neal want?"

"You don't look pleased." Silas hefted a mug and took a long draught.

"Not at all." Flint leaned against the support, his mind awhirl with conflicting ideas.

A high piercing cry from above drew his attention to the sky. The Merlin soared in circles on the updraft, silhouetted against the azure heavens. Slowly the falcon descended, angling its wings to coast toward the porch. Unusual for the raptor to not be with Cassie. What was Allegro doing coming to him?

"Did he have good news or bad?" Giles asked, his fingers dancing over the strings.

"Both, I suppose." How had he let Neal talk him into doing the impossible? Flint frowned at his companions.

Silas set his mug down and dragged a hand over his mouth. "We could use some good news."

Allegro landed on the railing, cocking his head to aim one eye at Flint as he continued. "Sheriff Neal believes us, that the gang is behind the killings." Who else could it possibly be though? Of course he believed them. The rest of what Neal wanted worried him far more than whether the man agreed as to who was behind the murders.

Giles switched from picking to strumming, the sound familiar and eerie. "So what's the bad news?"

Standing still became impossible. Flint pushed away from the post and paced along the railing, four strides one direction and then back. The spooky music filtered into his mind, stirring up any number of possible calamities while attempting to satisfy Neal's demand. If he prodded the wrong person, accused the wrong man, his career as an innkeeper would end abruptly. He'd lose the trust of those he cared about. Everything he'd worked so hard to achieve would face ruination. He raked his fingers through his hair as he turned to address the two waiting men.

"Neal wants us to provide evidence or a witness before he can arrest anyone." He shook his head as his companions stared up at him. "I know. Not only does he want us to find the evidence but he warned me that those men have become emboldened of late and so be careful. Oh, and in his words, 'keep your loved ones close' as if we haven't already been doing so."

"Did he also advise how we're to find evidence against this secretive bunch?" Silas tossed back the contents of his mug and slammed it down on the table. "That's absurd."

The music stopped as Giles rested his hands on the body of the guitar. "They meet here in our own dining room in order to watch us all. I can sense that much."

"It's not against any law to come to a public inn and have a meal and ale." Flint began pacing again, the steady thump of his leather shoes on the wood porch floor punctuating his thoughts. "They don't do anything here but conspire together. How's that evidence when all they do in our sight is talk?"

Damnation. He'd tried to get out from the middle before by bringing the law into the matter. Now he was stuck right back in the center of things. Why should any of them be tasked with finding the dirt on those men? Putting the entire family, but mostly his future wife, at even greater risk of retaliation. After all, they ascribed her with the role of leader of the supposed Fairhope coven. Was that even true? Did they have a coven? Confusion and dismay whirlpooled in his mind. Those men wanted to harm, kill, annihilate them but how could he prove it?

"Well, why do you suspect them of the murders if you've no proof?" Silas drummed his fingers on the table several times. "There must be something."

"I see the danger sign, the attacking owl, hovering over their table but only I can see it." Giles set his guitar down and grabbed up his glass of whiskey to take a gulp.

"Invisible symbols won't work, obviously." Flint continued pacing, anger building inside. "It's impossible. We have nothing to link any of them to any of the dead witches."

"I feel so damn helpless." Silas bounced his fist on the arm of the chair. "Hearsay doesn't prove anything."

Flint gazed at him, his thoughts spinning. The threat to the family escalated yet again. Keep his loved ones close, indeed. He'd like to wrap his arms around them and dare anyone to hurt them. Cassie's pleading expression filled his mind's eye. A simple hug was all she craved. Not one to protect but to comfort. How much longer did Mercy have before her wandering spirit finally could rest in peace? He drew in a breath and let it go. How could he say no?

"I know we don't have anything. Yet." Flint raked his fingers through his locks and then fisted his hands on his hips. "But those men are guilty. They've been meeting ever more frequently here and eventually they're going to make a mistake. They'll tip their hand so we can see their cards."

Allegro hopped once and then sprang into the air, flying away. Flint gazed after the bird until it disappeared into the clouds. Odd how Cassie's familiar visited him while he shared his upsetting news with the others. Like he listened and then made his own plan. Was that even possible?

Shrugging off his silly musings, he fixed his gaze on the Guardian.

Giles lifted his guitar and began picking idly along the strings as he glanced between Flint and Silas. "When they do, we'll be waiting."

Silas leaned forward to clasp his hands together on the table as he glared at Flint. "We're going to stop them one way or another. We must."

"Yes, we must." And he must give Cassie what she wanted. What she needed. One last real moment with her ghostly mother.

The eerie guitar music filled the parlor and chilled Reggie's heart. The fact that the music conveyed such emotion and attitude showcased his son's talent. At the same time, he wished for a different tune, a happier one or at least one not as melancholy and spooky.

Reggie had wandered away from the dining room after his luncheon with Silas and Daniel. He carried a book into the familiar, welcoming parlor and settled near the fireplace to read for a short while. Ever since he'd returned home, to his haven, he'd been beset with one emotional reunion after another. A little private time to gather his thoughts seemed a fine way to spend a few minutes. The fire snapped and popped quietly as it burned, keeping the chill away. He opened the book and lowered his eyes to peruse the pages while trying to ignore the music from outside.

Footsteps on the stairs interrupted his reading. He kept his head down but peeked to see who might be invading his privacy. Faith and Hope. Perfect. If he concentrated, mayhap they'd not notice him and keep on walking out of the parlor altogether. He held perfectly still as the steps came closer.

"Oh, Reggie, how nice to see you." Hope's voice shattered the peaceful moment. "Are we intruding?"

Even if he had to pretend, he'd attempt to make amends with his wife's sisters. If the family had any true hope of reuniting, then they'd all have to make some compromises. Starting with Hope and Faith. He knew why they'd encroached on his property but they needed to understand the complete situation and their role in settling the conflicts surrounding them.

Stifling an annoyed sigh, Reggie lifted his head. "No, of course not. Won't you join me?" He closed the engaging book and laid it on the table at his elbow to pick up after he confronted the two women.

"If you're sure?" Faith hesitated to take the seat opposite, her eyes flashing with suspicion. "I'm sure we don't wish to interrupt your...reading."

He gazed at her with a slow smile creeping onto his lips. She was very uncomfortable around him, as well she should be. "Please, we have much to catch up on after so long."

Hope gathered her voluminous skirts and eased onto a chair, smoothing the indigo fabric over her knees. "It has been quite a while. I am relieved to see you home safe and sound."

Faith sank onto the chair farthest from the fireplace, perching on the edge as though she didn't intend to linger. "Was it a very difficult journey?"

"Indeed. I have no intention of repeating it, but I believe the effort yielded significant benefits for the inn's clientele." Reggie crossed his legs and tapped his knee with a finger. "I'm much relieved to have come home in one piece despite all of our challenges."

"Scarlet mentioned you insisted on not letting her assist in easing the hardships. Why ever not?" Hope peered at him, curiosity in her expression.

"Call me old-fashioned I suppose." He could have relented and allowed her to help him transport everything and everyone with a whisper and a flick of their wands, but explaining the sudden disappearance in one place and then appearance at the inn would have been difficult. "As it is, we worked to achieve our goal instead of taking the easy way. I didn't want to misuse my magic for personal gain like some might."

He pinned his gaze on Faith, waiting for her to meet his eyes. He lifted one brow in a silent query which made her flush pink and glance away.

"I see. That's very sporting of you." Hope nodded at him even as she flicked an inquiring glance at her sister. "Now that you're home, I suppose things will go back to normal."

"I doubt that will happen. Flint has made some impressive strides in improving the business." He wouldn't penalize Flint by snatching his authority away from him. Rather he'd encourage him to continue acting as an associate innkeeper, working together. A shiver wiggled down his spine as he realized a part of him didn't want to take back the reins as much as he once thought. But he must gather them in hand since Flint and Cassie would marry and strike out on their own. He'd take her away from the inn to start their new life together. Then what would Reggie do? "I don't know how I'd have managed without his vision and his oversight."

"He has a good business sense." Hope shifted in her

seat, crossing her ankles. "I've been quite impressed with him since our arrival."

"Yes, I'm sure. Speaking of your stay, how long do you intend to occupy your accommodations?"

Hope tensed, her gaze sharpening on him. "Until Cassie agrees to be part of our trinity as is her destiny."

"She must accede to our demands." Faith crossed her arms over her chest, eyes glittering. "We need her just as our father decreed."

"Ah, yes. Your father." He stood to stare down at the two witches. "Let us speak about his ideas and his aims, shall we?"

Faith shrank back in her chair but glared at him with malice shining in her eyes. "He had his reasons."

"And they became yours, didn't they, Faith." He strode toward her but stopped short of towering over her. "That's why you were at the swimming lake that summer day, isn't it?"

Hope leveled her gaze on Faith. "You never told me you'd been to the lake."

Faith dropped her arms to grip the armrests with white-knuckled hands. "I didn't."

"Now, Faith, please. I saw you by the tree that afternoon, but I didn't have chance to speak to you because of everything else going on. Poor George. If only he hadn't gotten the silly idea of diving into the lake. Where do you think he got such an idea?"

"He wouldn't dive into the lake." Hope clutched her hands as she glanced between Reggie and Faith. "He knew better than that. It was far too shallow to dive in."

"Then I can't imagine why he would have done such a perilous thing. Do you?" Reggie angled his head as he watched Faith squirm in her seat.

"Faith?" Hope stared at her with growing alarm. "What did you do?"

"Yes, Faith, what *did* you do?" He smirked at her, goading her toward revealing the truth.

She lifted her chin and glowered at him. "I'm sure I don't know what you're referring to."

"Oh?" He smiled softly at her, enjoying her discomfiture. "I think you do."

Faith rose slowly to her feet, her face flushed with anger. "I don't have to listen to accusations from someone like you, Reginald Fairhope. I'm going to my room."

She marched away, her back straight and stiff, and up the steps without a backward glance. Reggie watched her go, knowing her secret festered in her soul. In time, he'd help her excise the guilt-ridden boil but not quite yet.

Chapter Eleven

llegro's preening presence in the family parlor helped center her emotions. Cassie grasped her hands together as she crossed the floor to stand by Flint. Despite the anticipation of what Flint had agreed to on Cassie's behalf, she simply vibrated with excitement. Her betrothed had approached her with the idea mere hours after he'd refused, saying only that he'd changed his mind. She sensed he'd had some kind of revelation to enable him to agree. She didn't want to ask too many questions as to why. Better to accept the remarkable gift with her heartfelt gratitude.

"Are you ready, Cassie?" Scarlet stood by Flint, poised as if to prevent him fleeing from the room. Her maroon dress swirled about her black shoes, her dark tresses cascading down her back. "I'll guide Flint through the process once you are."

The anxiety and love emanating from him blended with Cassie's nervous anticipation. She desired to feel her ma's approbation toward her marriage within the loving circle of her arms. Her dream wedding, the one she'd planned since a girl, always included the tender moment of approval and blessing prior to her pa giving her away to her new husband. She smiled at Aunt Scarlet and then pushed reassurance out to Flint, until his frame eased against the chair back. The time had finally arrived and she couldn't help but smile.

"Ma, I need you." She called out to her mother, never sure if she would respond. Especially now that her ghostly form seemed more insubstantial each time she appeared.

Scarlet shifted to stand in front of Flint, resting a hand on his shoulder. "That's right. Relax and open your mind and your heart to accept the spirit of the person you want to host."

"She's not here. Will that matter?" Flint let go of the chair and draped his arms on the armrests. "I mean, she's welcome but I don't want any other random ghosts taking up residence."

Scarlet chuckled as she leaned closer to him. "Focus on Mercy and invite her in. Cassie, if you can summon your mother again, please."

She nodded as she perused the room, waiting and hoping for her mother's ghost to materialize. Flint reclined in a chair by the fireplace, attempting to follow Scarlet's instructions. His emotions ran high, one of those being a fierce purpose. Nothing would prevent him from hosting Mercy. She could only wonder as to the cause of his resolve.

She skimmed her gaze around the room. "Ma, please? I need you now." How much longer Flint would wait was hard to gauge. His inner struggle between complying and running remained strong. "Where are you?"

Mercy shimmered into view by the doll's house, an

inquiring expression on her face. "Did you want something, dear?"

"Thank you for coming, Ma. I do want something." She motioned toward Flint's strained expression. "We do, in fact."

"What might that be?" Mercy tilted her head and floated closer to Cassie.

She half smiled at her mother, pulling in a long breath before letting it out. "A hug from you." Saying the words made the concept all the more real. The last motherly embrace she'd experienced had occurred way back in June, four months earlier. She'd thanked her mother for the beautiful dresses and hats she'd purchased for her in Nashville with a long, grateful embrace. An eternity ago.

"A hug? I don't know that I have the strength any longer." Mercy shifted side to side as she regarded Cassie with growing eagerness. "You know something, don't you. Is it really possible?"

"Yes, Mercy, it is." Scarlet beckoned to her, inviting her closer. "Flint will host you long enough for you and your daughter to have one last embrace. If you want to, of course."

"I would love a hug." Mercy slid her surprised gaze to Cassie. "But do you really want to? After all I've done?"

"Maybe partly because of everything that has passed between us. I want to put all of it behind us, forgive and forget."

Her ma stared at her with a gentle expression. Allegro flew to Cassie and landed with an easy grasp of her shoulder. The last several months they had clashed over Cassie's need for freedom, as well as Flint's role as fill-in innkeeper and then as her beau and betrothed, until finally he had won Mercy over to believe in his fine character. Now they were to marry in a few hours. So much had happened in a relatively short span of time. Her mother's demonstration of approval would be the icing on the proverbial wedding cake.

"There is much I wish I could take back." Mercy shimmered, her spectral image dimming as she squinted at Cassie. "I hope you can forgive me."

Her ma verged on transparent. They should hurry. "I do. Flint, are you ready?"

He swallowed, a grim smile on his lips. "Come on, Mrs. Fairhope, I'm sure you're as anxious as Cassie."

Allegro flapped his wings twice before he launched from Cassie's shoulder to alight on the back of a chair across from Flint. The falcon must understand what they said. There simply was no other explanation. She shook her head slightly and then met her ma's gaze. "I'm ready when you are."

Flint nodded but remained silent, concentrating on opening himself to host Mercy's spirit.

Scarlet beckoned to Mercy to approach Flint, and then looked at the soon-to-be ghost host. "Relax and open your mind, welcome her spirit inside."

Mercy floated to Flint, hesitating in front of him before she leaned toward where he sat with his eyes closed in anticipation of her merging with him. Her ma disappeared at the same time Flint jerked in his seat. Cassie flashed a look at Scarlet, who nodded in reassurance, then looked back to Flint. His eyes flew open and he darted his gaze about the room, finally landing on Cassie as he pushed out of his chair.

"My dear, come to me."

Cassie blinked, hearing not the masculine voice she expected but her ma's dulcet tones. "Ma?"

Hearing her mother's voice from her fiancé's mouth took a moment of adjustment. She tried to picture her ma's features, her light blue dress, her slim figure instead of Flint's afternoon shadow on his jaw, his crisp white shirt, dark vest and trousers, and his muscular frame. Like when Abram shifted into her form, she needed to pause to accept the switch. She focused on the emotional state of the person inside of the outer shell of the human form, recalling her ma's eagerness and abiding love despite her tendency to be overly protective and judgmental. Cassie looked beneath the surface to see the spirit inside.

Mercy smiled and stepped toward Cassie. "I don't know how long we have, but like you I've longed to comfort you, to show you how much I care and that I support your decision."

"Thank you so much." Without further thought, Cassie hurried into her mother's open arms, relishing the feel of her embrace tight about her shoulders. Tears smarted in her closed eyes, forcing themselves out from behind her lids to course freely down her cheeks. "I love you, Ma. Thank you for everything you've done for me. I'll never forget you."

"I trust you will have a long and happy life with Flint." Mercy squeezed her tighter. "He's proven his worth to me many times over. Knowing he will be looking out for you makes leaving you easier."

She couldn't think about her mother departing and never returning. Not now. She'd grown accustomed to having her ghost around. Once she moved on to whatever other realm lay ahead, then Cassie would never again have the chance to speak to her, to seek her guidance and wisdom. She'd be motherless for all time.

Holding on for a few moments longer gave her time to compose herself. With a sniff, Cassie lifted her head from her ma's shoulder. "I love you."

Footfalls interrupted the tender moment between mother and daughter. Cassie glanced over her shoulder at her aunts striding into the parlor. Hope entered first, with Faith trailing behind her. She pulled away from her ma, ending their final hug.

"Isn't that too sweet for words?" Faith chortled as she drew closer to Cassie.

Cassie stiffened, turning to face the two witches, as the warmth of her mother's embrace dissipated with each passing moment. How dare they belittle her precious time with her mother? They were hateful and evil. She bristled as they stopped beside her. "You're just jealous of the relationship I've had with your sister. The sister you pushed away, threatened with unspeakable retaliation. Then came after me."

"My sister? What has she to do with you hugging your betrothed?" Startled, Hope peered closer at her and then at Flint, her eyes widening. "Ah, he's allowed the witch inside of him. How brave of the man. Or how foolish."

"I'm very surprised at you." Faith arched her brows at Cassie. "Why would you want your mother to inhabit your betrothed? Ever?"

Bewildered curiosity filled the air around Cassie as her aunts regarded her. Hope tried to hide her intrigue under a layer of contempt while Faith struggled to mask her own dislike for the situation beneath sarcasm and dismissal. As the two powerful witches detected her probe, though, they shielded their emotions behind a defensive wall.

"I needed a real hug from her before I marry Flint this evening. Is that so hard to fathom?" She'd recall the special feeling of her ma's arms for the rest of her life. No matter what the witches might say next, they couldn't steal the treasured memory away.

From the puzzled gazes aimed at her, she'd say they didn't understand at all. She glared at them, silently daring them to continue their spiteful tirade.

"All right, Flint, Mercy, that's enough." Scarlet broke the standoff with a sharp tone. "Flint, sit down before you fall down, and Mercy, you need to vacate his body."

Flint moved back to resume his seat as the haint of Mercy appeared beside the chair, nearly invisible this time. Flint slumped, eyes glazed with fatigue.

Cassie rushed to smooth hair from his eyes, inspecting their depths for any signs of trouble. "Are you all right?"

"I-I think so. That was more draining than I'd thought it would be." He rubbed his face with a hand before meeting her worried gaze. "She loves you far more than she ever told you. All of you. Knowing now how deeply she loves her children, and her family, makes her decisions and actions even more meaningful than I've given her credit for. She suffered greatly by sending your brothers away, by not having her sisters around for support."

Exactly what she'd always suspected. Her ma would never have admitted to feeling such a depth of emotion toward anyone, presuming it showed weakness. Obviously, her sisters believed the same thing. Cassie probed their emotions, running into the wall surrounding them. Not this time. She needed the truth. Summoning her powers, she silently called on Giles to augment her abilities with his strength. She concentrated on her aunts and brick by emotional brick broke through their barriers. She sent acceptance toward them, relieved when they didn't fight her influence. Their belief in their sister's guilt with regard to their mother's death wavered, flickering toward understanding what had truly happened in the past.

"I always thought there was more there." Cassie straightened to address her aunts surrounding her. Aunt Hope and Aunt Faith leveled stoic looks at her, but she could tell the exchange gave them something new to consider. "Now I know for certain."

She turned back to Flint to plant a kiss on his mouth. "Thank you for sharing the truth of the depth of my mother's love with me. I'll always treasure that revelation."

Perhaps seeing for themselves the reality of their sister's love would have a positive impact on Faith and Hope. She could only cross her fingers and see what they'd do next.

Being bested by a younger, less experienced man never set well with him. Reggie roamed the Fury Falls property, poking around to see what Flint had changed, added, improved in his absence. Flint had gone and done exactly what he'd asked him to do. Work on identifying and improving the inn's offerings before his special guest visited in November. Turned out, he'd managed to do much good in a short amount of time. Not that Reggie was surprised, but seeing it laid out so nicely gave him pause.

He'd started his solitary tour of the property behind the inn, glad to be outside on a fine fall afternoon. He had a short amount of time before he'd need to go in for midafternoon dinner or miss out on Sheridan's scrumptious shepherd's pie. Pausing on the back porch to survey the outbuildings arrayed across the stretch of lawn between the inn and the forest, he noted the extra-tall fence protecting his daughter's large and bountiful garden at the far right. Her love of gardening pleased him beyond words. She tended to each variety of flower and vegetable like a loving parent. Seeing to their needs and ensuring they grew tall and proud. She'd be an excellent wife and mother.

He strolled off the porch, thumping down the handful of steps to the grassy expanse and on toward the dirt path up to the hot springs and falls above. The white crushed stone on the carriageway glinted in the sunlight as he crunched across the expanse. That innovation may be Flint's best improvement to the property. Removing the quagmire that formed at the entrance after a hard rain made arriving passengers happy. Reducing the billowing clouds of dust on dry days made everyone tasked with cleaning the inn happy, too. The boy was indeed clever and capable. Now that Reggie had come home, he'd have to find some way to properly acknowledge Flint's contributions to preparing for the senator's upcoming visit.

The stable, too, had been spruced up. The front of the barn boasted flowering bushes on either side of the freshly painted red and black doors, the sides of the barn gleaming red with black trim. One of the stable lads whitewashed the fencing around the pastures, white paint smattered on his work pants and tan shirt. The dogs kept him company, sunbathing in the grass. Reggie smiled at the sight, glad in his heart he'd acquired the dogs. He enjoyed having the canines around as both watch dogs and companions.

Leaving the flatter part of the property, he began the climb to the falls. Breathing deeply, he savored the familiar scents of pine and sun-warmed earth. He'd been gone from home far too long. The tranquility of the property had enticed him to put down roots the first time he'd set foot on it. He'd sensed the love and care of those who'd once lived on the land. Likely Indians and transient types, fur trappers and hunters who had helped discover the wealth and riches of the land itself. That discovery brought more and more people from the east, looking for land and the wealth it yielded. His friend John had come in search of greater wealth, despite having already made a fortune in the Carolinas. He'd brought with him both the knowledge and the luck required to continue to build his fortune, both of which he'd readily shared with Reggie.

The view of the foothills, covered in an array of reds, golds, and browns with shades of green woven between, made him breathe more freely. A few fleecy white clouds drifted across the azure sky. A perfect day for the triple wedding in a few hours. His thoughts drifted back to when he'd married Mercy. Another beautiful day, one replete with hope and love.

They'd married at her parents' home, saying their vows before the local minister in the decorated formal parlor. She wore a cream satin gown with a pale pink lacy hat, holding a bouquet of red roses and daisies. He'd never forget the love shining in her eyes as they faced each other while the minister performed the ceremony. Only the family attended, as they'd wanted to keep the event intimate. Reggie wasn't much for being around a lot of people, and Mercy had said she didn't want to make a fuss. Neither admitted to their real concern: how the neighbors would react to having two powerful magical families join forces. What neither of them had anticipated was that the neighbors had every reason to worry.

Putting one foot in front of the other, he made his way slowly up to the fragrant hot springs. There he found other improvements, a small hut built where guests could change into bathing outfits. The surrounding of the springs had been cleared of rocks to enable an easier approach on foot to the steaming waters. Several stone benches flanked the waters, giving people a place to sit and relax. He took a minute to survey the area, the bucolic scene easing but never erasing the pain in his breast.

His homecoming had been far more distressing than he'd ever let on to his family. Especially Cassie. The first night he'd spent in his bedchamber proved how much coming home broke his heart. Though he suspected Cassie already sensed his dismay. Burdening her or anyone else with his loneliness would be unfair and unfatherly. It was his burden to shoulder. His grief to bear. But, oh, how he missed his wife.

Shakespeare's line about counting the many ways of loving someone flowed into his mind. What about counting the ways of missing the one you love? Of the longing, the desire, the futile hopes? Was there an abacus for counting those? Maybe he'd make one for the purpose. Red beads on a black rod, his heart pierced through and left to bleed dry. On the road heading home he'd wondered what state he'd find her ghostly form. How vibrant would her haint be? An indication of her remaining time on earth. What he found confirmed his worst fears.

Not only Mercy but the other spirits lingering around the property had some unfinished business in need of resolution before they could rest in peace. Each ghost harbored a secret need or desire which must be satisfied. Only then would their restless roaming end and their spirit find eternal rest. He'd suspected a few spirits lingered on the property when he'd purchased it, but now many more haunted the place. The land seemed a gathering place for ghosts, as if the spot marked a crossing point. Over time, perhaps they'd finish their business and move on without his help. He could hope.

Maybe he should find out for himself. He scoured the vicinity until he spotted the perfect area. Positioning himself in the middle of the small level clearing, he spread his arms wide and lifted his face to the sky. Chanting his summoning spell, he slowly pivoted in place, scanning his surroundings for signs of spirits. The air around him quivered, opening to receive haints from another dimension. Shadows shimmered and formed into translucent beings.

"Welcome and greetings, my friends." Reggie kept his arms wide as he nodded to each of the spirits in a ragged circle around him. "I wish only to know why you are here. Do you need help crossing over?"

They must have a reason for staying nearby. Even without realizing it herself, Mercy had told him why her presence had dimmed. She'd been waiting for him to come home and make things right. Despite Allhallows providing spirits the ability to revisit the living, her time to cross neared with each passing moment. As long as he was away, she'd remained to protect the family to the best of her phantasmal ability. Now... He swiped a hand over his brow, closing his eyes against the pain in his chest. Now, she had begun to let go, to find her way to her grave. The very thought shafted pain through his heart. The piercing cry of a red-tailed hawk circling high above opened his eyes again. The lighter underside of the bird's outstretched wings contrasted against the blue heavens. Contrasted like the hope and the devastation warring inside of him.

The ring of spectral forms began to spin around him, slowly at first, then building up speed until they whirled around him. Their demands and needs tumbled into his brain, piling together into a steady stream of anguish. The onslaught threatened to defeat him with the emotional power aimed at him. He flung his arms wide and shouted into the maelstrom snatching at his hair and clothes. "I hear you and will do what I can. Now leave me be!"

Crossing his arms at the wrist, he flung his arms outward and sent a force of his own to empty the clearing of all beings but himself. As the wind died down and silence settled around him, he dragged in a shaky breath. The haints had lingered to avenge their murders. The dead witches sought out the Fairhope coven's assistance to end the threat against their kind. They would not rest until the culprit was caught and punished.

He straightened his clothes, tugging down his vest and smoothing his hair into place. Glancing at the sun, he determined he must make his way back to the inn. As soon as his heart stopped racing and he could breathe steadily again. He sat down on a bench to compose himself, searching the edges of the clearing for any last vestiges of the spirits.

Almost time to go back, to go on with the rest of his life. But how could he without his beloved at his side? He would never find another woman like Mercy. No other woman could ever measure up to her. Yet he'd failed in his marriage vows. She'd died without him there to protect her. Her precious things tossed about, broken, stolen. If Greg's ghost had been telling the truth, the precious locket was still on the property. If Reggie and Cassie worked together, surely they'd locate it. Reclaim one piece of her past, of her connection to his parents. Before they'd been taken from her. He could do that much.

The wedding was set for only a handful of hours from that moment. He looked forward to sending three of his children on toward their future lives with their spouses in grand style. He'd conjured some ideas of appropriate gifts for each of them. Gifts which would help them start their new lives in fine style and on a firm footing.

He didn't need things as much as he once thought. Not while living on his own without a wife. He faced years ahead of being alone. Without a spouse to share his day, his worries, his fears. He'd put on a brave front for the sake of his family, but his children's sweet concern simply didn't compare to that of his loving wife. Still, he owed them his protection and that he would certainly do.

He squared his shoulders as he watched the hawk circle above, salty tears slipping from the corners of his eyes. He may never be whole again, but he'd be strong for his family if it was the last thing he ever did.

Chapter Twelve

Where could it be? Cassie had already searched her bedchamber. Her ma's missing locket had reminded her of the missing pearl earbob. Her favorite one she'd lost while trying on dresses for the looming nuptials. She'd tossed the bed linens and quilt. Dug through the bureau drawers. Poked her head into the depths of the wardrobe. Rummaged through the shallow drawers of the writing desk and reached into the row of pigeonholes along the back edge. All while Allegro snoozed on the back of the bedframe, his beak tucked under his wing. She didn't want to wake him but she did want to find her earbob.

She needed a finding spell. A quick one that would be easy to recall. Mayhap it would also help her locate her mother's locket. She still had some time before Mandy would arrive to primp and dress for their joint wedding ceremony. Haley had gone home to nap and refresh herself before the big event. A nap sounded heavenly. Unfortunately, Cassie couldn't have laid down to sleep if her life depended on it. She'd rather keep busy.

Perched on the edge of the chair in front of the writing

desk, she tapped her pen against her cheek as she stared at the blank sheet of paper before her. Something short and direct, simple and memorable. But what? A cool breeze pushed the light curtains toward her and then let them fall back. Dogs barked and horses whinnied outside. Teddy's voice floated on the breeze, indistinct urging words which suggested he herded chickens toward their roost.

If something were indeed lost, what words would have the power to call it out from hiding? She mulled over phrases before jotting down words which seemed to convey her will.

> *Day or night, by star or light*
> *Reveal the place, shine on its face*
> *Restore the lost to its true home.*

Not bad for a first attempt. But place? Restore? Was there a better, more precise word? She needed help with her writing.

"Hey, sister, what are you doing?" Silas strolled through the open door into the bedchamber. His easy grin and loose stride suggested he'd settled into life at the inn, at least for the time being. But she sensed his wandering ways still lurked in the recesses of his mind.

She leaned back in her chair and welcomed his presence with a smile. "You have perfect timing." She handed him the paper with a flourish of her hand. "What do you think of this?"

He scanned the page and then lifted quizzing eyes at her. "What is it?"

"A finding spell. I hope anyway."

He studied the spell with pursed lips as he took her

pencil and scrawled on the page. Scratched out a phrase and rewrote it. Then handed the paper to her. "How's that?"

She took the paper back and scanned the new spell. "That's much better. Thank you."

"Will you sing it?" He crossed to sit on the bed, jostling the falcon awake in the process.

Poor Allegro couldn't even take a nap without being bothered. He blinked at her and then flapped his wings, resettling them along his sides. He perused his surroundings with a sleepy sweep of his head. Then he dozed off again.

She looked back to the paper in her hand. "I am not sure yet." Which had more power, singing or chanting? Did her voice have more force, more effect when she sang? Something to tinker with to understand the nuances between the effort used for speaking versus singing. While she preferred singing, not every situation needed song. A quick chant may be more useful.

"What do you plan to sing?" Scarlet halted at the open doorway. "Sorry if I'm being nosey but I couldn't help but hear as I was looking for Reggie. Have you seen him?"

"He went out to see if he might spot where the locket was hidden, and to survey the state of the property in general." Silas rested his palms on his knees, a knowing glint in his eyes. "More so, I believe he needed some time alone."

Cassie had sensed the same thing from her father before he'd gone off on his rounds of the property. Giles had completed his security walk but her father struggled with an overwhelming amount of emotional revelations. He tried to hide his disquiet from her but she'd snuck around his defenses more than once to find out for herself how he fared. His emotions ran high. Coming home to find his wife a ghost being the most weighty reason for them.

"I've written a finding spell. I've misplaced an earbob so I thought it might help me find it. If so, it might be useful with locating the locket as well." She motioned to the page. "Silas helped me improve it. Shall I try it?"

Scarlet crossed her arms and nodded. "Let's see what it does."

Cassie stood and moved to the center of the room. She centered herself, closing her eyes and breathing deeply for several moments. Then she read the spell, chanting it several times as she slowly spun in a circle.

Day or night, dark or light
Expose the site, shine a light
To return the lost to its true home.

As she pivoted she saw a flash of blue light in the far corner of the room. She hurried over to bend down and poke into the corner where the floor boards met the molding. A crevice hid between them, the pearl set in gold wedged into its depths. She pried it out and inspected it, relieved no damage appeared to its surface.

Turning around she held it up in triumph. "I found it. It worked!"

Silas and Scarlet applauded, grinning at her success. Cassie dipped a curtsy as she chuckled. "Now to see if it will help us find the locket."

She gazed at the pair, a happy smile on her lips. Her aunt and her brother were now part of her life. How had she endured life without family around? Musing over the last few months as compared to the last few years highlighted the vast differences in the forces and harmony surrounding her. Knowledge of her true nature, her abilities, and her expanding family all combined to enrich and empower her life. Her family grew and stretched in both capacity and capability. Her heart swelled with pleasure.

"I am so grateful to have you both here." Family must come first.

Scarlet glided closer, snaring Cassie's hands in her own. "I'm glad I decided to come here with my brother. To meet you and your brothers. I only wish I'd been allowed to know you sooner."

"We all lost out on that opportunity." Silas slid his hands into his trouser pockets. "At least we can correct the oversight."

"I understand Reggie's reasons but truly wish it hadn't been necessary to keep the family apart." Scarlet released Cassie's hands, exploring her expression with sparkling eyes. "We'll need to spend all the more time together to make up for what we've lost."

"Agreed." Cassie pulled her into a hug, one nearly as satisfying as the one with her mother earlier in the day. As she eased back, she caught sight of her mother shimmering into the room. "Ma, what brings you here?"

"I'm delighted to see you getting along so well. It warms my soul to have the family reunited." Mercy's diaphanous form flickered by the writing desk. "Just be careful to not let your guard down where my sisters are concerned. They may act all lovey dovey, but they can still do damage."

Her pushy, powerful aunts were not nearly as supportive as Aunt Scarlet acted in the short period she'd been at the inn. Why couldn't Hope and Faith see how much their efforts forced a chasm between them? Yet, they had hesitated more than once recently as their way hadn't yielded the results they'd aimed for so arduously. Lessons learned?

"I don't believe they feel quite so strong about their previous demands." At least, she hoped so. She'd tried to dissuade them from strong-arming her into working with them. Instead, providing other ways they could all work together for different aims. Hers, in fact. "But I'll take what you say to heart."

Time had a way of flying even when he wasn't having fun. Flint only had a couple of hours to complete the new bedchambers. They already boasted the new furniture hauled so carefully hundreds of miles, but the finishing touches still needed for the door frames and floor moldings glared at him. He rubbed a roughened hand over his jaw, grimacing at the stubble rasping against his fingers. The sleeping arrangements would need to change after the wedding ceremony in mere hours. He'd already moved the aunts to their new room in the family residence. Sheridan and Pansy were safely settled in an upstairs former guest chamber, with Zander and Matt across the hall. It seemed only right to keep that long-separated family together. But he needed to finish the guest bedchambers ready to receive the influx of tired travelers on the morrow for the open house and Allhallows festivities. But the detailed finishing work proved more than he could handle.

"What's the matter, Flint? You look to be under some strain." Beck's deep-throated chuckle pulled Flint out of his musing.

"I need a carpenter now but they're all booked for the next few weeks. Just look at that." The gap between the rough surround of the door and the swinging door itself allowed anyone tromping past to peek inside the room. Nobody would want to change out of their dusty clothes into fresh ones let alone climb into the comfy bed with such a lack of privacy. He shook his head as he met Beck's gaze, eyes dancing with mirth. "You think it's humorous?"

"You do know I'm a carpenter by trade, don't you?" Beck eased closer to the door to examine its state of completion. "This won't take long at all to finish."

"Wait. You're a carpenter?" How had he missed such an important bit of information? He must have been preoccupied with other concerns to have overlooked that aspect of Beck's abilities. "What have you made?"

The disbelief in the other man's entire expression gave Flint pause. Beck raised both brows as he swept the room with an arm through the air. "All of this furniture that my brother ordered, for one thing. And don't forget the doll's house he had me craft to his exacting specifications for Cassie."

The miniature house had fine detailing, exquisite gingerbread style decorations around the roofline as well as gracefully carved porch posts and railings. Flint had been impressed with the fine workmanship when Cassie had opened the surprising gift on her eighteenth birthday back in July. If Beck possessed such fine capabilities, then Flint would gladly turn over the remaining finishing to his expertise.

"She has come to appreciate that house. It is a fine example of your talent." Flint peered at him, rubbing his jaw as he considered his options. The tapping of hammers on slender nails echoed from above and around him in the rooms of the addition. But he had to see to the rest of the preparations before he prepared himself for the wedding. "Might you lead the remaining efforts to finish up the addition? I have some other tasks I need to tend to before the ceremony. Daniel can help you for a bit, as he's expressed an interest in working with his hands as a result of working on all this."

"I'm happy to help. I don't want to lose my touch." Beck quirked a brow. "Though I don't need to only use my hands to work my magic with wood, if you get my drift."

"Your magic, you say." Flint searched the other man's sly countenance, recognizing the subtle implication of his words. Given they stood in the very public part of the inn, his precaution was appreciated. "Yes, I understand."

The warlock used his hands and his magical vision to enhance the appearance of the finished product. No matter whether it was furniture or floor boards. Just what he put into the finished product was a matter of conjecture. Or perhaps conjuring. He glanced around, ensuring they weren't overheard.

"I'll leave you to it then. And just in time, there's Daniel to lend a hand." Flint beckoned to Daniel to hurry closer. "Daniel, Beck here is a fine carpenter and would like your help to make the final touches. Are you willing?"

Daniel shook hands with Beck and then nodded. "I have some time, so that is fine. But I'll need to be putting the finishing touches on myself ere long."

"Why, you're not getting married." Beck smirked at him, teasing humor in his eyes.

"No, but I want to set a good example for this guy here." Daniel punched Flint on the shoulder. "You look pretty rough at the moment. I can't let you marry my sister in such a state."

"He better not appear in such an aspect of disarray to marry my daughter." Reggie strode from the inn's passage leading from the entrance hall past the dining room. His sharp gaze surveyed the four new rooms flanking a short hall off of the main passage with intense interest. Then he leveled his sober gaze on Flint. "The addition looks fine, Flint. You've done well, just as John told me in his weekly reports. I'm very pleased with all of the improvements you've made. I just came in from touring the property to see for myself what you've done."

Sweet relief flooded Flint's soul. He'd worried himself into a state on more than one occasion wondering about and fearing his employer's reaction to the many unapproved changes he'd wrought on the property and its amenities. Having Beck help with the final tasks with the addition took the last weight off his shoulders as well. Since Reggie had returned to take over management, the addition and the gathering the next day may well prove his last efforts as interim innkeeper. Then he would need to find another position. Going back to work for his own father didn't entice, but he'd prefer to do so than have no employment. Especially needing to support a wife.

"Thank you, sir. I appreciate your kindness." Add retrieving his stack of architectural and hostelry magazines to his list of things to do. He'd had offers from other hotels over the last few months, ones he'd declined but now he'd need to revisit them. "The inn is ready for you to take over control again."

Reggie inhaled slowly and let out the breath. "Right. For now, I must excuse myself to help Cassie with an urgent task. One she wants to accomplish before she'll don her wedding garb."

"What sort of task is so important?" Daniel hesitated before turning to follow Beck down the short hall to the next room in need of attention.

"We're going on a treasure hunt." Reggie grinned before he spun around to hurry back into the main section of the inn. "Don't be long."

"Right behind you, sir." Flint's future wife had some strange timing if she needed to go in search of hidden treasure before she'd dress for their wedding ceremony. Then he paused. The locket. She desired to find it, perhaps to wear it to the ceremony. He poked a finger at both Daniel and Beck with a warning look. "Don't take too much longer on this addition for today, men. We need to be ready after the supper rush to gather at the gazebo."

"Do not fret." Daniel punched him on the shoulder again. "Relax. We won't make you wait one more day to claim my sister."

Flint rubbed the aching joint. "I'll be glad when the addition is all finished and everything in its proper place. The senator will be here in a few days, probably tired from his trek across country. He'll want a hot bath and a comfortable bed. Then I'll relax."

Beck guffawed. "So you're anxious for everyone to find their new beds, especially the newly married, is that correct?"

Heat crept into Flint's cheeks. His growing eagerness exposed to the jaded light of day left him feeling vulnerable. Why shouldn't he anticipate the pleasures of wedded life with a beautiful, intelligent woman? He opened his mouth to put them in their place and then hesitated. Better remain circumspect with her brother and uncle. "Just finish your job and I'll see you later."

The sun hung low in the sky as she gathered with her father, Aunt Scarlet, and Giles in front of the inn. Time was running out to complete the task of finding her ma's locket. Time was also running out for her ma to witness her daughter's wedding. Urgency sizzled inside her veins as she observed the others. Allegro soared above, his wings outstretched against the darkening sky. Sunset came earlier as autumn leaned toward winter, bringing darkness earlier along with it. She dreaded the longer nights ahead, but this year she'd have Flint to share them. A happy thought.

"Are you ready?" The somber expressions aimed at her echoed her own determination. "We need to hurry."

"I hope we can find it." Her pa gazed at her, his brows drawn. "The minister will be here in a little under two hours. You best begin."

As her time of being a child, a maiden, drew closer to ending, her womanhood reached out to welcome her. The locket bridged both worlds, an heirloom of her mother's that would carry memories into Cassie's future as a wife and eventually a mother. A twinge roiled her stomach. Children of her own. Wards to rear and teach. She swallowed her sudden unease. While not ready for all that came with becoming a mother, her role in marriage included bearing her husband's children, his heirs. She'd manage. For now, she simply needed to find a small piece of jewelry on a large expanse of property.

"Here we go." She steeled herself for possible failure but resolved to do her best. Chanting her finding spell, she strolled around the area in front of the inn.

Allegro circled above, slowly lowering his circuit. Drawing closer as he also kept an eye on possible hiding places for the locket.

Giles paced beside Cassie, his gaze scanning restlessly. Scarlet stayed close to Reggie as they searched in every nook and cranny of the inn's exterior. Surely it hid somewhere easy to stuff a small item in quickly.

She pictured the locket in her mind as she chanted, focusing entirely on its oval frames folded closed with a tiny clasp. The pictures inside, miniatures of her grandparents, displaying two people without smiles. Their fine attire, carefully arranged hair, and somber countenances her only clue to the people she'd never met. Would never meet, since they'd both passed on long ago. Her ma hadn't told her much about it, only showing it to her years before when Cassie had surprised her in her room, staring at the pictures.

"Say it with me, Giles." Adding his voice to hers should increase the power of her spell. Extend its range and strength.

Maintaining a rhythmic chant of the spell, she prayed it would work. The vast acreage covered with trees, bushes, and the river itself stretched in all directions. What if he'd hidden it in the barn, in a knot hole in a board somewhere? How would they ever find it? Doubt would only hinder her effort, so she resolutely pushed it aside. Her spell had worked earlier to find her earbob, it would work now. It must.

A flash of blue light jerked her attention toward the verge of the forest stretching beyond the gazebo toward the highway. She'd seen a similar light in her room before discovering the earbob. Could it be?

"Over there. That oak, maybe?" She pointed to a young oak tree several yards into the forest.

"Klee! Klee!" Allegro dove toward the tree, wings back to increase his speed. Swooping up to brake his careering flight, he landed on a branch near a small opening in the side of the trunk. He angled his head toward Cassie, his dark eye gleaming in the dimming sunlight, then dipped his beak into the narrow slash in the bark. When he pulled back, a glint of gold made her gasp.

"He found something. Thank you, Allegro!" What a clever bird she had as a friend and familiar. She ran across the grassy expanse to the base of the tree, her heart pounding. The falcon leapt into the air and then flew down to drop the object into her upraised hands. She turned the locket over to inspect both sides, fine filigree flowers on one side and the inscription "With you always" engraved on the other. "Look!"

Giles skidded to a halt beside her. "That's amazing. You're amazing, Cassie."

Scarlet and Reggie hurried to join Cassie and Giles. Scarlet leaned in to peek at the locket. "I remember that. It's been a long time since I saw it last."

Reggie huffed a sigh. "Too long, truth be told. But we didn't want to risk anyone asking questions so she wouldn't wear it. Instead, she kept it in her box, close to hand, where she could look at it when she missed my parents."

Cassie startled. "Your parents? Why?"

"Because they gave it to her upon our marriage. Carrying a token of love from them provided protection as long as she wore it." Reggie grimaced as he stared at it for several beats of her frantic heart. "Obviously, since she wasn't wearing it at the time of her death, it must work or she wouldn't be a ghost now."

The memory of the violent end to her ma replayed through her mind's eye. Finding her body bleeding from a head wound on the carpet in her bedchamber. Alone. Cassie hadn't been there to comfort her as she lay dying. She closed her hand over the locket, holding it close. If only her ma had worn the talisman, even if she'd kept it hidden from others' eyes. Perhaps she'd still be alive.

"Why don't you keep that as my engagement gift to you." Her pa wrapped an arm around her shoulders and squeezed. "I want you to have it."

"You could replace the pictures of your grandparents with ones of your parents." Scarlet rubbed her hands together. "I'm sure they'd approve."

Cassie clutched the locket, sensing the spirits of her grandparents echoing in the fine gold casement. "I think that's a fine idea. I'll need to have some commissioned..."

"No, let me." Scarlet rubbed her hands faster and then stopped to splay them toward the sun and sky. With a light clap of her hands and some mystical words, a pair of miniature portraits lay on her fingers. "My gift to you as well."

Scarlet handed the pictures to Cassie with a flourish. The small squares of paper showed the images of her mother and father, carefully stern expressions in place. Mercy wore her favorite blue gown with her blonde hair artfully arranged on her head. Reggie appeared in a dark suit, vest, and white shirt with a refined hat snug on his gray-tinged dark hair.

Opening the locket, Cassie memorized the faces of her grandparents Fairhope. "How do I put them in?"

"If you'll allow me..." Reggie snapped his fingers and the

small squares disappeared from her hand and reappeared within the tiny frames of the locket. "All set."

She snapped the locket closed and then lifted the chain over her head to allow it to hang around her neck. "Thank you both. I'll treasure it always."

She'd wear it every day, knowing in her heart how her family loved her and she them. Knowing no matter what else befell her or any of them, they would always have each other. She'd grown more capable, more intuitive, and more aware with the arrival of her brothers and then again when more of her family joined the others residing at the Fury Falls Inn. Her abilities exceeded her hopes and with the talisman in place, she'd be protected on another level as well.

"Now that we've found the locket, what say you to going inside to ready yourself for a certain ceremony?" Reggie winked at her.

The rhythmic sound of a horse trotting up the lane distracted Cassie for a moment. Approaching the inn a lone figure of a man rode a white horse. The minister.

"I better hurry so we don't keep the good preacher waiting." She grinned at her father, aunt, and brother as she turned toward the front steps of the inn. "Or my groom."

Chapter Thirteen

Impatience tensed every muscle. The minister shouldn't dilly-dally with the marriage ceremony. Stewing, Reggie stood at the front of the assemblage of family and friends gathered around the base of the gazebo. The feeling of being watched, judged, condemned wouldn't permit him to simply enjoy his children's wedding day. Giles stood by Haley on the left, Flint and Cassie in the middle, and Abram and Mandy on the right. The black-clad minister had his back to Reggie but the man's nasal voice droned on interminably with the sacred words. Hate warred with the love flowing from the trio of couples in the gazebo. Somewhere nearby someone didn't want the ceremony completed. He could feel it.

The girls wore elegant gowns in a variety of gem colors: turquoise, emerald, and topaz. Cassie's deep turquoise gown had a cream lace overskirt and matching neckerchief. Mandy's dark green skirt was topped by a white blouse with lace-edged sleeves, emphasizing her sparkling eyes. Haley's gold gown glittered with silver threads throughout the fabric and rhinestones scattered across the bodice. The men had opted for more subdued suits of dark gray or blue, providing a refined backdrop for their women to shine beside. If only they'd had time to have a portraitist paint them, then they'd have this fine showing for all to see in years to come. Instead, he would have to capture the image in his mind to recall later.

Mixed feelings made his pulse thump in his ears. Seeing his beloved daughter resplendent in her fine wedding outfit, her smile dazzling despite the underlying worry about the other feelings invading the quiet evening air, should be a joyous moment. Instead, he fretted about all of the blissfully happy young people standing out in the middle, in full view. An easy shot. The longer they lingered together, the higher the risk.

At the same time, his sons deluged his soul with pride. Just looking at the four of them, all confident, mature, strong, and determined, made his heart sing. Each displayed unique and useful qualities and skills. More important than their appearance and their usefulness, though, was their commitment to family even after the hardships they'd endured in order to survive and thrive. He could never put into words the depth of his pride and love simply knowing they'd come home to their sister in her time of need. And didn't run off again but stayed. They had guts and courage to spare. And yet, his unease ratcheted up another notch.

The niggling worry bloomed into an encompassing concern. Reggie casually looked away from the couples listening intently to the minister, seeking the source of the ill feelings. He kept a pleasant smile on his lips as he searched the faces of those around and behind him. His brother and sister clustered with Daniel and Wilma, young Teddy keeping close, all watching the proceedings with happy grins on their lips. Mercy hovered near them, barely visible any longer. She had begun her final journey, away from him, from the family, all but tearing him in two at the thought of losing her forever. Behind her, Hope and Faith enjoyed the advent of their niece and nephews marrying. How fortunate for them they could witness the happy occasion despite the reluctance with which the rest of the family tolerated their presence. He'd need to have another word with them soon. His staff had gathered off to the other side, Sheridan with Pansy dabbing her eyes with a kerchief, Matt and Zander meeting his perusal. He inclined his head to the men, attempting to relieve their concern. At least for a moment.

Beyond them, the inn's guests slowly strolled toward the inn or perhaps stopped for a few minutes to enjoy the sight of a triple wedding under the idyllic flower-draped gazebo. Scarlet had stepped in and worked her magic to decorate the gazebo with white flowers and also conjured a large white tent nearby where Sheridan's wedding feast waited for the minster to finish his duty. Chafing dishes kept warm the roasted turkey with cranberry relish, specially prepared eggplant, and pumpkin bread until they were ready to celebrate the weddings. Eventually. At the rate the elderly minister lingered on each word as if it carried the meaning of eternity and good fortune all wrapped into a few syllables it might be a while.

He continued to skim the audience, silently thanking them with a nod for their support. Then Reggie's gaze stopped at sight of the gang of men Flint had warned him about. No happy countenances among those witnesses. He probed their emotional state and found the source of the hate he'd detected earlier. He clenched his fist, tempted to eradicate them with a wave of his hand. Opening his hand, he forced calm in. Not in front of so many witnesses. And not when it would interrupt the wedding. But they were the threat. He'd keep a very close eye on them on this special day.

Shifting to survey the entirety of the property, he contemplated his big wedding gift to his daughter and new son. The idea had inserted itself into his mind as he'd explored earlier, taking note of the many changes Flint had made. The man had a knack for assessing the situation and seeing what needed fixing to better serve the guests. Having Flint take charge had benefited his business far more than he had dared hope.

"Do you, Giles Fairhope, Flint Hamilton, and Abram Fairhope, take, respectively, Haley Baker, Cassandra Fairhope, and Mandy Crawford to be your lawfully wedded wives?"

Pivoting back to continue observing the ceremony, he linked eyes with Giles. His oldest son nodded, his gaze shifting to rest on the gang behind Reggie. Between them, he and Giles could monitor their actions. Giles scanning the area behind Reggie, and Reggie keeping an eye on things behind the couples uniting for the rest of their lives. As long as he had a say in the matter, that would be a very long time, too.

Which brought up the fact he hadn't settled on an appropriate gift for his sons upon their marriages. They were beginning new phases of their lives, now with a wife and before long a family to provide for. With good fortune, that would be true for all four of them, whether getting married on this day or not. One thing they'd all need he could give them.

A chorus of "I do" in strong masculine tones rang across the front lawn of the inn.

"Do you, Haley Baker, Cassandra Fairhope, and Mandy Crawford, take Giles Fairhope, Flint Hamilton, and Abram Fairhope, respectively, to be your lawfully wedded husbands?"

The three women agreed, their melodic voices saying "I do" as one voice.

Memories of his marriage to Mercy swam in his mind's eye, the small supportive gathering of family. A raucous celebration followed with plenty of roasted hens, free-flowing punch, and sly jokes regarding his marriage bed that night. Mercy had been shy and hesitant after the ceremony, anticipating consummating their new marriage. She had less experience in such matters and therefore more to fret over. She'd worn a gossamer nightdress with a satin bodice, but not for very long. A smile toyed on his lips at the memory of their first night together.

Exploring her fine body had taken all of his attention for some time. He'd put her at ease first, softly telling her of his love, how much he wanted her to enjoy being together as friends, as family, but most importantly as lovers. He would never hurt her. Rather, he'd do all in his power—personally and magically speaking—to ensure she had everything she could need or want. As long as they had each other, he'd be content and happy.

"I now pronounce you husbands and wives."

Cheers from the observers around him startled him out of his reverie. Mentally shrugging away his recollections, he cheered along with the rest. His only daughter and two of his four sons were now married. His family grew by leaps and bounds as a result.

The couples trotted down the steps and into the grassy yard to congratulatory kisses and hugs from friends and family. Then they led everyone to the tent to begin the feasting and toasting. A side table displayed a large, white frosted, multi-layered cake decorated with a variety of frosting flowers and fresh berries. Reggie scanned the interior of the tent, angled his head at the bare white canvas, and decided it needed more pizzazz. He snapped his fingers and winked an eye. Bursts of light flickered along the ceiling of the tent, adding gay sparkles to the festive venue.

"A nice touch, dear." Mercy shimmered at his side, staring at the colorful sparkles with delight.

"Oh, Pa, that's lovely!" Cassie grasped his arm and gave him a kiss on the cheek. "Thank you."

"Congratulations on your wedding." He planted a kiss on her forehead and then clasped Flint's roughened hand, evidence of the months of labor he'd done to benefit the property. Solidifying Reggie's decision. "I haven't given you my gift yet."

"It's not necessary, sir." Flint pulled Cassie into his side and wrapped a possessive arm around her waist. "You've both given me the greatest gift in your daughter."

"True, true, but I—or rather, we—do have something for you both I think you'll like." The curiosity in their eyes hurried him to reveal the present. "Mr. and Mrs. Hamilton, the inn is yours to do with as you like."

Flint gawped at him, his mouth hanging open as he processed the enormity of the gift. "The inn, sir? That's unexpected."

"But wonderful. How generous of you, Pa." Cassie

glanced askance at her husband and then moved to embrace Reggie. As she pulled back, she extended her hand toward her ma. "Thank you both for your support."

"Yes, thank you." Flint nodded, stunned pleasure in his eyes. "You will stay with us though, won't you?"

Reggie glanced at his wife, her tired smile piercing his heart.

"For a time. Until I can build a cottage nearby." The memories embodied in the dog-trot structure behind them haunted him as much as his wife had haunted the inn for the last few months. Far better for him to start fresh than to relive the past day after day. "I don't want to be in your way as you begin your new life together. You deserve your own home. And Flint, you've earned the right to own the inn you've worked so hard to make flourish."

"You've done a fine job. Congratulations all around. I fear I must go for now." Mercy flickered. "Love to you all." Then she vanished.

"What's going on over here?" Beck strode up beside Reggie, tapping him on the shoulder as he peered at him.

It took Reggie a moment to gather his composure after his wife left so abruptly. He couldn't grasp where she went or how but he always dreaded he'd never see her again. Like she'd died over and over. He drew a steadying breath.

"I'm going to need a new house. Interested?" His brother would probably insist on every possible refinement he could muster, which would take longer than Reggie would like, but the results were always worth waiting for.

"Sure. I'll get Daniel to help me, so I can teach him how to go about it." Beck waved at the man in question.

Silas noticed the motion and tapped Daniel's shoulder, before the pair walked over to join the conversation.

"Did you want me for something?" Daniel peered at Beck and then took Wilma's hand as she sidled up next to him.

"Help me build this guy a new house, will you?"

"I'd be happy to." Daniel placed a kiss on Wilma's head. "Then we can talk about where we're going to live after we're married in a couple of months. Perhaps I'll need to build one of my own."

"So there will be room for me to stay on for a short while, right?" Silas glanced between the three men. "Until I sort out my future plans, I mean."

"Indeed." Flint nodded. "As long as you'd like."

"With the new rooms added, we have plenty of room for everyone."

"Including me." Teddy raced up to grab hold of Flint and Cassie's hands. He bounced on his toes as he glanced between them with an excited grin. "Now you're married, and have your own place, can I adopt you as parents? Please?"

"Adopt us?" Cassie grinned down at the lad, and then shot a look to her new husband. "What say you?"

"I'd like nothing better than to call you my son, Theodore." Flint gravely shook the boy's hand. "Welcome to our family."

"Now I have a grandson as well as a new son. What a day for the Fairhope clan." Reggie gazed at the happy countenances around him, highly pleased and very emotional at the splendid turn of events. He swallowed the knot in his throat and blinked away the threat of tears. "We should enjoy Sheridan and Matt's fine meal and then I'd like to speak to my sons in private." Four pair of quizzical masculine eyes aimed his way but he only shook his head.

"Later."

Meg sauntered up carrying a tray of champagne flutes. "Perhaps a toast first?"

"A fine idea." Reggie selected a glass and waited until everyone had one lifted and ready. Their future stretched before them. Years ahead to love and laugh, to have children of their own if the Fates allowed. Like he'd enjoyed with the love of his life. His joy dimmed as he recalled that the end of his wife's haunting approached with each passing minute. But now was a time of celebration not grief. He bit back his sorrow. "To long and prosperous lives for all the newly married couples!"

He swallowed a large mouthful and then stiffened. The hate and fear flowing through the early evening air nearly choked him. Cassie frowned as she glanced sharply around. Giles and Scarlet tensed, detecting the same emotional tsunami dousing their enjoyment of the moment. The threat to his family had reached a new high.

How dare those witches and warlocks flaunt their existence? To blatantly use magic and cavort about as if they had any right to exist. I want nothing more than to annihilate them now but my men have assured me everything is prepared, waiting for the big festivities on the morrow. Waiting for the perfect deadly moment on the witches' most revered high day, Allhallows Eve, to rid the region of their scourge. I'll bide my time, but only for one more day.

After the festivities ended, Reggie went to the dining

room to grab a nightcap. He didn't imagine he'd sleep on this special night for the happy couples. Their marriage night reminded him of his own and the memory of his wedding night contrasted too much with the lonely bed waiting in his room.

He slipped behind the bar and grabbed a shot glass and a bottle of fine whiskey. Then he moved to a table and plunked down to splash the dulling liquid into the glass. Tossing back the shot, he grimaced as it burned down his throat.

Beck ambled in, his tie loose about his shirt collar as he shook his head. "Drowning your sorrows, brother?"

"Grab a glass and join me." He refilled the glass and set the bottle down.

He didn't want to think about his own wedding night. The images of Mercy as she approached him with cautious curiosity, wearing her beautiful nightgown. He'd avoided going to his room where he'd be reminded of too many nights with her. Nights he'd never enjoy again. Reliving those memories knowing they were forever in the past proved painful indeed.

Beck soon occupied a chair at the table, dragging the bottle closer to fill his glass. "It was a nice ceremony."

"If it weren't for the gang lurking at the back, I'd have enjoyed it more." He tossed another shot and swallowed. "They're planning something and soon."

"And that worries you, of course." Beck sipped his whiskey and thumped his glass onto the table. "What can we do about them?"

"Giles is watching them, says they'll find a way to prove it's them behind the killings."

"What if they don't?"

Reggie lifted both brows, recalling his experience in the clearing that afternoon. "If the living witches cannot finger the killers, the deceased witches want to take a stab at it."

Beck blinked rapidly at him and then gaped at him as understanding lit his eyes. "You've seanced with them?"

"In a manner of speaking." He quickly relayed his earlier encounter with the spirits. "I think they want to help us nab them."

His wife had been murdered, too, just not by the same gang of men. He understood their need for justice, for vengeance. Their deaths came about at the hands of men, not natural causes. Their lives cut short for no sound reason. No wonder they lurked and lingered waiting for the moment when their deaths were avenged.

"That could be an interesting sight to see. How many spirits are we talking about?" Beck refilled his glass.

"A dozen or so. They have spoken with Mercy, seeking her out precisely because she haunts the inn. They asked for her help."

"A spectral contingent to our growing arsenal." Beck tapped a finger on the lip of his glass. "Do you sense the growing tension in the air? Like forces are gathering which we have no control over?"

Reggie nodded. "I can't sleep because of it."

Beck eyed him with a knowing look. "I see."

"I mean it." Not only the memories of his first night with Mercy kept him on edge. "After absorbing what the witches' spirits relayed this afternoon, how could I relax? Something is coming and soon."

"Is that all?"

Reggie dragged in a breath and let it out slowly through his nose. "Of course not. You don't need to know specifics."

"I know you're probably thinking of your own wedding night while the couples are settling in for theirs. It's only natural." Beck lifted his glass in salute. "To good memories worth making and remembering."

His recollections of the life he created with Mercy flipped past in his mind. Building their first home. The births of their children. Family celebrations for holidays and other special occasions. Then starting over at the inn, worrying about his sons every day, praying for their safety and good fortune. Watching his daughter grow and mature into a fine young woman oblivious to her powerful magical abilities. All the memories mingled into a morass of feelings.

Reggie hefted his glass. "To good memories."

He swallowed his whiskey and prayed the good memories would combat the bad ones.

The mere closing of the bedchamber door, the soft thunk of the latch closing under her new husband's hand, fractured her equilibrium. Cassie had never been in Flint's bedroom before, especially with him so close and so manly. She had a vague notion of what occurred behind closed doors but not much else. Her heart fluttered, vibrating the edging of her carefully embroidered night shift. She'd stitched the delicate flowers, a pastel rainbow of colors against the white linen, preparing for her wedding night. With each pierce and tug of the needle, she'd imagined Flint's expression when he saw her wearing the garment. She swallowed the nervous saliva gathering in her mouth. What she hadn't expected was the gleaming appraisal in his hungry eyes, his examination of her from her brushed hair down her trembling frame to her bare toes.

"My love, you have nothing to fear." Flint tugged the string tie loose from his shirt collar and dropped it on the dresser.

Easy for him to say. She wasn't ready. She hadn't spent as much time as she'd wanted to prepare herself for the mysterious happenings after the ceremony and reception ended. Whenever she'd thought about marrying, she'd focused on the dress, the shoes, the location for the ceremony. Would it be a private affair inside, in the parlor perhaps? Or in the dining room so others could attend? The gazebo served the purpose on a fine autumn evening with her family and friends surrounding the three couples. Including the inn's guests was an afterthought but it had worked out. Other than the gang's presence, staring and glaring at them as if they flouted custom and the law both. Her pa and brothers acted with restraint but kept their guards up as the ceremony progressed. She'd also kept an eye on the men, ready to use any defensive tools in her own magic arsenal. All so this moment could happen. She moistened her lips as her musings ended as she regarded her new husband.

Methodically, he removed the remainder of his suit until he stood before her in nothing but his night shirt. Dark gold chest hairs with a hint of red curled over the vee opening. As he slowly approached, the heavy linen brushed his thighs with a faint rasping sound. She'd never seen a man in such a state of undress. Without a shirt, vest, trousers, let alone shoes. His bare legs and feet were sparsely covered in red-gold hair as he padded toward her, his expression that of a hunter pursuing a nervous doe. A nervous bride. Her pulse beat in her ears, her throat, while she wiped her damp palms on her shift.

"Flint..." Steeling herself to not retreat from her husband, she kept her feet rooted to the spot on the floor beside the thrown-back quilt on the bed.

He'd readied the room for this very moment. Several candles flickered around the room in lieu of the more utilitarian oil lamp. The curtains hung limply at the window, shielding them from the night sky outside. Finally, the time had arrived for them to consummate their marriage, an act necessary and highly anticipated. If only she didn't tremble so. Her ma had not prepared her for what might happen next. Her ma's encouraging hug had fortified Cassie for the choice she'd made, but yielded no insights into what would follow. She'd witnessed breeding between horses and the cattle. Surely, coupling between the farm animals wasn't the same as with man and wife. But she had no concept of what he expected from her, nor what she should expect from him.

"Cassie." He took her hands and held them against his chest, the heat seeping into her chilled fingers. "I love you. I'll always take care of you. We will take our time and learn what pleases each other."

"I—" What could she say? Humming her calming spellsong seemed immensely inappropriate. He might misinterpret her unease as reluctance to lie with him. She merely felt unprepared, not fear. Chiding herself for her doubt and insecurity, she inhaled a steadying breath. She would follow his lead with all the love in her heart. "I love you, too."

He let go of one hand to cup her jaw as he leaned close to kiss her mouth. She closed her eyes when his lips pressed hers, savoring their warmth, letting him ease her worry. When he broke off the kiss, she opened her eyes to his deep, dark pupils searching her expression.

"Today is the first day of our life together." He squeezed both her hands and leaned his forehead against hers. "No matter what else happens, who might be against us, we will always have us."

Mention of the lurking threats sent her thoughts skittering. A shiver raced down her back as a sense of impending danger invaded her. Alarmed, she pulled back from Flint and opened herself to the throbbing hatred surrounding her, long enough to identify its general location. On the property, close by but not in the room. Obviously it didn't come from Flint. Then from whom? She probed farther afield and felt the lingering presence flowing around the inn. The gang most likely. She shuddered but now was not the time to deal with them. At the moment, she didn't even want to think about them. Giles was nearby so she sent him a silent message of awareness, letting him know she was safe despite feeling disquieted, and then studied her husband. He deserved all of her attentions on this special night. Raising her inner barrier, she pushed away thoughts of anything, anyone, but Flint.

He studied her with anxiety in his eyes. Not something she wanted to see. "You are all I need, Flint. Except for maybe some idea of what to do next." She smiled coyly up at him as understanding dawned in his regard.

He kissed her lightly. "We will learn together as I do not have a lot of experience in this either. Enough to guide, though." He traced a finger down her jawline, resting it on her lower lip. "I love kissing you."

She lifted her mouth to accept a series of kisses, her eyes drifting closed as she enjoyed the building sensations inside. Half her mind engaged in kissing him, while half tried to fathom the inner experience. Not merely a physical trembling of anticipation, growing and insisting she relinquish control to his attentions to her body. But the burgeoning and overwhelming need to be closer to, to be consumed by, this man. Her husband. A shadowy but inviting path beckoned her with every kiss. Where the path might lead escaped her, but she'd follow him anywhere.

A silent acknowledgement from Giles along with a hint as to his own nighttime activities interrupted her concentration and thus her enjoyment. Followed by a silent query from Silas in response to her own unease. No. She couldn't deprive herself or her husband of the intimate, private moments to follow. The path they hurried down was reserved for them alone. She wouldn't allow anyone else to witness their first night together.

She closed her eyes, clutched Flint's upper arms, and imagined a glittering magical dome surrounding them. Infusing it with energy to prevent anyone from tapping into either of their emotions or thoughts, she whispered her will to reinforce it. Sparkling rainbows of light and fluttering colorful butterflies formed a huge globe and created an intimate world of their own.

Now nobody would know exactly what they did to consummate their marriage. As it ought to be. She opened her eyes to capture her love's undivided attention.

"Now, where were we?"

Chapter Fourteen

id you hear me?" Mandy plopped the tray of clean, folded napkins on the bar counter.

"What?" Flint startled at the clang of metal on wood. The sound vibrated through him like a tuning fork struck on metal. "My apologies. What were you saying?"

He couldn't help but glance yet again to the rear of the dining room. The gang occupied several tables at the back, eager to break their fast yet also keen on observing every tiny move Flint made. What brought them out to the inn so early on this morning of all mornings? He racked his brain for the last time they'd ventured out so early and came up empty. Suspicion soured his mood, and on the morning after his first night with Cassie. Some things just were not fair.

"Blast it, Flint, you need to listen." Mandy thumped the counter with her hand. "Sheridan needs your final approval."

He shot another glance at the group of refined men making a pretense at casual conversation around the cloth-covered tables. Finding out what they plotted in low tones became his priority. How to do that seemed pretty clear. He turned firmly away from spying on the men to address his hostess. "I will go talk to him in a little while. Right now, I'm famished. What I need you to do is get me something to break my fast while I sit over there to...have a short break."

Her arched brow disappeared into her hair. "A break? Now?"

"Off with you." He looked askance at the men, aware of their continued regard, then marched around the bar to drag out a chair at a nearby table.

Those men planned some kind of mischief. He could feel the weight of their eyes as they continued to watch him. By their every action he discerned a coiling of their muscles, anticipating enacting their devious plan. But what exactly did they plot over their morning coffee? Curiosity and fear mixed into a burning, seething morass in his gut.

"Can I pour you a cup of coffee, Flint?" Larry hovered at Flint's elbow, his eyes alight as he looked down on his boss.

"Yes, thank you." The man's obsequious attitude irritated him, in line with the agitation the gang stirred in his gut. He had to do something to alert the others and he knew what. "Can you send word to Zander that I'd like to see him, please?"

"Of course. I'll return shortly." Larry tossed a penetrating look at the gang of men before he spun on one heel and strode out of the dining room.

With Larry out of the room, the gang seemed to pay even more attention to Flint. He hoped it wouldn't take long for Larry to locate Zander because the sense of urgency in Flint had escalated so high that even Mandy kept shooting him concerned looks. Flint gripped his cup, sipping the hot liquid with jerky, impatient movements. Zander could be spared to ride into town to bring the sheriff or the deputy. Giles wouldn't go too far from Cassie's side, so Flint would rely on his right-hand man to handle the task. Next he'd need to alert Giles to the situation, but how could he do that without leaving himself?

Sterling Nelson strode into the dining room without hesitation, going to the group of men conversing at the back. He'd dressed in his usual distinguished three-piece suit, but instead of his usual ivory vest he wore a tan one with his dark brown coat and trousers. A nice ensemble for a workday morning. He tipped his beaver top hat to Flint as he passed, an easy confidence in his gait. The man enjoyed a stellar reputation in the region, known for his intelligence and charity. Ever since he'd first visited the inn, Flint had counted his blessings to have such an esteemed customer. His patronage meant he'd spread the word and others would also come out to see what the inn offered. Business had grown quickly after he became a regular customer.

Cassie sauntered in, a quick flick of a look over her shoulder toward the entrance hall where Larry had since disappeared suggesting she sensed something amiss with the waiter. Grimacing briefly before easing a smile on her lips, she surveyed the people seated at tables about the room. Her eyes met his, lighting knowingly as she lowered her gaze and went to the piano.

Their first night together had been magical without any magic involved. Other than the security of their private bubble of loving. Within its enchanted shield, they'd spent time truly becoming acquainted with each other's sexual preferences. Just as he'd planned and prepared for before they tied the knot, uniting their lives until death parted them. An entire life together. A very long time in the future if he had anything to say on the matter. Pressing his lips together, he averted his gaze from the pairs of eyes aiming at him from the back of the room. He couldn't allow those men to threaten his wife and her family. But he wouldn't give them the satisfaction of knowing they'd put him on defense. Let them wonder what he was up to for a change.

A guffaw from the gang drew his attention to where Sterling had joined the group. He'd taken a seat near the window so he could see the doings of the entire room. Sterling's stern, inquisitive gaze swept the others, finally landing on Flint. The dozen men around him seemed deferential to the banker. They looked to him for direction. But how could it be possible that such an upstanding, respected citizen could lead a gang of refined men acting as thugs, or worse as murderers? Yet all signs pointed to Sterling Nelson as the man dictating their actions and maybe even committing the murders. If only he had evidence to present to Sheriff Neal.

"You wanted to see me?" Zander slid onto a chair beside Flint, his long legs folding under him as he leaned forward to keep their conversation private.

"Coffee?" Larry set two porcelain cups on the table and held the silver coffee urn between them.

Flint lurched back to avoid bumping into the hot vessel. He shot a warning glare at the waiter who should know better by now how to properly serve a guest. "Please. And remember your training."

Ignoring the reminder, Larry poured the steaming dark liquid into the cup, then glanced at Zander. "Sir?"

"Thanks." Zander pushed the cup closer to Larry.

"My extreme pleasure." Larry smirked as he lifted the spout to stem the flow, drying the tip with a towel. "You enjoy your meals."

The waiter's tone dripped with sarcasm as he spoke to them. Shocked, it took Flint a moment to marshal his wits. "Larry, I'm warning you. Remember your training or you won't have a job."

Larry's mouth tightened into a sneer. "I shall try to keep that in mind."

Zander frowned at Flint as the waiter left. "What did he mean by that?"

"I can only guess." Flint drew a breath but it didn't relax even his little finger. Cassie's sweet voice floated across the room as she played her version of Greensleeves to calm the tensions even he could feel without empathic ability. "Those men are up to something. I need you to ride to town and bring Neal or Parker back with you. They need to look into this before someone gets hurt."

Zander shot a furtive look at the men and then whispered to Flint. "Maybe Daniel can help me...pop in on the sheriff?"

"Good idea. The faster you can get word to them, the sooner they can do as they promised and deal with this situation." Daniel could bounce to town with Zander and return in minutes instead of hours. Time mattered. Flint stared at Zander as reality struck a deep chord in his heart. Everything had changed upon marrying Cassie. "Tell Giles before you go. I'll stay here and try to figure out what is going on. I have far more to fight for now than ever before but I cannot do it alone. Hurry."

Without another word, Zander pushed away from the table. Flint tried to pretend to relax in his seat, tried to sip his coffee as if nothing was wrong. Cassie glanced his way occasionally, her concern reflected in her eyes as she sang one song after another. The men at the back continued their quiet, serious, perchance deadly conversation. Mandy delivered a plate of eggs and bacon, a crisp waffle with maple syrup, and a reassuring pat on his shoulder. Flint focused on eating his cooling meal, sipping his cold coffee, straining to hear anything incriminating he could pass along. Maybe he could glean something from Larry.

He beckoned to the waiter who strode over. Flint studied his features, searching for clues as to his motivation and intentions. "More coffee." Larry poured hot coffee into the cup while Flint perused his mannerism. The man's edginess made him nervous. What bothered him so much to make him repeatedly flash his gaze around the room? Sending him into the thick of the men may prove enlightening. "You might ask those gentlemen if they need a refill as well."

"Of course." Larry scurried across the short span to offer coffee to the group of watchful men.

The waiter made his way slowly around the three tables of men, pouring and talking, smiling and nodding. Getting along famously with the suspicious lot. What did Larry know? Or... Flint drummed his fingers on the table, lifting his cup to sip as he considered a new angle to the people involved. Could Larry and Isaac be working *with* the gang? Working *for* Sterling? Spies within the inn to report back to the leader of the crimes, to the leader of murdering innocent women. The pair of men who had frequented the dining room had arrived very conveniently after Flint had spread the word of needing male waiters. Suspiciously so, in fact.

A ruckus at the arched doorway announced the arrival

of Deputy Barney Parker along with Zander and Giles. Zander ushered the deputy toward him, but Flint rose to cross the room to meet him halfway. Away from where the gang could hear their conversation. Cassie continued to sing and play, her melodic voice working its magic.

"Hey, Flint, what's the matter?" Barney met Flint in front of the bar, resting a hand on the counter. "Zander said it's urgent. Even insisted Daniel bring me out with him."

Flint peered closer at him, aware of his reluctance to take advantage of the magical abilities of his family. Acknowledging magic existed was one thing, but experiencing it quite another. "You bounced?"

"Is that what you call it?" Barney gave a shaky chuckle as he rolled his eyes. "If you hadn't warned me about his...um...talents I might have objected. But I figured whatever it is must be important for you to ask him to come get me."

"It is, but I don't know if we want to talk here and now." He indicated the gang and Sterling's intense observation. "We should take this discussion to my office."

"The timing is good because I was going to come see you, to tell you about another killing not half a mile from your doorstep." Barney pulled his hat from his head and clasped it to his chest. "The poor woman didn't stand a chance. It was horrid what they did to her."

"We must put an end to this." Giles raked a hand through his hair and then swept the room with his severe gaze, pausing as he reached the gang. "The owl is right there pointing its talons at the gang."

"Anyone in particular? Is it over anyone?" Flint refrained from turning to stare but kept his gaze on Giles. "Surely it's telling you something."

"Hm, yes, I do believe so. It's over Mr. Nelson in fact."

Barney scowled. "I don't see any owl. What are you blathering about?"

"Magic, my friend." Flint bopped Barney on the shoulder. "You'll have to trust Giles as the family's Guardian to tell you the truth."

"Klee! Klee!"

A collective gasp swept across the guests in the room as Allegro shot through the rear window to dart about the room. Flint looked more closely at the falcon as it circled around him and headed toward Cassie.

"He's got something." Flint started toward Cassie as the bird soared over the piano and dropped a small object on the mahogany lid. The Merlin flew over to the blanket rack along the wall beside the piano and landed. As Flint drew closer to the piano, the pale object glinted, reflecting the lamplight as it rocked back and forth before coming to rest.

Cassie reached for the small disc, holding it up to examine it with a slight frown on her pretty face. She looked at him as he stopped by the bench. "It looks like a button but why would Allegro bring me this?"

"May I?" Flint held out a hand and Cassie dropped it onto his palm. The off-white button featured an embossed rose. He'd only ever seen this style on one article of clothing. Sterling Nelson's fancy vest. The one he wasn't wearing for a change. Perhaps it was missing a button or two? It could be the evidence they needed, but not without context. "Allegro, where did you find this?"

"Klee!" The bird tilted its head and then launched into the air and flew around the room before heading toward the arched doorway.

"He wants us to follow. Come on!" Flint gestured to

Barney and raced out of the room.

They ran after Allegro down the hall and out the propped open front doors, then along the lane. Flint and Barney stayed with the falcon as he flew toward a small abode tucked beside the Winchester Road not far from the inn. The cottage hunkered at the edge of the forest, its windows dark in the early morning sunlight. Flint trotted closer, scanning the yard for any signs of life but detecting only silence. Allegro flapped up onto the front porch railing, facing the ajar door.

"He wants us to go inside, I think." Flint gasped for breath after running so far, hands braced on his thighs. "Think it's safe?"

"This is where we found that poor creature last night who was killed." Barney panted beside him, but didn't struggle for every breath like Flint still did. He yanked open the door so they could tramp inside. "Show us, Allegro."

"Klee!" The falcon flashed past Barney and into the dim room, heading straight to the cold hearth of a large cooking fireplace. A black cauldron hung from a metal hinged rod, away from where a fire once burned. Signs of a scuffle as well as drag marks on the dirt floor suggested the scene of the attack.

Flint eased into the room, glad the body had already been removed. With good fortune, the bird had located the evidence in a simple fancy button that would see the arrest of the killer. How the bird knew to find such a thing was a mystery to him. But he'd learned the falcon seemed to understand what they said, what they needed. He recalled Allegro listening to him on the front porch when he'd told Giles and Silas they needed evidence. Smart bird, indeed. "See anything?"

"Not yet, but give me a minute." Barney searched the stone floor of the hearth, sweeping a hand over the uneven surface. Then stopped to pry something from a crevice between two stones where the chinking had failed. Holding up a matching button, he grinned. "Well, look at that. Mr. Nelson seems to have dropped something in his hurry to vacate the premises last evening. I'll just hang onto this if you don't mind."

Flint grinned back. "Not at all."

"Good." Barney held up the rose-embossed button, glee and righteous determination in his eyes. "We have proof that Sterling Nelson is our man. I'll go relay what we found to Sheriff Neal and meet you back at the inn later."

Flint breathed a sigh of relief. "Finally we can put an end to this once and for all."

Reggie stepped back as the pair of men raced out the front doors after the falcon. He probed their emotions and found their intent to catch the killer. Flint's certainty they soon would have the evidence they needed to stop the witch hunter. They could use his help all right. So he hurried to follow them, stumbling over the threshold as he ran onto the front porch. Catching his balance, he stared after them running down the lane, debating whether to join them with all his powers and his anger flaring inside. As he hesitated, Scarlet appeared at his elbow, laying a restraining hand on his arm. His anger had alerted her to his intent.

He glanced at her hand and then at her worried expression. "What's that for?"

"You shouldn't get involved right now."

"They could use my help." His fingers sparked with

anticipation of flexing his magical muscles. "You can't stop me if I choose to go."

"No, I can't." She squeezed his arm and then dropped her hand away. "You know what happened last time you went off in such a state."

"I have learned to control my temper." He didn't look at his sister, preferring to stare at the customers approaching the inn in their carriages and on horseback. Another busy day loomed ahead, but all he could think on was satisfying his need for revenge. He'd ignored his ire but now it surged to the forefront of his being, obliterating the gentle façade he'd worn like a costume. He took a step but stopped, pondering what he'd accomplish by following his instincts to find the killer and rip him to shreds. He slid a glance at Scarlet. "You don't believe me, do you?"

She crossed her arms over her chest, the long, belled sleeves hanging in points down the front of her dark red skirts. "You'll have to prove it to me."

He bristled at the doubt in her voice. "I choose my actions with care. You should know that by now."

"Then why are you dawdling here? You know you want to race after them, to find the men responsible for the witch hunt and annihilate them with a flick of your little finger." She waved an elegant hand toward the carriageway. "Go on then. Have fun. I'll be here to pick up the pieces of your family when they learn about the cruel side of your personality."

He pivoted to glare at her for a long moment. How dare she tempt him to do exactly what he wanted to do despite knowing the ramifications? "You want me to?"

She shook her head in disgust. "Of course not, silly. I want you to cool your heels right here and let Flint handle this his way. The right way. You don't want to be responsible for killing another human being again, do you?"

Not again, no. Images of the blood splattered across the walls of the dungeon where he'd taken out the man who dared to try to confine him against his will made him cringe. He'd been young and high-strung with a temper to match and no self-control. Now he repented most every day for the spontaneous, deadly actions of his youth. He had learned to manage his response and his white-hot temper, but certain threats triggered his instinctive lethal reaction. Like witch hunters. But his sister was right.

"Fine. I'll just sit here on the porch and wait for them to come back. Is that acceptable?"

"I'll join you." She took his arm and led him over to the pair of chairs flanking a small table to one side of the doorway. "Just to be sure."

Chapter Fifteen

One more look. The senator would arrive on the morrow according to the note a messenger handed him a short while before. Flint prowled through the halls of the upstairs addition, examining the finish work and the arrangement of the furniture. After one last inspection, he'd have no more time to fix anything amiss. The Allhallows festivities were set to begin in just a few hours. Before he'd endeavor to have fun, everything must be ready.

Pausing in the central axial hall, he trailed his gaze over the fine carved woodwork Beck had completed. Not content with plain framing, Beck had indulged in finely carved rosettes at each corner of the doorframes. The trim also benefited from his artistic touch, boasting raised edges suggesting ancient columns. His magical style blended well with the rest of the more rustic appearance of the inn. Perhaps Flint could persuade him to work a little magic on the rest of the property.

The newly waxed oak floors gleamed as they flowed away from him down the hall and into the four new rooms, the honeyed grain providing a welcoming sight. A plush runner would dampen the noise of shoes on the hard surface. He contemplated what kind of carpet, whether a design or a plain sturdy weave. Covering up the fine wood seemed a shame though. For now, he'd leave it alone, then reconsider in a week or two.

He sauntered down the hall, turning right into the first room. In pride of place stood the four-poster bed, its highly burnished wood declaring its elegance and quality. The specially made indigo and ecru overshot patterned coverlet graced the stuffed mattress. He'd employed several women to weave the blue dyed wool and cream multi-strand cotton into geometric patterns suitable for either a masculine or feminine occupant of the accommodations.

Beside the bed, a matching night table held a waiting decorative oil lamp centered on a lace doily. Strategically placed around the room were a writing desk and chair, two stuffed seats and small table by the window, with matching thick rugs on either side of the bed. He wiggled his toes inside his shoes at the tempting lushness of the rugs, imagining their comfort on a cold morning. With a nod of satisfaction, he left the room to peek into the other three rooms on the upper floor of the addition.

Emerging from the last room, he took a minute to verify the door to the fire steps outside remained unlocked. He opened it and drew in a breath of fresh air, the bustling yard outside reminding him of the ticking clock. Best he moseyed on downstairs for a final inspection. He pulled the door shut and spun around only to jerk back when he caught sight of Mercy shimmering in the middle of the passage.

"Mercy, you startled me." He pulled himself together and pasted on a small smile. "Did you need something?"

"I've been looking for you, Flint. I have something I must say to you." She held her hands together in front of her light blue skirts as she studied him in silence for several long moments.

The longer she hesitated, merely staring at him with a prim expression, the more anxious he became. What could she possibly want to tell him? She'd berated him for months for everything he did. She had little good to say to him so perhaps he didn't want to hear whatever troubled her now. Although hosting her had given him new insight into her feelings, he still didn't really know her. Would never have the opportunity to truly know his mother-in-law.

He couldn't wait any longer. He had much to accomplish in order to be prepared for the start of the gathering. "Mercy?"

"I'm sorry, Flint. I should have been kinder to you. You've done some fine things around here and I never told you how much I appreciated your efforts on my husband's behalf."

Surprise dropped his mouth open. He'd never expected gratitude from her. "Thank you. That means a lot."

"And..." She drifted closer to him, letting her hands fall to her sides. "I wanted to affirm how glad I am that you married Cassie. I'm proud to call you my son, her husband."

Shock replaced the surprise bouncing around his gut. "Thank you again. I promise to always love and cherish her, and do my utmost to provide for her."

Mercy smiled at him, her image flickering. "I know you will. I will watch over you both."

Then she was gone. Flint blinked, stunned into immobility for several seconds. Thinking about her surprising message and her blessing. Finally, he was truly accepted into the family. The boost to his confidence buoyed his spirits higher than the clouds. Whistling, he hurried down the hall to find his wife and share the startling news.

Flipping through the stack of neatly penned papers, Cassie kept her eyes down. The wary contemplation by Hope and Faith chilled her shoulders. Pausing at one page where Silas had noted a special bit of family history worth relating to them, she read the familiar words. The reason she'd invited her aunts, all three of them, to the parlor for a little...talk. What Silas had learned probably had been family lore among the three older witches for some time. Not thinking it a revelation at all. Another secret brought to light.

"Now that you have us here, why don't you enlighten us as to why you are ignoring us?" Faith marched back and forth in front of the blazing fireplace, each stride an exclamation mark of her irritation.

Scarlet spread her arms wide as she pirouetted by the doll's house, her ankle-length jade green skirts swirling around her legs. "Isn't it grand to be reunited, ladies? Far too much time has passed since my brother married into your family. Be happy."

Hope huffed from her stiff perch on a cushioned chair by the fire, her chin up and pointed. "A long time indeed."

"Enough. I will tell you why I've asked you all here." Cassie stood, clasping the stack of paper between her hands. "Or rather, Silas, will you please tell them what you found?"

Faith stiffened and halted her aggravated pacing to examine Silas. "Found where?"

"In Ma's trunks." Silas studied Faith and then reached for the pages. "May I?"

Cassie handed him the family history so carefully documented and presented for the family to read and comprehend. A rich and surprising history. "I wish for you all to listen to what Silas has to say. Your attention is imperative."

"I can't imagine—" Faith shot a glare at Cassie.

Cassie blinked at her, a flash of panic from Faith betraying her aunt's dismay at Cassie's insistence of paying attention to what her brother had discovered. Interesting. What was she afraid of?

"Be still." Hope shushed her sister with a stern flick of her hand. "Continue, Silas."

"Very well. I've spent the last few weeks reading everything my mother kept in the trunks upstairs. Very enlightening reading." Silas turned pages as he spoke, finally stopping at one with a series of asterisks down the right margin. "In particular, a few events in our family's past that shed a bright light on certain questionable activities."

Faith moved woodenly to sit on the cushioned chair opposite Hope, summoning her familiar to her lap and stroking Malachi's fur with quick motions.

Hope and Scarlet both glanced sharply at Faith as if they sensed the same worry and dread with a hint of defiance as she detected. The closed expression on the witch's face provided no hint as to her thoughts. Her tense posture, though, suggested she hid deep concern about what Silas might have uncovered in his reading. Cassie had skimmed the penned history but mayhap more hid within the words on the pages than she'd surmised. High time to shed some light on all of the family's past.

Cassie rolled a hand. "Go on, Silas."

Nodding, Silas pointed a finger at a marked passage. "For example, here's mention of a letter from Grandfather to Ma suggesting he'd make her pay for disobeying his demand she work with her sisters. He said, 'If you continue to be stubborn, then you leave me no other recourse but to punish you until you realize the error you've made.' Then later, he writes to her, 'See what happens when you deny your father? Your sisters have sided with me, agree with me that my way is best for the expansion of this family's territory to ensure our continued dominance in the region. Relent or a terrible price must be paid.' I don't know what exactly transpired between you two and your father, but he seems to feel he's won."

Surprise widened Hope's eyes. "I had no idea he'd punished my sister for not following his lead. I thought he'd simply let her go and then lashed out at us for not doing enough. When all along..." She trailed off, her gaze turning inward. "How stupid of me."

"Stupid?" Faith jumped to her feet, bristling with emotion. "Never. Our father was the most important man in southern Alabama if not the southern states. His intellect and foresight enabled him to lead most effectively. Nothing could be allowed to stand in his way. Nothing!"

Heated anger washed into Cassie from her aunt's rigid form. Conflicting emotions battled in her trembling frame as she glared around her. Then a hint of doubt, of remorse reached her, suggesting her aunt had done something for her father she regretted. But what?

"Aunt Faith, whatever is the matter?" Cassie raised her

inner barrier to block out the swirling angst from her aunt.

Faith stifled her outburst with a hand to her throat. "What do you mean?"

"Yes, Faith, what did you do?" Scarlet grabbed her skirts in her hands and inspected Faith's stony features. "I can tell you did something. Confess."

Faith slowly raised her chin, looking down her nose at the group surrounding her. "What I had to. What Father said would ensure our family's future and he was right! I'd do it again in the same situation."

Hope frowned at her, slowly gaining her feet to meet her eye to eye. "What...did...you...do?"

"Removed the distraction like Father wanted." The confidence in Faith's eyes wavered the longer Hope studied her. "It worked."

"What distraction, sister?" Growing anger echoed in Hope's voice. "Just tell me and we'll work it out. We're family, after all. And family forgives mistakes. Right?" She glanced around the group of women, all nodding in agreement, and then pinned her gaze on Faith.

Faith flattened her lips together before she swallowed. "George."

Cassie gasped, covering her open mouth with her hand. No. "What do you mean?"

Everyone froze into a tableau of horror as realization descended like a dark gray fog. Scarlet stood near Cassie, alert and on edge. Silas slowly stood as if preparing to move between his aunts. Faith clenched her jaw and spun away, stalking to the fireplace only to turn and glare at Hope.

Hope stared at her sister, fists at her sides, eyes glittering stones, her wand suddenly in her hand. "Be careful, sister."

Faith's defiant stance withered under her older sister's

condemning look. "With George out of the way, you concentrated on creating the trinity he'd always strived for us to form. Until Mercy fled..."

"You...what?" Hope took a step closer to Faith. "What did you do to George to get him 'out of the way'? Did you hurt him?"

"I never laid a hand on him. I-I merely suggested he dive into the lake." Faith backed up as Hope moved closer step by step. "He did the rest."

A wail of despair and anguish erupted from Hope's mouth as she lunged at Faith, aiming her wand at her as she glared and flicked the wand. Faith grabbed her throat, wrestling with an invisible adversary, gasping for breath. Hope inched closer, wand aimed at Faith, concentrating on attacking her sister. Cassie stared in horror, overcome by the emotional tidal wave from the struggling women. She staggered and Silas steadied her with an arm about her waist, supporting her as their aunts fought. Hate and anger, grief and disbelief, woe and regret all swirled about the parlor until Cassie feared she'd vomit. She struggled to strengthen her inner barrier, finally shielding herself enough to attempt to intervene before Hope killed her sister.

"Stop!" Cassie crossed her wrists and then swept them apart, sending a wave of energy that knocked the two witches off their feet and broke the deadly spell. "Enough."

Hope turned on her with blazing eyes. "She killed my son. She can never atone for her crime."

Faith held out a hand toward Hope, then let it fall. "I did what our father demanded. You'd have me defy him?"

Hope spun around to glare at Faith, her wand pointed toward her heart. "He'd obviously lost his mind if he thought murdering my son would help me focus. How dare you? I cannot believe you could be so naïve and stupid."

"Put away your wand, Hope, that's not necessary." Scarlet leveled her own wand at Hope, but kept a grim smile on her lips. "We can work through this revelation."

"Just like all the others." Cassie eased closer to her aunt. "Please, Aunt Hope, no more fighting or manipulating." She motioned to her to lower the wand pointed steadily at Faith. "Please."

Silas eased closer to Faith, slowly putting himself between the sisters. "Aunt Hope, you don't want to kill your sister."

Hope blinked at his statement, then slowly slid her wand into her skirt pocket. "I don't want to waste a good spell on her. But that doesn't mean I forgive her."

Faith's shoulders slumped as she dropped onto the chair behind her. "I thought I was doing what was right for the family. For all of us."

Mercy shimmered into the middle of the grouping. "What is going on here? I could hear the shouting all the way from the other end of the house."

"I understand now, Mercy, why you fled home." Hope twirled around to pace over to the dining table, putting distance between herself and Faith. "Our father had turned evil and selfish, thinking only of his own ambitions and revenge."

"The truth finally emerges." Mercy flowed toward Hope, hovering a few inches above the floor. "That's the past, sister. We must put it behind us and move forward as a family."

Cassie glanced between her three aunts and her mother. "It's time we all learned how to work together, combine our strengths and bolster each other's weaknesses."

"I agree." Scarlet sidled up to Cassie and laid her arm over her shoulders. "We witches must defend each other, not defeat each other. Who is with me?"

Hope crossed her arms over her chest as she glared at Faith. "She can't possibly think we'd want her help."

Faith flinched at the disdain and dismissal in her sister's voice. "I thought I was doing the right thing. But...now I see Father lied to me. Tricked me into believing his twisted logic. Hope, can you try to forgive me? I am sorry for my failings."

Slowly drumming the fingers of one hand on her crossed elbow, Hope studied Faith for several moments. "In time, it is possible."

She sensed a change of heart around her. Cassie lowered her barrier, testing the emotional states of the other witches. Hope's guarded yet optimistic heart beating steadily. Scarlet stood ready to intervene but also open to welcoming the other two witches more firmly into the family. Even Faith appeared contrite and willing to listen. Time to play her best card.

"Please? Won't you both join with me to defeat those who wish to kill us?" Cassie moved to tug on Faith's hand, encouraging her to rise. "We need to come together and unite our powers for good, not for evil or ambition."

"Sisters, listen to Cassandra. She speaks the truth. You've seen how her powers have increased and expanded as her brothers and father have returned along with you, Scarlet, and Beck, too." Mercy held out a translucent hand to Hope. "Instead of Cassie joining you two, you both need to join her. Be the aunt to her she needs in my place. I'll rest easier knowing you're supporting each other, looking out for each other when I can no longer do so."

Her ma's image flickered and then stabilized but Cassie could tell she'd grown weaker since the last time she'd seen her. How much longer before her ma no longer had the strength to appear and offer her advice? She squared her shoulders, firming her resolve to stay strong as the time approached for saying a final goodbye to her mother.

Hope nodded slowly, extending a hand toward the ghostly appendage of her sister. "I understand, Mercy. Finally. I agree to work with Cassandra, to help her defeat the threats against the family—all of the family—once and for all."

Mercy turned to Faith hesitantly standing beside Cassie. "Will you as well?"

"Yes, I promise." Faith's eye glittered with tears, a thin wet trail down one cheek. "I am sorry, Hope."

Hope took hold of Faith's hand with a long sigh. "As our sister wisely said, that's in the past. Dead and buried along with our father." She firmed her lips and then peered at Mercy. "I'm sorry I blamed Reggie and Giles for my son's death. I know now they did what they had to do to protect their family. All of it. Father is ultimately to blame for everything, my son, your family breaking up and leaving, and our sisterhood shattered."

"Now let us make it official." Cassie held out her arms in welcome. "Join with me to unite our powers into a more powerful force than we could ever be on our own."

The witches and warlock formed a circle, clasping hands. Cassie slowly scanned their faces, seeking their acknowledgement of a future together. One stronger together. Now let those who wanted to kill them come and get them.

The Fairhope coven stood united and ready.

The ruckus in the kitchen did not bode well for the Allhallows Eve feast. Reggie pushed resolutely through the swinging door and right into the fray between the two cooks who were arguing about everything from how much vinegar went into the turnip greens to how fine to chop the beets for the orange-sauced dish.

"Silence!" Reggie clapped his hands together several times to emphasize his command. "You sound like fish wives bellowing at each other in here. Our guests will hear."

"Sorry, sir, but my son is—"

"Enough, Sheridan." Reggie held up a hand. Men shouldn't squabble so. Doing so was unseemly. "Calmly, tell me what has you both up in arms?"

Matt harrumphed. "According to him, I can't do anything right." Fists on hips, Matt glared at his father. "Then why did the number of meals I serve double while you were gone?"

Sheridan crossed his arms over his chest. "They were desperate, no doubt."

Matt stuck the point of his carving knife into the skinned hare on the worktable. "No doubt they heard you'd left and the food was better as a result."

"Boys!" Reggie wanted to throw his own temper tantrum as the two grown men acted like children before his eyes. "You have people arriving shortly for the feast you're supposed to be preparing for their enjoyment, not fighting over."

The door swung open and Cassie marched in, a tentative smile on her lips. "Something smells good in here." She pinned her reproachful eyes on each of the cooks. "So why can I hear you two shouting way out in the dining room, hm? You need to work out whatever differences you've imagined and get busy."

"Sorry, Miss Cassie." Sheridan shook his head and grinned ruefully at her. "We're trying to make sure we give you the best we can."

Matt pulled the knife from where he'd stabbed the hapless hare and began making a slit in the side to hold the savory stuffing waiting in a nearby wooden bowl. "Everything will be ready before you know it."

Reggie gaped at the effect his daughter had on the two antagonistic men, calming them into working together with a few words and a smile. Fatigue settled on his shoulders. Since returning to the inn he'd felt tired more often than not. Everything that went into running the place seemed overwhelming instead of challenging. Once he had possessed the energy to build his business, but now...he didn't seem to have the heart to do the work any longer. But what else would he do if not help at the inn? Sure, he'd given Flint and Cassie the entire enterprise, but he'd fully anticipated helping from time to time. They'd need his input and guidance for some little time. He raked a hand across his jaw. Or would they? Flint had done a fine job in his absence, so Reggie had no real need to hang around.

A swoosh of the door opening lifted his eyes to see Pansy sashay into the kitchen wearing a sprigged cotton day dress and a tentative grin. "Ah, there you are, Cassie. I've been seeking you."

"You're just in time to tell your husband to behave himself and stop fighting with your son." She grinned at Pansy, softening her command into a joke. "What can I do for you?"

Pansy swished over to Sheridan and swatted his arm. "Hear the lady? Get yourself to work and quit this foolishness. I have business to discuss with her."

"Yes, ma'am." Sheridan pecked her cheek and winked at her. "Whatever you say, ma'am."

A couple in love. Finally reunited. Reggie stifled a sigh. He'd done what he could to bring them back together, to bring them back home to the inn. They'd stuck to each other like a mating pair of eagles, parting for a short span but always returning to nest together. Reggie had returned to the inn but not to his wife. Not in a true sense. Sadness layered over the fatigue on his shoulders, weighing them down more.

"What did you wish to speak about?" Cassie picked a piece of diced apple from a bowl on the table and popped it into her mouth.

"Hey, those are for the acorn squash not your stomach." Meg pulled the bowl away from Cassie, a mock look of horror on her sparkly features.

Coming home to find the kitchen maids were both elves had taken Reggie a while to digest. Both Meg, or Megara, and Myrtle Marple glowed with magic and vitality. The women he'd originally hired had seemed sedate and mature, their gray hair suggesting their age. But when he came back he'd learned they were not merely women but elves. Their gray hair had transformed into silvery tresses full of sparkle and light. Their skin glowed. They moved with grace and elegance but also were sturdy and prepared to defend themselves and others.

In fact, everywhere he looked now he saw a magical creature of one kind or another. With various abilities and approaches to aiding and defending the people who lived and worked at the inn as well as the guests and diners. The atmosphere of the entire property had shifted from merely welcoming to inviting people to trust their surroundings and enjoy themselves. Just look at how quickly Pansy had settled in with so many strangers to call family.

"Well, Miss Cassie, I'd like to offer my seamstress services to the guests here." Pansy rested a hand on the work table. "I need something more to do with my hands rather than sit about staring at them. If you get my drift."

"I love that idea. You did such a lovely job with the wedding gowns, I cannot thank you enough. Right now, I've a mess of mending piling up in the parlor waiting for someone to take care of." Cassie grasped her hands together. "When I started offering such service, I had no idea how popular it would become. Are you interested in simple mending jobs as well?"

Pansy clasped Cassie's joined hands and shook them once. "Indeed. That's fine. When would you like for me to begin?"

"Now, so you'll get out of my kitchen with all your irrelevant blathering." Sheridan shooed them away with a wooden spoon and a grin. "If'n you don't mind, that is."

"We're going, Sheridan." Cassie waved him off, flashing an amused glance toward Reggie. "Come on, Pansy, we can talk about how you can expand the mending to include full seamstress services."

Reggie witnessed the exchange with deep humor and amazement. Cassie had grown and matured in his absence far more than he'd realized. She handled herself, and everyone around her, with easy charm and good humor. Not only had she maintained her impressive garden, and helped to manage the dining room and entertain the guests, but she also had a side business of mending. All while learning how to be a powerful witch.

Mercy shimmered into the kitchen by the still swinging door, beckoning him to follow her, pointing up, toward their private bedchamber. She'd grown so translucent he could clearly see the grain of the wood in the door behind her. Best to find out what she wanted to speak to him about, in the privacy of their room. He nodded and she vanished.

"Sheridan, Matt, we're expecting the guests to arrive soon, so please work together to make sure everything is ready. Understood?"

"If'n he'll do as I—" Sheridan snapped his mouth closed when Reggie pointed a finger at him.

"No arguing, just cooking. Got it?" Reggie narrowed his eyes, reflexively reaching for his wand. Not that he needed it, but it made a fine impression on those who didn't know the extent of his limitless magical ability.

With their silent nods of understanding, Reggie smoothed his pocket, touching the length of ebony secreted inside, then headed toward the door and the dreaded answer to his question: what did his ghostly wife wish to speak to him about?

Chapter Sixteen

Flint smiled at Cassie as she stopped with Pansy by the open front doors, where clusters of dried cornstalks and orange pumpkins welcomed guests inside, to exclaim over some whispered conversation. The smell of hot spiced cider perfumed the air and made his mouth water in appreciation. The girls pointed to the pumpkins while mischievous grins erupted on their lips. He didn't have time to investigate further, since he was in urgent need of Reggie's advice. Only then could he relax. He'd been looking for the man but hadn't yet found him. He would look in the kitchen next and see if he was hiding in there.

Cassie pulled Pansy a few steps closer to the side door leading to the residence, then stopped, giggling. Her inner joy bubbled from her ever since they'd married. His own pleasure increased with the cheering realization of her happiness. As he'd promised Mercy, he would spend the rest of his life ensuring she remained happy and content.

Reggie burst through the kitchen door, leaving it to swing to and fro as he marched into the entrance hall. "Hey, Flint. Everything ready?"

"Nearly. I was looking for you. Do you have a minute?" Flint stopped in front of him, expecting his assent as he blocked his progress across the entrance hall.

"Not really. I need to go upstairs." Reggie glanced at the side door and then sighed as he met Flint's surprised gaze. "All right. What do you need?"

Composing himself, Flint peered at him. He seemed anxious to leave. What Flint had to say would only take a minute. "I've walked through the entire inn and the property outside. I believe everything is ready for the senator's arrival tomorrow, as well as for the gathering festivities this afternoon. I was wondering about how best to greet the senator? Like any other esteemed guest, or with some fanfare, a band perhaps?"

Reggie swung his head from watching the women hustle out the side door to aim his gaze at Flint. "While the senator is of some importance within his usual sphere, here he's just another guest. Perhaps an influential one with the potential to further bolster the reputation of the inn, but nothing more than that."

"So no band?" Flint rubbed his jaw with his roughened hand. "Perhaps Giles could play his guitar just to create a welcoming atmosphere."

"I'm sure whatever you decide will be fine." Reggie widened his stance as he crossed his arms over his chest. "You're a fine innkeeper, son. You simply need to trust your instincts."

"I worry that I'll miss something important." Like not having enough of something desired by their typical guests, but more concerning was failing to pass muster for the senator. "You will let me know if you notice anything amiss, won't you?"

"There is no need." Reggie gripped Flint's upper arm and shook him. "You've done an impeccable job. Now, I must go."

Reggie's kind words so firmly stated reinforced Flint's own confidence. He surveyed the entrance with pride in his heart. No matter what might happen next, whether good or bad, he was ready for it.

"You'll manage all of this far easier than I could." Cassie lifted a white linen shirt with a tear in the sleeve, poking her finger through the hole to emphasize the extent of the necessary repair. "I'm not a seamstress like you."

Pansy took the shirt and inspected the ragged edges of the hole. "A few tiny stitches and a new set of cuffs to hide them and he should be happy with the result."

"That particular guest can be very persnickety." Cassie chuckled as she reached for another article of clothing from the pile on the table in the parlor. "Not all of them are so picky, mind."

"You gathered quite an array of clothes in need of attention." Pansy sorted through the mess of pants, blouses, aprons, and more. "I'll be busy for sure."

"As you let folks know about your ability to sew fine clothes for them in addition to making minor repairs, you'll be very popular." Cassie slipped her hands into her apron pockets as she spied her pa walk into the parlor. "Hey, Pa, do you need anything?"

"No, thanks. Just going upstairs." He smiled wanly at her and trudged on across the room to the steps. The thud of his shoes on the treads grew fainter up the stairwell but his angst remained in the room.

Cassie stared after her pa, longing to go to him. To ease his disquiet. Yet she sensed he desired privacy. He'd shielded his emotions as he'd gone up the stairs so she no longer could tell exactly how he felt. But the glimpse she'd had hurt her soul. Grief and pain filled him, pushing out the hope and joy he'd felt at the wedding.

Pansy lifted a dark blue blouse and fingered the fabric. "This cotton is so soft. It would make a comfortable and sturdy dress. Shall I ask Flint to order some from town?"

Should she go to him? Ask him if she could help him. She had sensed his conflicting emotions on more than one occasion since he'd come home. Since the wedding and with the big visit by the senator approaching, he'd grown more distant, quieter. She didn't know what bothered him, though his grief over Mercy's death and the anger of how she died both remained obvious concerns. Maybe she could sing her calming spellsong to ease his pain. Using her magic on her father may not be the most proper idea. But what could she do?

"Cassie? Did you hear me?" Pansy lowered the blouse as she leaned closer.

"I'm sorry." Cassie shook off her misguided tendencies in order to focus on the conversation at hand. "I would love a dress made from that fabric. Would you mind?"

"No, of course not. Have Flint purchase the material and I'll whip it up for you. No problem at all."

"Thank you." Cassie kept her eyes on Pansy but her thoughts strayed upstairs to her pa. Up to where she surmised he struggled with his own very personal problems.

The silence within the room unnerved him more than

any arguing could. Reggie stood in the middle of the bedchamber, eyes closed and senses open. Life pulsed all around him. The daily sounds of people going about their day: horse-drawn carriages and oxen-pulled wagons rattling and jouncing on the lane, the shout of greeting from a man clomping up the front steps, the melodic singing of a washerwoman accompanied with flapping of sheets as she hung them on the line. Animals pursuing their needs: a barking dog greeting new arrivals, the nicker of a horse from the paddock, the crow of a rooster out back herding his hens. But in his bedchamber, where he expected to have a conversation with his wife of so many years, silence.

Exactly what his future would be after her ghost took to its final resting place. A future alone and lonely. He opened his eyes, blinking against the bright late morning light flowing through the glass at the window. A life ahead filled with pity because his wife had passed on. Pity? He shouldn't feel pity for himself. Not when he could do anything he desired with his magic. Squaring his shoulders, he inhaled and surveyed the room. No one would pity him. Not even himself. He would start anew. Build his cottage, and leave all the possessions surrounding him right where they stood. He'd make a new bed, wardrobe, everything, and never look back.

And yet... Without a wife to come home to, talk with, love, what was the point?

His shoulders sagged as he sank onto the tree of life quilt, the stuffed mattress crinkling beneath him. Head in hands, he cleared his mind. Or tried. Memories seeped into his consciousness of his time with Mercy, of the decisions they'd made together, of the fights over petty disagreements he couldn't even recall, and most of all the love shining from her eyes when they had quiet moments together. In this very room.

"Darling, are you all right?"

He raised his head, drinking in the translucent vision of the love of his life. "I am now."

She stood silently for a long moment, then drifted closer to hover near him. "I have loved you with all of my heart ever since I first saw you at the annual gathering."

They'd been so young and wild back then. She'd dared him to race her to the big oak tree, flying on horseback across the rolling fields. Uncaring of the risk, only the race and winning. His powerful stallion won against her sturdy mare, naturally, but she'd won his heart with her challenge and spirit.

He stood up to face her, reach for her hands only to pass through her cool, wispy fingers. Couldn't even touch his wife any longer. Fighting back a burning pressure in his chest, he grimaced and then tried to lighten the mood with a shrug. "I've loved you since that day as well, my dearest. I always will."

"Reggie, I wish we had more time together now that you're home."

"I should have listened to Cassie and come home sooner."

"It wouldn't have changed anything if you had." She shrugged one shoulder. "My time here is coming to an end because you've come home."

"I'd hope with Allhallows nearing, we'd have a bit longer." He frowned at her. "I don't under..." Yes, he did understand. He'd known it for some time. "You were waiting for me."

"I hadn't realized it myself until recently. I needed to

know you'd be here to look after the kids." She shifted to one side, shimmering and then steadying. "I've been doing what I can to instruct our children with their rediscovered powers. Now you've returned, I can let go and rest in peace."

"They've learned well but there is always more to know." Even at his age, he discovered nuances to his powers. "You can't leave...yet."

"I don't want to, but my time has come." She held out her hands to either side. "Now that you and your brother and sister are here to teach them, to ensure they know what they need in order to use their powers wisely, it's time."

"But your sisters. Don't you want more time with them since they're not trying to steal away our daughter?" Any possible excuse to keep her at his side, even in her ghostly form, he'd cite as reason for her spirit to stay. "You've wanted your sisters back for so long."

"I leave them to you. Look out for the family and live a good, long life." She tilted her head to one side and smiled sadly at him. "Tell them goodbye for me. Now, I want to give you one last hug, if I can."

Nothing he said would make a difference. She wouldn't stay. Couldn't. He needed to be a man, or at least behave as one, and let her go. Nodding, he stepped toward her. She shimmered and then solidified for a single beat of his heart and then faded even more.

"I'm so sorry, but I can't. I love you and always will, Reggie." She held out her hand to him.

Holding his over hers until her ghostly hand chilled his palm, he tried to give her a reassuring smile. "I will always love you and only you, sweetheart."

"Goodbye, my love." She stared at him with glittering

eyes. Slowly, her spirit shimmered into nothing.

"No." The lone word wrenched from him. He dropped onto the bed, sobbing at losing her yet again. For good. She'd never appear to him again. The mattress crinkled with the jerking of his body in anguish as he cried, pressing his hands to his eyes.

"Pa, what's wrong?" Cassie asked, suddenly at his side. "I sensed you were upset and came to see if I could help."

He hadn't heard her approach but he lifted his head to see her concerned expression. She probed his emotional barrier and he strengthened his defensive shield. Some moments he couldn't share with anyone. "Ma has gone."

"Oh, Pa." She settled onto the bed beside him and wrapped her arms around him. "No wonder you're upset."

"She said goodbye and then just...vanished." He snuffled and palmed away the tears on his face. "She told me to tell you all goodbye."

"When will she be back?" The bed trembled beneath them, their combined emotions barely contained.

If only he had a different response than the painful truth. His daughter had said goodbye to her mother once, while he was away and left her home alone to deal with the tragedy. To face doing so again would be doubly difficult.

He shook his head, shifting to put his arms around her before he answered her question. "I'm not sure. But I think... Never."

"Oh." Tears ran down her cheeks as she leaned into his embrace.

His earlier determination to move out of this room returned with a vengeance. He could not sleep in this room, in this bed, without Mercy tucked into his side. He wanted to fly away from the entire building, leave it all behind so he wouldn't be surrounded by so many memories. Never be forced to look upon objects which recalled their life together. Remove himself from the ache those memories would cause in his heart.

Cassie's quivering shoulders as she cried over the loss of her mother anchored him to reality. His family still needed him. He had the power and the strength to end the threat posed by the witch hunters. When they'd been stopped, he'd leave it to the next generation to actively protect the family. Then he'd do as he'd promised and watch over the family, only from a distance. That would have to suffice.

"Pull yourself together, Cassie." He eased her away, lifting her chin with a finger. "The party is only a couple hours from now."

Sniffling, she nodded. "I should dress for the occasion. Will you be all right?"

"Go on. I'll be fine." He helped her stand, holding her hand for a moment. She'd been through so much in her short life, but she'd done so with grace. "Put on a smile and let's have some fun."

Chapter Seventeen

Children's laughter filled the air in the dining room. The unusual, happy sound lightened the heavy feeling slowly being replaced by the festivities in honor of Allhallows Eve. Cassie took her place at the square piano, lovingly trailing her fingers across the burnished surface as Giles settled onto a nearby chair. Mandy supervised the youth carving their Stingy Jack lanterns, wielding sharp knives to slice through the hollowed out pumpkin shells. Funny faces, sad faces, scary faces: the array of lanterns spread across several long tables at the back wall, between the two open windows where rain-scented gusts swayed the curtains. A dreary late afternoon created a fitting atmosphere for the day. Cassie signaled to Giles with a brief nod and then pressed the ivory keys, singing a haunting melody to help set the mood. Despite the minor key of the song, Cassie did her best to add levity and fun into the tune.

Flint's efforts to promote the festive gathering had yielded a crowd unlike any they'd ever hosted. All of the accommodations welcomed guests for the special weekend, every bed taken by at least one if not more visitors. A point of pride for her husband. Additionally, a significant number of families had ventured out on a rainy afternoon to partake of the food, drink, and many fun activities they'd devised for the children. Aside from carving pumpkins, they'd set up a barrel for bobbing for apples, a favorite among the younger guests. Myrtle had pulled together the bits and pieces needed for the ladies to fashion fall wreaths to hang on their gate post or front door, setting up a trio of tables near the fireplace for them to work and chat. The men moved about, greeting each other and striving to not show how much fun they were having. All in all, the room exuded peace, happiness, and an expectation of fun ahead.

A few months before, on her eighteenth birthday in fact, she'd dreamed of escaping the Fury Falls Inn. Plotting her escape had consumed her mind for weeks. Then she'd met Flint Hamilton and devised the idea of marrying him so she wouldn't be under her ma's overprotective thumb. Never had she dreamed of falling in love with the big, handsome, caring man. Knowing him had changed her perspective and her heart. Her pride in being Mrs. Flint Hamilton filled her entire being with a warm, fuzzy feeling. Her ma had also expressed her satisfaction with their marriage, as had her pa and brothers. To add new sisters to the family, as well as an aunt and uncle, all combined to fill a void she hadn't realized existed. Having everyone gathered together seemed magical in its own right. Tonight's happy events celebrated not only the special day but also her growing, thriving family.

Meg carried in a large tray ladened with tempting dishes for the grand feast about to commence. All of the kitchen staff had worked long hours to prepare the special dishes for the highly anticipated day. Stuffed roasted hare, scotched and colloped venison steaks, and glazed ham. Gazpacho soup, turnip greens with bacon, stuffed eggplant, sweet potato pudding, beets in orange sauce. For dessert, tea cakes, molasses gingerbread, pound cake, pumpkin bread, burnt custard, and a specially decorated layer cake ready for her father to slice as the witching hour approached. The two cooks used their natural competitiveness to put on quite a banquet. An outcome which pleased everyone.

Her moment of happiness faded as anger and fear crashed into her inner core. She shielded herself against its onslaught but probed the flowing mass of people around her for the source. Or rather sources. Uncertain as to what she sensed, she looked to her brother. Giles squinted his eyes as he continued his strumming, a slight nod acknowledging he sensed her unease.

"All right, children. Let's take your Stingy Jack's pumpkins out to the front porch and light them, shall we?" Mandy's clear, strong voice rose above the murmurings and laughter in the room. She clapped her hands together and ushered the chattering children out of the room, each with arms wrapped around their prized creations.

Pansy hurried into the room with a large, sweating pitcher, carrying it over to Flint at the bar. She wiped her wet hands on her apron as she greeted the guests with a shy smile. Pansy's past would take time to overcome, if she ever did. But she had begun to relax her guard after only a few days at the inn. Over time, perhaps she'd fully blossom and share her true personality with everyone. Cassie vowed to herself to help her bloom as much as possible.

"Is everything ready?" Flint slid the pitcher to one side, then dried the counter with a swipe of a white towel.

Pansy spun back to face him. "Yes, sir. Matt is bringing the last of the meats out in a moment." She motioned toward the door with a wave of her graceful fingers.

Cassie wrapped up the song she played, knowing her part was done. She lifted her fingers from the keys as Giles made a few more strokes on the guitar strings. Daniel escorted Wilma into the room, lingering on the edge of the clusters of families and couples enjoying themselves. Such a sweet pairing. They'd make a fine married couple. For the moment, it was time to join the rest. She rose from her seat to blend with the crowd, beckoning to Giles to come with her. The party was beginning and Cassie wanted to be in the midst of the fun. After all they'd been through over the last few months, she needed one day of lighthearted good times.

Sheridan and Matt entered in grand style, carrying platters of steaming dishes with a sway and flourish as they crossed the room to the waiting banquet tables lining the side wall. The crowd clapped and cheered as the men set the trays down and then took a bow, grinning ear to ear.

"All right, folks." Flint held up his hands, waiting for the cheering to stop. He nodded to several men close to him, apparently accepting their compliments. Then he motioned to the gathering. "Thanks for coming out to help us celebrate the opening of our new guest rooms, all of which are filled thanks to you." More cheering and clapping made him motion for silence yet again, but he did so with a huge smile of appreciation. Mandy shooed the children back into the dining room as Flint waited for everyone to settle down. "And to celebrate Allhallows Eve in style. As you saw when you arrived, we invited the children to carve Stingy Jack's lanterns to use as decoration out front to welcome the spirits on this night. Let me tell the children about our friend, Jack."

The children huddled in front of the adults, close to Flint and his tale, Mandy standing close by. Cassie enjoyed the Irish myth of Jack and his lantern. Stingy Jack worked as a blacksmith who once invited the Devil to have a drink with him. But he didn't want to pay the tab, so he convinced the Devil to become a coin with which Jack would pay then he walked out of the tavern. The coin he put in his pocket next to a silver cross so the devil couldn't change himself back. Only after bargaining with the devil to not seek revenge did Jack release the devil from where he'd kept him in his pocket. But after Stingy Jack passed away, his spirit could not rest.

He wasn't allowed to enter heaven, and the Devil honored his promise not to take possession of Jack's soul in hell. The Devil, instead, gave him a glowing coal to find his way in the dark. Jack put the glowing coal into a carved out turnip to guide him in his eternal wandering. Thus the mysterious lights seen at night in the Irish wetlands were said to be Jack roaming about. When the British came to America, they brought along the tradition of making lanterns from turnips, beets, or potatoes, then putting coal, embers, or candles inside to celebrate the fall harvest. Cassie thought of the strange lights and sounds the Bakers had described earlier. Perhaps Stingy Jack wasn't only a legend after all.

"If it weren't for the early settlers in the 1600s relying so heavily on pumpkins, then we'd be carving turnips tonight instead. But as the old Pilgrim verse goes:

'For pottage and puddings and custards and pies

Our pumpkins and parsnips are common supplies,

We have pumpkins at morning and pumpkins at noon,
If it were not for pumpkins we should be undoon.'

The crowd clapped as Flint bowed exaggeratedly. Cassie joined in, grinning at her husband's happy antics. He'd earned the right to entertain the people who came to enjoy everything he'd created. He'd turned the complacently rustic inn into a vibrant, thriving destination. The crowd honored him with their continuing applause. Her pa's pleased expression with the entire event iced the cake of her pride.

A spike in hatred made Cassie freeze in mid-clap. Startled, she swept her eyes over the cheerful group until she spotted Sterling Nelson glaring at her. The hatred and anger braided into a whip that flicked at her defenses. She raised them higher, denying the loathing flowing from Sterling toward her. Every nerve rang in alarm at what she saw before her. Arrayed around Sterling, the rest of the gang of men stared at her as well. Eyes glittering and jaw clenched, Sterling started toward her. She spun back around, sending a silent alarm to Giles. Her pa and Silas turned at the same time as Giles to assess her state of near panic. Allegro swooped into the room, flapping his way straight toward her only to pivot midair and change course with an accusing "Klee!"

An iron hand grabbed her arm and pulled her around to face Sterling, tall, dark, and dangerous as he leaned toward her. "I've got you now and I'm going to take care of you myself."

"You're hurting me." She stiffened, pulling her arm away but he proved far stronger. Only then did she realize her locket missing. She'd forgotten to put it on after washing up before donning her party dress. But surely he wouldn't harm her in the middle of so many witnesses. "Mr. Nelson, please."

"Silence, witch." He yanked on her arm and started hauling her to the back of the room where his men eagerly waited.

Allegro dived at his head, but Sterling fended him off with an angry jerk of his other arm. Even if she had both hands free, she didn't dare use her powers in the midst of so many innocent people. Someone, maybe even the children, would get hurt and she couldn't allow that to happen. He yanked on her, dragging her with him back toward the gang who leered at her in anticipation. No, she couldn't let him take her back there. She screamed, beating at his iron grip, Allegro circling the man's head.

The cheering and clapping stopped abruptly as the crowd became aware of the altercation behind them. Cassie called out silently to her family, catching Mandy's eye as the hostess moved among the guests, whispering calmly to each of them, her eyes wide and worried. Cassie hummed her protection spell, creating an invisible shield around her. But Sterling shook her into silence before slapping her across the face.

"None of your magic, witch. You be silent. I'm going to make sure you never sing another note." He shook her again and then continued dragging her toward his men.

They meant business. Primal fear welled up inside her gut. She gasped for breath as her heart thudded in her ears. Nobody moved to intervene as if struck dumb by the scene.

"Help! Please!" She struggled, trying to pry the man's fingers from her arm. If only she could free her hands, she'd blast him away from her.

With a growl, Sterling swung about and hit her again,

sending stars bursting into her vision. He shifted his hold on her, his muscular arm around her throat, dragging her across the floor. As her consciousness faded and her jaw throbbed, she heard Allegro's angry cry overhead. Her eyelids flickered, but she saw Flint and Giles stalking toward her, closing in on Sterling.

The man had lost his ever-loving mind. Rage consumed Flint as he marched toward Sterling. He'd kill him with his own hands, with his pistol, with anything he could in order to rescue his woman. Cassie's eyes remained closed, her body limp, as Sterling dragged her toward his men. What they intended to do with her did not matter one tiny bit. The mere fact he'd laid hand to his wife in such a barbaric manner meant the man would die an ugly death.

Giles paced beside him for several strides then slipped off to one side, weaving through the people gawping at the horrific scene. Reggie stayed near, tense, alert, continually assessing the situation. The warlock fisted his hands, crossing his wrists as he stalked toward his daughter. Haley took hold of her mother's arm and hurried her out of the dining room to join those in the entrance hall and front porch. Daniel and Silas appeared in the crowd, helping to usher them from the room. Daniel used his bouncing skills to quickly remove people two at a time from the dining room, bouncing in and out repeatedly while Silas raced others out of harm's way. Flint tracked the brothers' actions peripherally, keeping his focus on Sterling and his thugs. Scarlet and Beck conferred by the bar, their gazes fixed on everything unfolding around them as they gripped their wands. All the while his heart had essentially stopped beating, his breathing shallow, the longer his wife didn't move.

"Sterling, you know you won't get away with this." Too many witnesses. Too many brothers. Too many times Flint had worried he wasn't enough but in this very moment he was going to stop the threat to his family. Barney should arrive with the sheriff at any minute. If Flint could delay long enough, perhaps he could prevent any bloodshed. But he wouldn't wait very long before he'd act. "We have your fancy-ass button as evidence of your involvement. Now we have people who can attest to the fact you've assaulted my wife. You've accused her of being a witch and revealed your intention of 'taking care' of her which we all know means you'll kill her like the others. Or you'll try. But I won't let you succeed. No, sir. You'll pay for your crimes."

The banker cackled with a hint of hysteria in the sound. "No, son. You and your...coven of witches will pay. We'll see to it." He glanced at Larry who nodded once, a grim expression on his face.

So he'd been right to suspect the two convenient waiters. When they'd first approached Flint about the job, he'd noticed how Larry seemed to lord it over Isaac. Dictating his response, his actions. Mere days after Flint had spread the word that he needed more help to ensure a proper appearance for the burgeoning offerings of the dining establishment. To measure up to expectations of the more refined guests he meant to entice. The truth had indeed been revealed as to where their loyalties actually pointed. Well, perchance it was time they'd learn a lesson. They'd die for their boss, or if they survived find themselves out of a job because they'd be in jail. He'd settle for nothing less.

Larry and Isaac dropped their trays and rushed toward

Flint. He pulled his flintlock pistol and aimed at Larry, who shuffled to a halt, hands out, eyes wary. Flint cocked the pistol, silently daring the waiter to take one more step. Abram didn't give him the chance, but shifted into a grizzly bear. The immense beast roared, the sound scattering guests and gang members alike, as it lunged at Larry, a swipe of his massive paw raking across his chest. Blood flowed down the man's torso as he dropped to the floor in a writhing sprawl. Isaac backed away, shaking his head, as the bear roared again and prowled toward him. The man spun around and raced toward the door, but Scarlet shot magical ties at him, binding his feet in mid stride. He hit the floor hard and lay still, knocked out. The bear rose on his hind legs and roared again before dropping to all fours and pacing toward the other men in Sterling's gang.

Flint looked to Reggie as he marched toward Sterling, tense and prepared to explode in anger at the scene unfolding in the room. Scarlet raced up to his side, detaining him with a sharp shake of her head. Reggie ignored her warning until she moved in front of him, preventing him from proceeding. Reggie had the power to stop the attack with the flick of his hand, but so many others would be hurt or killed if he did. Scarlet understood Reggie's flash temper and how he needed to control and contain it before innocent lives were lost. While they argued about whether Reggie should annihilate the gang, precious time ticked away.

Flint didn't want to wait. Cassie stirred as he moved closer. Allegro seemed to sense her coming around and dove at Sterling, pulling up at the last moment with claws extended to leave long gashes across Sterling's cheek. With a yelp, Sterling swatted at the falcon who easily avoided the flailing hand. The sound brought Cassie fully awake and she struggled to free herself from Sterling's hold, but he pulled her around in front of him. Her terrified eyes flashed toward Flint, catching and holding onto his steady regard. He would not let her down.

"You coward." Flint leveled his pistol at Sterling's head, hesitating to fire with his wife being used as a shield. He'd refined his aim but flintlock pistols continued to have a range of variability in accuracy. He'd prefer a larger target than the evil man's nose. "Let Cassie go. This doesn't have to end like this."

"Ha. I've worked long and hard to get rid of the blasted witches around here." Sterling swept his free hand around the room, including the few remaining guests standing uneasily around the periphery. "You good folks need not be afraid. Join me and my men in cleansing our region of witchcraft once and for all. Come! I invite you to accept my invitation to stand up for your community, as we are."

Mandy stepped forward from where she'd been steadily consoling the remaining guests. She turned to face them with a somber expression. "You know which side you are on, don't you, good people?"

A few men shuffled their feet but everyone nodded. After several beats of Flint's heart, they quickly moved to stand behind him. He nodded his thanks for their support, then glanced to Giles on his right and then the bear on his other side.

John Baker broke away from the men at the back of the room, sidling up to Sterling with one hand extended. "Sterling, come now. Enough is enough."

"You traitor." Sterling shifted his stance to angle Cassie's taut frame to shield him from attack. "I should have never trusted you."

"Sterling, it's over. You can't win against so many." John shrugged off Sterling's fierce glare. "It's time to end this."

"Never!" Sterling grabbed a candle stick off a nearby table as he grappled Cassie toward the front corner of the room. "I'm going to make certain this witch cannot use her siren song to enchant fine people any longer." He shoved the candle into the heart of the mahogany piano as Cassie attempted to break free from his grasp. "Burn in hell, witches!"

Flint gasped despite himself as several men in the gang raced out of the room while others grabbed up the decorative candles and began to ignite anything they could find to burn. Tablecloths, curtains, even stoking the fireplace into a roaring, sparking inferno.

Sterling spun around and grabbed another candle, rushing to the table for wreath making and igniting the strands of pussy willow, reeds, holly berries, and other drying plants used to decorate for the season. Flames leapt into the air. Smoke billowed across the room. Shouts outside alerted Flint to more men joining in the attack. Cassie's vision of the inn burning flashed into his mind. No. He wouldn't let the entire inn burn to the ground.

"Flint! They've lit the outside. They've barred the doors so we can't get out." Beck stared at him, with his mouth hanging open. "We must get these people out of here."

Flint turned instead to Sterling. "You've gone too far to go back." He raised the gun, pointing it resolutely at the man's ridiculously narrow nose.

"We need to get my daughter away from that rogue and then I'll deal with him myself." Reggie sidestepped around Scarlet, marching toward Sterling. Scarlet shook her head slowly, but didn't interfere with his progress again.

Flint heard footsteps to his side but kept his aim. Then a wooden chair flew through the air and hit Sterling on the head, knocking him to the ground. He looked sharply at the source and saw Myrtle standing grimly glaring at Sterling. But the chair worked to free his wife. Cassie scrambled toward Flint's outstretched hand when the man's arm released her, but Sterling snared her ankle and dragged her back toward where he lay prone on the floor. Flint lowered his weapon, unable to find a good line of fire.

Reggie rushed up beside him. "I just need a moment when he's not holding her hostage to disable him. I just need a moment."

"I could shoot him but I'm afraid I'd hit Cassie. What do we do?" Flint stared at Sterling, unwilling to take his attention from him while he had Cassie in his grasp.

In the next second, Beck appeared at their side and settled the indecision with a magic thunderclap that knocked everyone standing down to their knees.

Chapter Eighteen

Thunder boomed overhead, rain lashing the side of the building. The two open windows allowed for water to spray the floor inside the dining room in fits and starts. Reggie struggled to his feet after recovering from the deafening thunderclap in the room. Beck had bought them some time, but not much. He wanted to snap his fingers and end the man endangering his daughter. That was all it would take, a quick snap and he'd vanish. However, his sister's dire warnings echoed in his head. Others would be injured. Innocent onlookers. He couldn't risk harming people who had the misfortune of standing too close to his power. He'd learned that lesson decades ago.

The gang of men had recovered as well. Loyal to Sterling, they scattered to do his bidding. Starting fires. Breaking furniture. Wreaking havoc. Only when Sterling fell would they stop their mischief. But stopping Sterling could mean hurting Cassie. He had to do something even if it meant laying his own hands around the madman's neck and snapping it in two.

Reggie strode toward Sterling, reaching him in time to

grab hold of him before he could recapture Cassie. He pulled the older man aside, giving his daughter a chance to escape. Giles restrained Cassie from engaging in the ongoing battle. Sterling punched Reggie in the jaw, annoying Reggie no end. How dare he strike him? Several bolts of lightning flew past him, Faith and Hope doing their part, to burn into Sterling's torso and head. Sterling swatted at the smoldering spots as Faith's cat joined the fray, hissing and scratching at his legs and hands. Quite a family affair to stop the witch hunter.

Sterling kicked the cat away and then pulled a powerful pistol from his coat pocket. "You don't know when to abandon all hope. You must die, witch, in order to save everyone else." Sterling pointed the gun at Cassie.

The man endangered her life. He inched closer, searching for a safe way to rescue his daughter. Without warning, spirits of the murdered witches joined in the fracas. Swooping at the remaining members of the gang, sending them shrieking from the room. Reggie grimly chuckled at the sudden turn of events before facing the leader of the gang.

Despite the warnings, he had to act. He summoned all of his power and focused it on Sterling, glaring at him. Pinpointed all of his magic on the evil man holding his daughter's life in his hands. Then he snapped his fingers and chanted his banishment spell, the one that not only made a demon vanish but ended the life of the person targeted. As Sterling dropped to the floor, freeing Cassie in the process, Reggie felt his life force snap inside. He struggled to remain standing but couldn't keep on his feet, crashing to the floor with a cry of pain.

"Pa!"

Thunder rolled outside, lightning flashing both inside and outside the windows. Pain and coldness raced through him as he struggled to breathe. Faith and Hope stepped up to defend him. His life ebbed as chaos exploded around him like hail on a tin roof.

Giles moved to check Sterling's pulse, only to look up at Flint with a quick shake of his head. Hundreds of footfalls announced the return of the guests to help in ending the battle. He heard Sheriff Neal's distinctive bass voice directing his deputies in quelling the fight. The avenged spirits hovered around the room, ending their harassment with a grim smile of thanks before vanishing. Cassie sang her calming songspell softly as she approached him, dropping down beside him with worry in her glittering eyes.

"Pa, are you all right?" She felt his forehead, examined his body and then paused when she sensed his broken spirit. "Oh, Pa."

"It's all right." Saying so made it so. He let his eyes close for a moment, let the wave of weakness flow throughout his tired body.

Hope's voice sounded above him. "I'm glad you managed to take care of the witch hunter."

Reggie opened his eyes, his wife's sister stewing above him, wand at the ready. "Hope, it's over. The leader is dead and the others will be easily identified now."

Flint appeared at her elbow, a shake of his head endorsing Reggie's words. "It's up to the law to do their job. Barney will round them up and haul them off to jail."

"Just say the word..." Hope lowered her wand, her eyes hard as she looked at Reggie. "Pull yourself together, Reggie. Your family still needs you."

His family. They clustered around him where he lay on

the hard floor. His sons all so fine and handsome. He searched out each of them, looking into their eyes as he probed their inner emotions, content with their confidence even while sad to cause them worry as he lay dying. He'd used up his power in order to save everyone else, and he'd do it again if necessary.

He tried to nod to Giles, but couldn't move his head. Instead, he blinked at him before shifting to consider Cassie, close at hand, her emotions laid bare for him as she tended to him in his last moments. His loving, beautiful daughter, now married and secure in her future with her husband. Behind her stood Flint. A very good and decent man. Flint's hard work and attention to the details of both the business and the people living and working at the inn had all culminated in a fine place for everyone to enjoy.

Reggie released a deep sigh, closing his eyes again. So tired. He'd carried so many of his own burdens, his family's secrets, for so long. He'd lost so much in the process: time with his family, seeing his sons grow and mature, the last moments of his loving wife's living presence. He'd gained much as well in a growing family, one full of love and hope for their futures. Perhaps the time had arrived for him to finally lay down all of his burdens. Let go of everything.

"Pa, Pa!"

He struggled to open his eyes again, seeing the anguish and terror in Cassie's distraught expression. With an immense effort, he reached a hand out to rest on her arm. "I am proud of all of you. You've all grown into fine young people with an amazing future ahead. Now go on and live good, productive lives."

"Pa, no." Cassie sagged against him, reaching out to him with her senses.

He smiled at her, a weary expression of his profound love. He sensed her awareness of what he meant to do. Her reluctant acceptance. Sensed Silas joining in the private conversation, the unwilling agreement with Reggie's chosen path. Giles stepped closer, lending his silent strength and support for all. Cassie's tears fell on his cheek.

"Take care of them." He weakly squeezed her arm and then let his hand fall away.

Over Cassie's shoulder Mercy hovered in her light blue dress, her flaxen hair flowing about her shoulders as if caught in the stormy wind blowing through the windows. His wife. His love. Reggie let out another sigh, closed his eyes, and then eagerly went to join his beloved wife.

The storm from the previous night left clouds masking the sky above the family cemetery behind the inn. Flint stuck the point of the spade into the soft earth and stepped on the back edge to scoop dirt out of the growing rectangular hole. Cassie's grief had left her weak and trembly, her aunts gathered around her to console her after cradling her beloved father as he died. Flint flung the shovelful of dirt on the pile beside the hole, Giles and Abram mirroring his motions from the other side of the man's grave. Daniel and Silas had gone to the barn with Beck to build a decent coffin, Reggie's brother grieving nearly as much as his daughter. How Flint hated to see a grown man cry, but he'd shed tears of his own. The whole situation seemed unfair. After finally reuniting they'd been parted forever. Tears seemed vastly appropriate. He jabbed the tool into the ground and hefted another heaping load onto the pile.

The men responsible for murdering so many innocent women were in jail. The aunts had joined forces with Cassie. Thus all the threats had finally ended. Life could settle into a normal routine and everyone breathe easier. Yet sadness weighed down his spirit.

Murmuring up on the rear porch reminded him of the inn's guests who'd surprised him with their devotion and support upon the tragic conclusion to the happy festivities. If it hadn't been for the quiet efforts by Mandy, dropping a word here and a comment there, the guests would not have come to realize how much the Fairhopes had done for them. How much they'd done for the community at large. How much they cared for each individual person who walked through the front doors. So when the true threat posed by Sterling and his men came to light, they stood their ground and stood up for the people and place they'd grown to care about. What a wonderful realization to carry inside him. He needed to thank Mandy properly for her dedication.

"I think that's enough." Giles leaned on the handle of his shovel and regarded Flint. "I'll let everyone know we'll have the funeral now."

"It's kind of them to linger to pay their last respects to Reggie." Abram leaned his shovel on a nearby tree and wiped mud from his hands. "Do you want me to inform Beck and the others?"

Flint grasped the shaft of his spade, balancing it in his hand, horizontal to the wet ground. "I guess I should be happy for them."

Giles lifted one sardonic brow. "I'm not sure I follow."

They'd dug Reggie's grave within a few feet of his wife's final resting place. Now that she no longer haunted the inn, having him lie next to her seemed a fine ending for him as well. He'd want to be close to her in death since he'd been apart from her for the last few months. If he were in Reggie's place, he'd wish to have his grave as close as possible to the woman he would love forever, even beyond death.

Flint leveled his gaze on Giles. "They'll be together for all time. Nothing will come between them now."

"I see." Giles walked over to take the shovel from Flint. "Let's wash up and get Sheridan to lead the service like he did for Mercy. She'd like that."

"Meet back here in twenty minutes and we'll get this over with." Although truth be told, he wasn't in any hurry to lay his boss, his new father by marriage, to rest. Yet the senator had sent word he and his entourage would arrive by early evening. With his imminent arrival, they had no option as to whether to accept them or turn them away. The group had traveled too far, and everyone at the inn had worked too hard, to deny them. "We have much to accomplish before this afternoon is over."

Flint went inside, heading toward his bedchamber in hopes of a minute of quiet reflection before facing everyone graveside. As he entered the family parlor, however, Cassie lifted tear-drenched eyes to silently plead with him to come to her. Wearing the same black mourning gown she'd worn at her ma's funeral months earlier. The one he'd hoped she'd not need again for years to come. Hope, Faith, and Scarlet surrounded her like ladies attendants, their concern blazing from their eyes as they also met his gaze. A shaft of distress zinged through him at Cassie's obvious anguish. He crossed the room to her in four strides, taking her hands and lifting her from her seat.

He tucked her close to his chest for a moment, and then pressed his forehead to hers. Her body trembled in his embrace. Her pulse beat slowly against his fingers. Too many eyes weighed on them, on her. "Come with me, sweetheart."

Without a murmur, she followed him upstairs to the privacy of their bedchamber. Her slow steps and tight grip on his hand conveyed her distress more readily than words. She'd lost both parents now. Both during violent episodes within the walls of her home. He clasped her hand firmly, willing his strength to flow into her. Willing her to not blame herself as she'd done after her mother's untimely death. Willing her to find comfort in knowing her parents were together again as they'd wished.

He closed the door to their bedchamber, and then turned to face Cassie as she barreled into him. Wrapping her arms around his waist, she clung to him, sobs rocking through her chest. He held her for a long moment, struggling to contain the grief welling inside of him. He'd be strong for her. She needed him and deserved nothing less than his complete support and devotion.

After a few minutes, she sniffled and eased her hold on his person to look up at him. "I will always miss him."

He pulled a clean handkerchief from his vest pocket and dabbed at her tears. "We will always miss both of your parents, Cassie."

"He sacrificed himself for me, and I'll be forever grateful for his selfless act." She sniffed, the last of her tears coursing down her cheek. "But he wanted to die, to be with Ma. I've sensed his grief ever since he came home. He'd let me see, let me *feel* how very much he craved her."

The man had definitely grieved for his lost wife despite

the only way for them to see each other was because of her haunting the inn. Perhaps she stayed precisely so she could see her husband upon his return. Well, why not? Flint clasped Cassie's shoulders and kissed her lips, relishing the ability to do both. Imagine being close to his wife and not having the ability to touch her, to feel her within his hands, the satin of her skin beneath his fingertips. The feelings from the more intimate caresses Flint had only recently experienced for the first time. To not have the chance to repeat such a tender moment would be its own kind of torture. The love Reggie and Mercy shared served as a fine example, one Flint intended to learn from, expand on, and enjoy for many moons to come. Loving Cassie would serve as his tribute to both Reggie and Mercy, and honor their trust in him and their daughter to follow in their footsteps toward a loving marriage.

"Now it's time for him to join your mother in their final resting place, side by side." He pressed his lips to hers, savoring the traces of her tears on his lips, drying them as he conveyed his sympathy and his love. He squeezed her fingers to lift her eyes to meet his gaze. "Are you ready?"

She inhaled slowly and nodded. "Knowing it's what my pa truly wanted, to be with her always, then yes."

The gathering of people encircling the grave, easily numbering close to a hundred, warmed Flint's heart. So many of the regular guests and some of the new ones who had ventured out to the inn for the festivities stood together to honor the original owner, the visionary, of the Fury Falls Inn. Flint escorted Cassie to the front of the assembly where Sheridan stood at the head of the grave, Pansy and sons standing by his side. Allegro silently flew to sit on Cassie's right shoulder, a somber attitude in the angle of his head and the set of his wings. Studying the grave site, Flint grimaced. A stone, engraved with an appropriate sentiment, would need to be sent for soon. Events happened too quickly to allow for the necessary refinements for the deceased but it would be seen to posthaste. In the meanspace, the family and friends surrounding the man's grave served to commemorate how beloved and respected he'd been in life.

Sheridan raised a hand to ask for silence. "We are gathered here today to say our farewells and fair journey to Mr. Reginald Fairhope. Mr. Fairhope lived to serve not only his Lord, but also his family and his community. If it were not for his decency and compassion, I would not be standing here before you a free man. If it were not for his caring and understanding, my wife of twenty-five years would not be standing here with me. My sons also owe their freedom to the Fairhopes for Giles Fairhope followed his father's example and used his resources to free them from a dreadful situation. Everyone standing here today owes some form of debt to Reginald Fairhope. Please join me for a moment of silence to thank him for everything he's done for each of us."

Lowering his head to stare at his shoe tips nestled among the grass blades, Flint clasped Cassie's hand. Sheridan's invitation to thank his boss for his help pulled on his soul. He had much to thank Reggie for. More than he could adequately put into words. First, the opportunity to escape his father's commanding presence to prove to his father and to himself he could run a successful business. Second, for the trust he demonstrated by putting the inn's improvements in his hands. Third, introducing him to Cassandra which opened new horizons for his future. But perhaps most of all for giving him the confidence he needed without realizing it. Flint had grown and matured in the months since he first rode Buck up the lane to the inn. Working at the inn changed him, improved him as he improved the inn.

"Amen." Sheridan waited until everyone finished their prayers and looked at him once more. He nodded to Flint and then glanced to where Beck and Cassie's brothers waited by the coffin resting on sawhorses under a blazing gold tree. "Gentlemen, if you will."

Flint squeezed Cassie's hand once and then hurried to help the others lift the coffin and carry it slowly to the graveside. With each step, he worked to keep the coffin level, to keep his emotions in check, to keep reminding himself of the rightness of his father-in-law's wish to die. The last goal remained elusive. Tears smarted his eyes but he blinked them away. He'd stay strong for his wife, watching him with glittering eyes of her own. She strove to control her emotions for the duration of the funeral, so he would as well. The six men worked to lower the coffin into the freshly dug earth, finally bringing it to rest with a soft thump. Giles and Flint by prearranged agreement picked up shovels and began covering the pinewood coffin with dirt from the nearby pile. After the ceremonial covering, they laid aside their tools as others would complete the task once the crowd dispersed. After exchanging a short nod, they found places among the surrounding folks sniffling and blinking with suppressed feelings.

"We commend Reginald Fairhope into the Lord's care." Sheridan held his hand up in benediction as he recited the Lord's Prayer with everyone solemnly joining in. "Amen. Go in peace."

The group seemed to heave a collective sigh as it broke up, heading toward their horses and conveyances and their distant homes. Pausing to say a quiet word to Cassie or one of her brothers as they drifted away from the cemetery. When the area had cleared of most of the remaining guests, Flint led Cassie, Allegro perched on her shoulder, inside the inn where some light refreshments were set out in the dining room. Allegro nuzzled her cheek before he left Cassie's shoulder to alight on his rest by the damaged piano, its charred surface black against the shades of deep red wood. The sight stabbed regret through Flint, knowing how much she enjoyed playing the instrument.

Beck sidled up to them with a tilt of his head to the piano. "I could help fix that if you'd like, Cassie."

Cassie slid a glance at Beck and nodded. "That would be lovely, Uncle Beck. Pa arranged for the piano from a passing piano maker who made it in exchange for his stay with us for several weeks. The man honed his craft as he worked his way across country, heading to New England somewhere to make a name for himself. I'd never be able to afford to buy one now."

"Then it will be my great pleasure to repair it like new." Beck flared the fingers of one hand in a slow, fanning arc. "It might take a magical touch, of course."

Cassie chuckled, the merry sound easing the tension in Flint's gut. "The aunts and elves have been busy using theirs to put the inn to rights, so why not?"

Indeed, as Flint swept his gaze around the room he couldn't tell there'd been a magical brawl the evening before. Other than a few missing chairs and the charring of the piano, the rest of the furniture and furnishings seemed untouched. Fresh candle sticks waited to be lit for the evening supper on every blue cloth-covered table. The chairs had been evenly spaced at each table in anticipation of the senator and his large entourage arriving most any time. A casual observer would never know of the utter chaos of the previous night's events. Thank goodness.

Giles joined the small group by the piano, the other brothers trailing in behind him. "Now that everything is calmed down, we've decided to do as Pa wanted and build our own homes on the land he gave us." He looked hesitantly at the others and then shrugged. "One other thing. We've been talking. We'd like to create a new community, call it Mercy, Alabama. What do you think?"

Cassie beamed, her eyes damp yet again. "Oh, guys, that's a lovely idea. Both that you'll stay close and that you'll honor our mother."

Flint held out a hand to Giles. "I think they'd both be very proud of all of you."

Giles returned the handshake with a nod. "I'll still be our family's Guardian, to keep things safe for everyone. Just not under this roof, which will give you more rooms to hire out."

"I think I'll need them now that word has spread of the fine accommodations as well as the stellar food." Flint shook hands with each of the other brothers in turn, ending with Silas.

"Keep a room here for me, will you?" Silas smirked at Flint with an amused chuckle, holding onto his hand for a moment longer than usual. "I still have some writing assignments that will have me on the road for a while but I'll come back from time to time to visit."

"One day you'll settle down right here in Mercy." Daniel nodded sagely then broke into a provocative grin. "Surely we can find a woman for you, too."

"Wait a minute..." Silas started to protest but a commotion at the door interrupted the banter.

"He's here, Pa!" Teddy came racing into the dining room, sliding to a stop beside Flint. "The senator has arrived, and man, what an entrance he makes."

The joy at hearing his newly adopted son call him his pa was overshadowed by the rest of what the boy said. Despite himself, panic shook Flint's composure. "Mandy, is everything ready? The menu..."

"Yes, calm down. We've double-checked everything." Mandy spun him about and pushed him toward the arched doorway. "Go welcome the man."

Flint took two steps and then halted, reaching behind him as he caught Cassie's amused expression. "Come with me."

She fell into step with him as he led her out of the room and onto the front porch. There he stopped, clamping his mouth shut and forcing a pleasant smile in spite of the enormity of the scene in front of the inn. Ten elaborate coaches drawn by gleaming teams of four matched horses filled the carriageway. The home dogs trotted about from vehicle to person to horse, inspecting and threatening in equal measure. The third coach in the cavalcade bore the insignia for the senator. The footman opened the door, and an elegantly attired man stepped carefully down to the crushed stone. Flint tugged his vest into place, then buttoned his coat, before hurrying down the steps to greet the esteemed man they'd been preparing to host for months.

"Senator Percy Graham, welcome to the Fury Falls Inn. I'm Flint Hamilton, the innkeeper." With the brothers' idea of building a new community, it might be time to change the name of the inn as well. Something to ponder after he settled the good senator into his rooms. Most definitely not while being appraised by the respected and regal man. "I hope your journey wasn't too taxing."

"Not more than expected." The pudgy man with silver-tipped brown hair and matching mustache examined Flint. "Where is Mr. Fairhope? I thought this was his establishment?"

Cassie sniffled at Flint's side and he reached out to draw her closer. "Unfortunately, sir, Mr. Fairhope passed away last evening. We've laid him to rest out back in the family cemetery this afternoon. This is his daughter and my wife, Cassandra Hamilton."

"I'm sorry for your loss, Mrs. Hamilton." The senator removed his beaver top hat and held it at his side.

"Thank you, sir." Cassie dipped a curtsy. "Welcome to the inn, sir. We hope you'll find it comfortable."

The senator took in Cassie's neat and trim appearance, and then skimmed the exterior of the inn. Finally meeting Flint's expectant and hopeful regard, he nodded. "I'm sure everything will suit beautifully. I've been eager to escape the strictures of the city for some fresh air and relaxation. Looks like I may have come to exactly the right place."

Memories of recent disastrous scenes played through his mind. After all the tragedy, the fear, and the bloodshed, the Fury Falls Inn could finally claim being a friendly, welcoming, and serene place. The Fairhope clan joined forces, creating an alliance worthy of the name. The coven aimed to promote peace and prosperity in the region, eschewing the grandfather's greedy power grab and domination of everyone and everything within his grasp.

This place, this inn, was his now. His dream of running his own hotel had come to fruition. He'd married the woman who completed him, filling in gaps he'd been unaware existed. The Fury Falls Inn had become his home and he'd never need to look anywhere else for contentment, as here in the inn he was surrounded by both happiness and love.

Flint shook the senator's hand again with a growing smile on his lips. "Indeed, I believe you have come to the right place."

The family supper gathering on All Saints Day brought joy to Cassie's very soul. Chairs crowded around Mercy's cherished dining table in the family residence. Her brothers, sisters, aunts, uncle, and husband chatted among themselves, the senator's praise still echoing in their excited conversation. Cassie had insisted on the family coming together to celebrate not only the end of the threats, the tensions, and the fears, but also the beginning of a peaceful coexistence. Love and hope filled her chest as she perused the happy faces surrounding her.

She stood and tapped her knife against her crystal glass filled with ruby-colored wine. "Settle down. I have something I'd like to say."

"No speeches." Silas put his hands together as if in prayer. "Please."

She smirked at him as she shrugged his plea away. "I've asked you all here to thank each of you for your help in defeating our enemies."

"Even when they were us?" Faith piped up from her seat at the far end of the table.

"Faith, really." Hope motioned for her to be quiet.

"We've put that to rest now, surely."

The change in her aunts surprised her most of all. "Especially since we came together to fight those who threatened us, so yes." Aunt Faith's entire demeanor had softened as a result of confessing her role in young George's death. Even her familiar, curled up on the chair before the blazing fireplace, had ended his hostile attitude. And Aunt Hope had become protective in a far more loving fashion. "You both have proved your merit and loyalty to the family. Which only proves..."

She paused to sweep her gaze around the expectant faces peering at her. Silas and his inquisitive nose for a good story. Abram's penchant for finding a different way to approach any situation. Daniel's logical analysis and insightful view of how people behave and the reasons for such responses. Giles' strength and compassion which supported the entire family. Flint sat at the head of the table, to her left, with calm confidence evident in his steady gaze. She smiled at him before continuing her survey of the family members at the table. Beck's serene yet serious gaze told her he listened attentively to what she had to say, but would he agree with her suggestion? And Scarlet's vixen-like features augured for some interesting fun in the future, now that they no longer worried about defending the inn and protecting its people. Yes, her family proved her mother's claim.

She nodded almost to herself as a sigh escaped. Allegro launched from his post and flew to her shoulder to offer his comfort. Stroking his feathered head, she cuddled his head against her cheek. The Merlin stretched his wings and then settled them along his sides, content with her increasing calm. Cassie returned her attention to her gathered family.

"As I was saying, all of you coming together as you have has proven we are stronger together as Ma always claimed." The future stretched before them, filled with hope and peace and uncertainty. "Now we need to find a way to use our combined strength for the betterment of this community."

"Agreed, Cassie." Daniel stood up, drawing Wilma up beside him. "We'd like to contribute by joining our forces in marriage the middle of December. Then we'll work to promote the idea of accepting everyone who comes to reside in our region."

Wilma clasped his hand and smiled around the group. "We'll move into the city so we can speak with the city leadership whenever possible."

"A fine idea. I'm glad you've set a date for your wedding, as well." Cassie probed the emotions in the room, seeking to ascertain how they received her comments. "I know my brothers intend to pitch their tents nearby, except Silas who will travel and spread the word of our fine inn and its offerings. Right, brother?"

Silas inclined his head with a wry smile on his lips. "Far and wide, but keep my room for me. I'll come back to check up on all of you."

"We promise. Right upstairs next to ours."

"About that." Flint held a finger in the air to indicate he had something to say. His eyes fastened on hers. "I believe we should move into the room at the other end of the hall. It's where the owner should sleep because of its location and the size of the chamber. Especially since there are two of us to share the space. Don't you all agree?"

Her parents' bedchamber.

Not only where they'd shared private moments together,

but also where her mother died. Could she? Sleep in their bed? Dress where they'd dressed? Which brought up the enchanted attic. She hadn't even investigated to see if it still existed now that her ma's ghost stopped haunting the inn. What about the trunks and the books and everything she'd treasured? She drifted her gaze around the others watching her.

A shimmering in the center of the parlor drew her attention. "Ma. Pa."

They'd returned, holding hands and smiling in the parlor. They really were together forever as they'd always desired. She grinned at their happy countenances, fully aware of the love flowing through them.

The others shifted to gape at the ghosts of Mercy and Reggie, hovering in the middle of the newly acquired flowered carpet.

Giles rose from his chair, fists resting on the table. "What brings you back?"

Reggie held out a ghostly hand toward those at the table as Mercy moved closer to them. "Your mother needed to say goodbye to all of you and I cannot deny her anything."

Mercy lifted the corners of her lips as she shifted side to side for a moment. "Children, sisters, I've come not only to say farewell and give you my hope for a wonderful life ahead, but also to tell you what I've done. I hope you'll approve."

Abram sat sideways in his chair, his elbow on the back of the wood seat. "What have you done, Ma?"

"I figured Cassie would be worrying about things by now, so I decided to solve her concerns for her." Mercy moved toward Cassie, her blue dress rustling and long hair flowing behind her until she stopped near the table. "I, or rather we, want you and Flint to have our room to refurbish as your own."

"But, Ma..."

"Your pa used his remaining powers to cleanse the room of our presence. You won't feel us in there, but will sense us in other parts of the inn. And..." Mercy turned to Faith and Hope with a grin. "He's also sent most of the family heirlooms back to your attic for safekeeping. I assume that's where you'll be heading now?"

Hope nodded, a slow smile splitting her face. "Yes, we were about to say as much. We'll protect them and they'll always be there for you when you need."

"We'd planned to leave this evening in fact." Faith sat erect in her seat, glancing around the group with shining eyes. "We'll miss you all. Please come visit from time to time."

"What about the attic, Ma?" Cassie frowned at her parents, grappling with the new revelations regarding her parents' abilities even after death. "Is it still there?"

Mercy canted her head to one side. "No, my darling. But the trunk of papers is now in the bedchamber waiting for you. I believe you may need them, if only to have a connection with your family's past."

Reggie surged forward to hover beside his wife. "We are extremely proud of you all and know you will do wonderful things for this community, and the new one you intend to build. But now, we must go."

"We love you. Farewell and live long, loving lives." Mercy blew a kiss to each of them as the pair slowly vanished.

She'd never see her parents again. The certainty weighed down her heart but also comforted in knowing they were together as they needed. "Now we know they will rest in peace for eternity because they've taken care of us as best they can." She scanned the somber faces as everyone resumed their seats and pondered what they'd experienced.

Flint, however, did not sit down but cleared his throat to gain their attention. "I have a proposition I'd like to make."

Cassie sank onto her chair, her quivering knees finally giving out. The last twenty-four hours had been emotional and draining. She peered up at her husband as he looked at the group clustered around the large table.

"What is it?" Beck leaned forward, clasped hands taut on the cloth-covered surface.

"I think there is no longer any fury at the Fury Falls Inn." His gaze inched around the table to assess each person's response to his statement. "I propose to change the name to Mercy Falls Inn, because of the new settlement my brothers intend to found as well as to honor the woman who brought us all together as a family."

Happy tears smarted in Cassie's eyes as she rose to her feet. "Oh, Flint, that's a lovely idea."

General agreement murmured from the family members. Cassie's heart swelled with love for her husband, his understanding and caring as well as his strength and fortitude. Where would she be without him at her side? Where would she be without her brothers, her aunts, and her uncle? Flint was right in saying her mother had brought them all back together. If she hadn't died, then Cassie wouldn't have reached out to her brothers to come to her, to pay their respects, and to be with her. None of the rest would have happened and they wouldn't be sitting around their mother's table facing a fine path into the future.

She raised her wine glass over the table. "I'd like to

propose a toast."

The others also stood, lifting their glasses as they waited for her to continue.

"To being reunited and at peace together."

"Hear, hear!"

She sipped from her glass as her family did the same. Her family united. No more secrets to reveal. No more threats to quash. No more questions about who they were and where they came from. Only trust and confidence to carry on, move forward, and support each other.

Flint came around the end of the table to draw her to face him, smiling softly down at her. "What do we do now, Mrs. Hamilton?"

She lifted her smile to meet his. "We do like my parents wanted. We live. We laugh. We love."

The End

Thanks so much for reading *Homecoming*! This story is the last one in the Fury Falls Inn series. I hope you enjoyed getting to know everyone at the inn.

To find out about new releases and upcoming appearances, please sign up for my newsletter via my website at www.bettybolte.com. I send out a monthly newsletter with book news to share with my readers, upcoming events and signings, and even a few favorite recipes, puzzles, and other doings!

I'd love to hear from you! Feel free to send me an email at betty@bettybolte.com, find me on Facebook at

AuthorBettyBolte, follow me on BookBub, or connect with me on Twitter @BettyBolte.

Thanks again for reading!

Betty

About the Author

Award-winning author Betty Bolté is known for authentic and accurately researched historical fiction with heart and supernatural romance novels. A lifetime reader and writer, she's worked as a secretary, freelance word processor, technical writer/editor, and author. She's been published in essays, newspaper articles/columns, magazine articles, and nonfiction books but now enjoys crafting entertaining and informative fiction, especially stories that bring American history to life. She earned a Master's Degree in English in 2008, emphasizing the study of literature and storytelling, and has judged numerous writing contests for both fiction and nonfiction. She lives in northern Alabama with her loving husband of more than 30 years. Get to know her at www.bettybolte.com.

Be sure to check out materials for book club discussions at https://www.bettybolte.com/bookclub.

www.ingramcontent.com/pod-product-compliance
Lightning Source LLC
Chambersburg PA
CBHW061226310726
48971CB00007B/1955